Threads That Bind

The Havoc Chronicles Book 1

Brant Williams

DEDICATION

For my father,
who could do this much better than I.

CONTENTS

CHAPTER 1

DMV DISASTER

Most people don't consider a trip to the Department of Motor Vehicles a life changing event – I certainly didn't. But the day I went to the DMV to get my driver's license was the day I discovered I wasn't like most people.

I paced outside the building with my dad, waiting for my turn to take the driving test. I shouldn't have been nervous. I had already passed my dad's unofficial examination, which he assured me was much harder than the DMV's. However, that didn't stop me from sweating profusely from practically every pore in my body. My palms felt clammy, and the sweat on my face made my heavy glasses repeatedly slip down my nose.

A thin man with a prominent nose and a bushy beard walked out of the DMV. "Madison Montgomery?" he read from a clipboard in his hand.

This was my big moment. A chance for freedom and mobility.

Once I passed this test, I would no longer have to depend upon the capricious whims of my parents to go where I wanted.

Clearly sensing my nervousness, Dad leaned in close. "You can do this, Madison," he said. He put one arm around me and gave me a small squeeze. Well, small for him. For me it bordered on rib crushing, but I was used to that. My dad was a big man with piercing eyes, and plenty of muscles. He complained about the encroaching gray in his hair, but both my mom and I thought it made him look distinguished – like Harrison Ford on steroids.

I pushed up my glasses and stepped forward. The man with the clipboard glanced toward me, and I saw the familiar expression of appraisal and judgment. It only lasted an instant, but that was all it took for people to see my physical appearance and dismiss me as something less than a person. After sixteen years, I had gotten used to it, but that didn't make it hurt any less.

I was very aware of what I looked like. For most of my life I had worn glasses. Not the cute, stylish glasses that some of my friends had. I would have been fine with those. No, my glasses had thick, magnify-my-eyes-to-the-size-of-Frisbees lenses.

I couldn't wear contacts - I have this touching my eye thing - and my ophthalmologist informed me that eye surgery was more likely to leave me blind than fix my vision.

To that beautiful image, add in braces, a propensity to sprout zits under stress, and the compulsive consumption of anything with sugar in it.

So yeah, I wasn't going to win any beauty contests - or be

nominated Prom Queen. But I was smart, clever, and quite a good actress. All of which were characteristics that had little value in high school unless you had good looks or a six figure allowance. I had neither, and it would be two more years before I could escape.

I gave the man with the clipboard a flat stare, showing him that I knew exactly what he was thinking. He at least had the good grace to look away.

"Is this your car?" he asked, pointing at my mom's Jetta.

I nodded.

I was about to climb in when a second car pulled up behind clipboard-man, catching my attention. Another man with a clipboard, this one shorter with a large forehead, slipped out of the passenger side door. I froze when I caught a glimpse of the driver.

Josh Lancaster.

My sweating increased from profuse to drenching. I'd pretty much given up on any guy at Woodbridge High being man enough to date someone for intelligence and inner beauty, but that didn't stop me from having a couple of fantasy crushes. And Josh Lancaster was the pinnacle of that list.

He stepped out of the car and ran a hand through his sandy hair. The DMV examiner ripped a piece of paper off his clipboard and handed it to Josh, who accepted it with a grin. His smile was so beautiful it almost hurt to watch him.

I sighed. What was it about this boy that gave him such power over me? I didn't like it, but I had no idea how to change it either. I had been in love with Josh since at least the third grade.

Josh looked up from the paper and began walking towards me. I stared like an animal caught in the headlights of a semi truck barreling down the freeway. I couldn't move; I couldn't even breathe.

A few steps before he reached me, Josh noticed I was there. "I did it, Madison!" he said, waving his paper excitedly. "I'm official!"

I opened my mouth to say something, but he had already walked past on his way to get his license. I stood there, a giddy feeling washing over me as I watched him walk into the DMV.

"Madison?" said Clipboard Man.

"Huh?" I turned back to face him, startled out of my obsessing.

He rolled his eyes and gestured toward the car. "Are you ready?"

I took a breath, deeply annoyed at myself. Of all the times to be distracted by a boy. I tried without success to push Josh out of my thoughts and climbed into the car.

Clipboard Man first had me test all the lights and turn signals. Then he asked me to drive through a series of cones. I'd practiced this with my dad and had it down - piece of cake.

When he directed me out of the parking lot and onto the roads, I made sure I did everything with textbook precision; it would be too embarrassing to fail my driver's test.

By the time we reached the Dairy Queen on Fifth Street, I began to relax. So far, I hadn't made any mistakes. Clipboard Man had me turn back toward the DMV, and I breathed a sigh of relief. Freedom was only a few minutes away.

That's when my vision blurred.

I'd never experienced anything like it. One moment I could see just fine, and the next everything looked like I had opened my eyes at the bottom of a swimming pool. I was so surprised that I accidentally pressed harder on the accelerator.

Admittedly, not my brightest move.

Once I realized my mistake I slammed on the breaks, causing the car to skid with a surprisingly loud squeal of tires. Under normal circumstances I might have been able to stay on the road. This was anything but normal. I tried to turn into the skid, but I panicked and did the exact opposite, causing the car to continue its out of control rampage. I did manage to avoid a tall brown blob – telephone pole? – and a blue blob – mailbox? – before hitting the curb and jumping the car onto the sidewalk. Several multicolored blobs that must have been people scattered as the car jerked to a stop.

My seatbelt locked up, keeping me from hitting the windshield, but my head jerked forward. The abrupt stop was too much for my heavy glasses on my sweat-soaked face and they flew against the dashboard. With a crack, one of the lenses popped out of the frames.

Once it was over, I sat up and looked around at a crystal clear world.

My vision was perfect.

"Are you all right?" Clipboard Man asked.

I turned to face him, every detail sharp and crisp. I could see each hair of his beard, the individual threads making up the weave of fabric in his shirt, and the drops of perspiration forming on his brow.

Looking out of the car, I saw the pedestrians I had almost hit glare at me as they walked away. One lady had on a large hat with fake flowers attached to it and the colors - bright reds, yellows, and greens - were so vivid that they seemed to wash out the color of everything else around them.

I was so distracted by the details around me that it took me a minute to remember to nod my head in answer to Clipboard Man's question.

"What just happened?" Clipboard Man asked. He bent over to pick up his clipboard from the floor where it had landed.

"An accident?" I said, still distracted by my suddenly clear vision. I picked up the glasses and held them near my eyes. Through the remaining lens, the world still looked blurry. I lowered the glasses, and everything was clear. How could this be?

"I figured that out," said Clipboard Man. "You were doing so well." He sighed and began writing on the clipboard.

Not a good sign.

Fortunately, the car appeared to have avoided any serious damage, and I was able to drive it off of the sidewalk and back to the DMV.

My mind raced during the drive back. What could have caused this? Part of me – ok, the majority of me – was ecstatic. I had been wearing glasses since I was two. This shouldn't be possible, but it somehow was.

Back at the DMV we got out of the car, and Clipboard Man handed me a ripped-off sheet of paper. A quick glance confirmed my fears: I had failed. That meant I would have to come back and take the test again. I groaned.

Dad saw me pull in and walked up to the car. He looked at me and cocked his head to the side. "Where are your glasses?" he asked.

I held up the broken pieces.

"What happened?"

"I didn't pass my test," I said matter-of-factly. I should have been more upset. This was something that I'd been looking forward to for years, and I was denied it at the last second. But looking at a world in perfect focus without glasses was so unexpected that I was still in shock, and my driving test didn't seem to matter so much at that moment.

Dad guided me into the passenger side of the car, clearly thinking I couldn't see without my glasses. I got in without protest, wondering how I was going to explain this to him.

Dad pulled out of the DMV and onto the road without a word. After a moment he spoke.

"So, what happened?" he asked.

I didn't say anything. How could I explain when I didn't understand what had happened myself?

When I didn't answer Dad continued. "Here's what I know: you left the DMV to take your test. When you came back, your glasses were broken, and the alignment on the car is shot." To demonstrate, he loosened his grip on the wheel, and the car veered to the right. He straightened the car and glanced over at me. "Well?"

"It wasn't my fault," I said, the words tumbling out in a rush. "One minute I could see perfectly, the next minute everything went blurry." I fiddled with the broken glasses in my hands as I told him what happened. "I know this sounds impossible, but I think my eyes healed themselves."

Dad looked at me and raised his eyebrows, clearly skeptical. Could I blame him?

"Honestly," I said. "I can see perfectly fine. The reason my vision went blurry is because I had on these thick glasses when my vision fixed itself." I held up the glasses. "You try to see out of these."

Dad didn't say anything immediately. I tried to read what he was thinking, but I didn't see any of the emotions I'd been expecting. He didn't look mad, or upset, he looked... thoughtful.

"Are you telling me the truth?" he asked.

"I am."

He pointed at a billboard down the road. "Can you read me what that says?"

My miraculously healed vision had no problem reading the words. "Accident? Injury? I can help. Call Richard Clayton, attorney at law." I frowned at my dad. "Not funny."

But Dad wasn't smiling.

***

That night at dinner, I discovered that it wasn't just my eyes that had changed.

Mom had made a big salad as part of her ongoing effort to help me eat healthy food. She didn't like what she called my "sugar addiction." Which, translated from Mother-ese to English, meant she thought I was fat.

She wasn't actually my biological mother. My biological mother had died shortly after I had been born, and Dad had remarried when I was five – I had a few fuzzy memories of the wedding. I knew some kids called their step-mom by her first name, but since she was the only mom I'd ever really known, I just called her Mom.

Usually, I choked salad down when forced to simply because I knew it was good for me. Unless I drowned it in ranch dressing I couldn't stand the taste of it, and Mom would only let me have a little on the side because she said that too much ranch dressing defeated the purpose of eating a salad.

But that night when I opened the ranch dressing, the smell was so overwhelming that just the thought of eating it made me feel queasy. Reluctantly, I decided to try eating the salad by itself and was shocked by the taste.

With my first bite I realized that I actually liked it. The flavors had somehow... changed. I could taste the subtleties of each vegetable. The lettuce seemed to be made up of several different tastes mixed together, the tomatoes had a hidden undertone of earthiness I'd never noticed before, and the green peppers practically exploded with flavor. I bit into a carrot, and it was as sweet as candy.

I ate my entire plateful and reached for a second helping. That caught my parents' attention.

"Madison?" Mom asked. "You want more?"

"Yeah, this salad is fantastic." I loaded my plate full and started eating.

Mom looked at Dad for a moment and finally shrugged. "That's great," she said. "I'm glad to see you enjoying vegetables." Mom didn't say anything else about it, but I caught her looking at me several times during the rest of the meal.

After dinner, I decided that since I had eaten such healthy food, and had survived my fiasco at the DMV, that I had earned some ice cream. I dipped up a big bowl of rocky road and sat down in the living room to eat. I took a bite and immediately spit it out.

The ice cream tasted like a combination of sweaty feet and rotten fruit. Ok, so I don't actually know what sweaty feet or rotten fruit taste like, but something was seriously wrong with it. Disgusted, I took my bowl back into the kitchen where mom was working on her laptop at the table.

"Hey Mom, this ice cream tastes funny."

Mom took my bowl and sniffed it. "It smells okay." She grabbed a spoon and tasted it. "It tastes fine to me."

"Really?" I scooped out another bite. Blech. I spit it out in the sink. "Are you kidding me? That tastes rotten."

Mom furrowed her brows in concern, and looked at me with that determined glint in her eyes she got when she had made up her mind about something. I didn't know what she'd made up her mind about, but it almost always meant she was going to make me do something she knew I wouldn't like.

***

I was right. The next day Mom made an appointment for me to see my ophthalmologist because, as she said, "Eyes don't just spontaneously get better."

I usually hated going to the eye doctor because I almost always came away with even thicker glasses than before, but this time I was all for it. Something strange was going on and I was just as curious as either of my parents to find out what it was.

The doctor examined my eyes and said she had never seen anything like it. She checked over my chart several times and was at a loss to explain how my eyes could have healed. She wanted to do more exams and write an article about me for one of the medical journals, but Dad stepped in and politely, but firmly, declined.

I was scheduled to see my doctor the next day, but after our experience with the ophthalmologist Dad put his foot down and said "no". I heard my parents arguing about it that night, something they hardly ever did – at least not when I was in the house. The argument gave me a sick feeling in my stomach, so I pulled the pillow over my head and did my best to shut it out. Unfortunately, it didn't work.

"What do you mean you don't want her to go?" Mom asked.

"This isn't something the doctor is going to be able to help her with," Dad said.

I pulled the pillow tighter over my head, but my heart was pounding, and I couldn't seem to shut them out no matter how hard I tried to plug my ears.

"We have to try," said Mom. "Something is wrong with her. What if it's some sort of brain tumor? Don't we owe it to her to provide the best medical attention we can find?"

"Look, you saw what happened with the ophthalmologist. The doctor will examine her and have no idea what is going on. Then he'll want to run her through a thousand tests only to come up with nothing."

"You can't know that for sure."

The discussion continued for another ten minutes, and grew in intensity and volume into a full-fledged shouting match. I couldn't take it any longer. I threw off the covers and stormed into my parents' room.

"Stop it!" I shouted. "Stop fighting about me!" Hot tears rolled down my cheeks. Whatever it was that had happened to my eyes hadn't affected my tear ducts. Mom hurried over and pulled me into a hug. "It's not that serious," I said. "I'll be fine." After a moment, Dad came over and wrapped his big arms around both of us.

The next couple of weeks went by in a roller coaster of events and emotions. It wasn't just ice cream that I couldn't eat any more. The sugary comfort foods I had once loved were now so overpoweringly sweet that I gagged when I tasted them. Even the tiniest bit of chocolate was too much.

A few weeks after my failed driving test, I got the courage to go back and try again. That morning as I pulled on my jeans, I noticed that they seemed to be rather loose. I buttoned them up and pulled at the waistband. There was a serious gap there.

I stood in front of the mirror and looked at myself from the side. I was thinner than before. My face seemed to be somewhat narrower, and as I checked myself out from different angles, there was no doubt about it: my butt was definitely smaller. To get proof, I went into my parent's bathroom and weighed myself on their scale. It was no illusion. I had lost ten pounds.

I put on a belt and had to cinch it to a hole I had never used before. A month ago, if I had lost this kind of weight Mom and I would have celebrated. Now, I didn't want to say anything to my parents because I didn't want to cause more problems. The less they knew about my changes, the better.

This time Mom took me to the DMV, and I passed the driving test without any problem. When it was time to take the eye test, I could easily read the bottom line of the chart, but I cheated and moved up a line just to seem more normal.

Over the next few weeks, I shed weight so fast that it became obvious my clothes no longer fit. Mom and Dad had another argument, but this time Dad agreed to at least see if the doctor could tell us anything.

The doctor poked and prodded me but after weeks of testing, just as Dad had predicted, he couldn't find anything wrong. My vision was perfect, my blood sugar was fine, the MRIs and other scans all came back normal. Even my complexion had cleared up. According to him, I was in the best health of my life.

For two months these changes persisted, and then everything seemed to level off. After dropping sixty pounds my weight stabilized, my vision dulled slightly (but was still better than twenty/twenty), and even my sense of taste seemed less acute. I still disliked sweet and fatty foods, but I could at least taste them without wanting to throw up.

As school approached, Mom took me shopping for new clothes.

Usually I considered shopping a painful experience bordering on psychological torture, but this time was different. Instead of hiding behind the racks while my mom asked the sales clerk if they had larger sizes in the back, I was easily able to find cute clothes that fit me. I didn't have to buy pants that were too small just because it was the closest they had to my size or pick between two shirts that I couldn't stand because they were my only options.

Mom went crazy and bought me anything that I wanted. She seemed to be enjoying the experience as much as I was, so I kept shopping with her. Who was I to ruin her fun?

Six hours later we came home with a car full of clothing. The trunk wasn't big enough, so we had piled bags of clothes into the back seat.

When we brought the clothes into the house, Dad's eyes grew wide, but Mom gave him a look, and he didn't say anything.

The next day my best friend, Amy Patterson, came over and we spent the morning trying on my clothes and deciding which outfits looked best on me. I thought Amy would be bored since she was too short to fit any of my clothes, but she spent hours helping me mix and match outfits. When I asked her about it, she rolled her eyes and said "That's what best friends are for."

In her own way, Amy had changed quite a bit this past summer too. My sudden dislike of chocolate and other comfort foods had affected her as well. Without me there to push her to eat my junk foods, she ate better and had lost ten pounds. Not only that, but she had worked all summer as a waitress and earned a big chunk of cash, the vast majority of which was going toward new clothes.

In the final two weeks before school started, I got my braces off to complete my transformation. When I came home and looked in the mirror, I hardly recognized the girl there. The heavy, pimpled teenager with thick glasses and braces was gone - replaced by someone I didn't know.

Yes, she was prettier. Yes, she was thinner. But who was she? My looks had been so much a part of who I was and how I interacted with people that I felt adrift without them.

I flopped onto my bed and stared at the ceiling. Wasn't this exactly what I had wished for so many times? I'd watched the pretty girls at school and had assumed that being slender and attractive would make my life easier. Now, with the looming reality of school in front of me, I wasn't so sure.

CHAPTER 2

AMONG THE BEAUTIFUL PEOPLE

I didn't sleep very well the night before school started. I had horribly vivid dreams about showing up to class in my underwear, looking the way I used to. Everyone pointed and laughed.

I woke up to a mixture of relief and annoyance: Relief that it was just a dream, but annoyance that it had to be such a cliché. I mean, underwear? Really? Didn't my subconscious have a more original way of telling me I was nervous? Of all the millions of things that could go wrong, my subconscious was afraid I might accidentally forget to get dressed? Not exactly a high-probability occurrence. Had anyone in the history of high schools everywhere, ever shown up in their underwear and not realized it until they got there?

I quickly showered and got ready. Fortunately, Amy and I had already picked out our first-day-of-school outfits, so I didn't have to agonize over that decision.

I ate a light breakfast – my stomach was too nervous to do much more – grateful that my sense of taste had dulled enough to let me eat a bowl of cereal without gagging.

Mom had already agreed to let me borrow her car for the day, so I got in and drove to Amy's house. She must have been watching because she ran out the door before I even came to a complete stop.

She got in the car and stared straight ahead. She took a deep breath and said, "Are you ready for this?"

If I didn't know better, I would have thought Amy was nervous. Growing up, Amy had always been the outgoing one in our friendship. When I was too nervous to go somewhere Amy begged, pleaded, and cajoled until I finally gave in and went along with her.

I shrugged. "It's just school," I said. "It's not the Bataan death march." Although, gym class did have that sort of feel to it.

Amy turned and stared at me. "Just school?" she said. "Do you have any idea how important today is going to be for the two of us?"

And then I realized the source of Amy's sudden cold feet - she had opening night jitters. To her this was not just the beginning of another year of school, but a chance to move up in the social hierarchy. New clothes and new looks meant that today was our audition for where we would fit.

"Do you really think that this year is going to be any different from last year?" I asked.

Amy pulled down the visor mirror to check her hair and makeup. "Madison," she said, "have you no vision? Of course this year is going to be different. Everything has changed."

We pulled into the student parking lot. Grabbing our backpacks and purses, we walked into the school. The familiar buzz of conversation punctuated by laughs and slamming lockers filled the air. The thick claustrophobic smell of too many people crammed into a poorly ventilated area wafted around me, occasionally interrupted by the overpowering smell of some girl wearing way too much perfume or a guy who had bathed in cologne.

Woodbridge High was a fairly small school, so all the students knew each other. But today, as I walked down the hall, I felt like a stranger. I knew I looked different, but seeing everyone's reaction made it more real, somehow.

Up until now I had been a known quantity in the school, boxed and categorized. Neatly labeled and then dismissed. Now I was something different - unknown.

As I walked down the hall, eyes that had once slid past me now lingered and even took second looks. Amy turned to me and raised an eyebrow.

"Feels good to be noticed, doesn't it?" she said.

We stopped by Amy's locker while she dropped off her books. I stood with my back to the lockers, watching people as they walked by.

Rebecca Alvarez had the locker next to Amy, so I moved out of the way as she came up. "Thanks," she said. She had never been one of our close friends – Amy and I were pretty isolated – but she had been going to the same schools and in the same classes with us for the past ten years.

"How was your summer, Rebecca?" Amy asked.

Rebecca glanced over at her and did a double take. "Wow, Amy. Clearly my summer was not as good as yours. You look great."

Amy beamed. "You think I look different? You should see Madison. Now, she looks different."

"Really?" asked Rebecca, clearly looking for some advance gossip. "How so?"

The smile on Amy's face got even bigger as she realized that her guess was right and Rebecca hadn't recognized me. She nodded her head in my direction. "Look for yourself."

Rebecca turned to look at me, an expression of incomprehension clouding her face. She was a nice girl, but not always the quickest to catch on.

"Hi, Rebecca," I said.

"Madison?" she said. "You're Madison?"

I nodded.

While Amy finished sorting her notebooks and folders, I gave Rebecca the ultra short version of the summer, telling her that I had eaten better and lost weight. I glossed over the mystery of my heightened senses.

"Wow. Well, you look great," she said, her eyes darting around, clearly bursting with the need to tell someone what she just learned. She spotted Carol Vaughn and quickly made her exit. Within seconds they were engaged in what looked like an intense conversation.

If there was any doubt about the topic, it ended when Carol looked over at me and her eyes widened.

Amy grabbed my arm and pulled me down the hall to my locker.

"Get used to that," she said. "By lunch you are going to be the talk of the school."

I took a deep breath. Clearly this was going to be a bigger deal than I'd thought. The idea of having everyone in the school talking about me – positive or not – began twisting my stomach into strange and complex knots. The kind that only boy scouts or crusty sailors knew how to tie.

I shoved my backpack into my locker and we headed to our first classes; Physics for me and American History for Amy.

In Physics class, Aaron Parker, who I had known since the sixth grade, sat down next to me and began introducing himself.

I felt myself blush, partly because I was embarrassed, and partly because he was very good looking. He had beautiful dark hair and large blue eyes with the longest lashes I had ever seen on a boy. We'd been in several classes together and a couple of times had been assigned to work as partners. We'd never been friends or interacted outside of school, but we were at least on a first name basis. I couldn't let this go on.

"I know who you are, Aaron," I said.

He blinked, clearly confused.

"You do?"

"Yeah," I said. "In sixth grade we did a report together on polar ice caps, and in freshman year you were in my English class and you, Peter, and I made a movie for our final project."

It didn't take him long to figure it out. "Madison?" His disbelief was clearly audible.

I shrugged. "That's me," I said.

"No way!" He hit the guys sitting next to him to get their attention. "Hey, check this out," he said and pointed at me. "Guess who this is."

And so it went for the rest of the morning. People I had known for years stared at me, baffled at how much I'd changed over the summer. Boys ogled and girls glared – that was something new for me. Apparently, I was now officially perceived as a threat.

By lunch time I just wanted to crawl into a corner and hide. For someone accustomed to being effectively invisible, this was too much attention and completely overwhelming.

Amy wasn't in my lunch period, so I planned on eating in a corner by myself, away from prying questions and uncomfortable stares. I grabbed a salad in the lunch line – it was one of the few options that my acute sense of taste would let me even consider eating - and scanned the lunchroom until I found an open table in the corner. I debated whether to sit facing the wall, so I could be alone and have a moment of normalcy, or sit facing the crowd, knowing that people stare and gossip about me. After a moment's hesitation, I opted to face the crowd. I was a compulsive people-watcher and the thought of spending the entire lunch period staring at a wall didn't appeal to me.

I carried my tray towards my chosen spot and noticed someone approaching out of the corner of my eye. Not wanting one of those collisions where two people walk into each other in the cafeteria and their trays fly up into the air, I stopped to let the other person pass.

But when I looked to see who it was, I found myself gazing into the beautiful eyes of Josh Lancaster. A familiar mixture of adoration and panic overwhelmed me.

Normally when I crossed paths with Josh he would keep walking. Sometimes he acknowledged me like he did at the DMV, but most of the time he hardly even noticed I was there. This time, he came to an abrupt stop and stared at me, a confused look on his face.

The confused expression only lasted for a heart beat before it was interrupted by Louis Packer, who hadn't noticed that Josh had stopped, running into him from behind. He knocked Josh forward and his food flew off of his tray in a graceful arc before crashing to the floor with a splat and the clatter of utensils.

The students in the cafeteria burst into enthusiastic applause. Josh stared at me with a horrified look of embarrassment on his face, something I'd never seen before from him. He quickly broke eye contact and scrambled to clean up his mess.

Not sure what to do, I continued to my secluded corner and sat down. I had a nice view of the cafeteria and was able to surreptitiously watch Josh while eating my lunch.

The janitor came in and mopped up the mess while Josh got back in line to get another lunch. He crossed the cafeteria – this time without incident – and sat at a table with his friends, looking sheepish. The guys slapped him on the back in commiseration and the girls all gazed intently at him and looked for excuses to lean close or touch his arm.

I tried not to be obvious that I was watching him, but a couple of times I saw him look at me and then lean in and talk to the people at his table. When five of them turned around at once, I knew they were talking about me.

Not wanting to be caught staring, I put my head down and concentrated on my salad. A few minutes later a shadow crossed my tray. I looked up to find Josh standing right in front of me.

"Madison?" he asked.

I had a bite of salad in my mouth and suddenly found it extremely difficult to swallow. I nodded to buy myself some time and took a drink. The wad of lettuce in my mouth felt roughly the size of Roosevelt's head on Mount Rushmore.

In my haste to swallow, I ended up choking and coughing. Fortunately, I managed to keep my mouth shut and not spray anything out, because if I had sprayed bits of chewed lettuce onto Josh Lancaster, the heat generated by my resulting blush would have caused me to spontaneously combust.

"Yes?" I managed to squeak out.

Josh pulled up a chair and sat down. I took a deep breath and tried to calm myself. He was just a boy. He was just a boy. He was just a boy. Oh, who was I kidding? He wasn't just a boy. He was the boy.

"I just wanted to apologize for nearly dumping my tray on you earlier." He shrugged and gave me a rueful grin. "I mean, I heard you had changed over the summer, but I didn't know what to believe until I saw you."

"Yeah," I said. "I'm still a bit in shock myself. It was... an interesting summer."

Josh flashed me his signature grin that always made my knees weak. "I bet," he said. He motioned over to the table where he had been sitting. "Why don't you come eat with us and tell me about it?"

Panic washed over me. Yes, I had changed physically, but it would only take a few minutes of conversation for them to realize I was a fake. On the inside I was still the same fat girl with glasses they had ignored or made fun of since middle school.

Why was I hesitating? This is what I had wanted my whole life – acceptance. Now it was being handed to me on a silver platter. If Amy were here, she'd yank me out of my chair and shove me towards Josh's table.

Hesitantly, I nodded and was even more surprised when Josh picked up my tray and carried it for me. We sat down and were greeted with mixed reactions. Megan Richardson a tall, thin girl with gorgeous blonde hair, gave us an impassive look. She was the captain of the girls' soccer team and was already being recruited by colleges. It took a lot to ruffle her. Selma Torres looked wary, probably wondering how my presence would change things.

The boys seemed more curious than anything else. Although they didn't say anything, I could see Mason Cross and Taylor Simpson trying to listen in while I talked with Josh.

At first I was extremely nervous sitting at a table talking with Josh, but I quickly discovered he had a talent at putting people at ease – or at least me – and I eventually found myself relaxing.

I gave him the entire story of what had happened over the

summer – almost crashing my mom's car when my vision changed, gagging on ice cream, and even about how worried my parents were.

Before I knew it, lunch was over and it was time to go back to class. Everyone else had left the table and Josh and I were the only ones remaining. For the first time since I sat down, there was an awkward pause. Well, awkward for me at least. Josh appeared completely relaxed and continued to smile at me. I wondered if he suspected how powerfully that smile affected me.

I took a last drink and put my cup on my tray. "Well, I should probably go to my next class."

Josh took our trays and dumped them. "Let me walk you back to your locker."

Our walk through the hallways generated quite a few stares. I could imagine the gossip racing through the halls, spreading like a wildfire fanned by a hot wind. While today was the first day I had actually ever had good gossip being spread about me, it still made me uneasy.

While I got my notebook out of my locker, Josh leaned against the wall and watched me, his deep brown eyes focused and intent. I grew so flustered that I dropped my history folder.

"Why are you doing that?" I asked.

"Doing what?" Although I didn't think it was possible, his grin grew even wider. He knew exactly what I was talking about.

I narrowed my eyes in mock anger. "You know exactly what I'm talking about, Josh Lancaster. You haven't stopped staring at me for the past half hour."

He reached out a hand and brushed a strand of hair out of my face. "I happen to enjoy looking at you. Is there something wrong with that?"

I bent my head down to let my hair obscure my face. It was an old, protective reaction to being watched, and this time I used it to help hide my embarrassment.

Josh reached out and lifted my chin. "What are you doing this Friday?" he asked.

My mouth grew very dry. Every ounce of moisture evaporated in the space of six words from Josh. Would I ever be comfortable around him? These involuntary nervous reactions were really starting to get old.

I took a deep breath and wished for something to drink. "Nothing," I said and to my surprise my voice sounded clear and confident.

"You want to go out?" he asked.

This was the point where I was sure I was going to wake up. Honestly, the limits of believability had been reached and reality had been stretched too far for this to be anything but a dream. There was no way Josh was actually asking me out on a date. Was I going to look down and realize that I was in my underwear too?

But there was no shifting of scene, no running in slow motion or even any underwear. It was one hundred percent scary-real.

It was time to use my acting skills. I took a long blink and used that time to imagine that I was in a scene in a play. When I opened my eyes, I was no longer awkward, shy, Madison. I was the quirky heroine being asked out by the lead male role.

"That depends on where we're going," I said. Did that really come out of my mouth? I watched his reaction with an outer façade of calm, but inside I was screaming at my own stupidity. What if he didn't like smart-alecky girls? What if he thought I was too rude and changed his mind? Oh, why didn't I just say "yes" and be done with it?

Josh chuckled. "I was planning an evening of hard labor and beatings, but since you appear to be so picky, we could try going out to dinner."

"Well, as long as there are no beatings," I said, and this time I was the one who smiled. As I did, I saw Josh's face light up, and I was so surprised by it that I almost lost my quirky heroine façade.

He hadn't been sure I would say yes.

This wasn't a pity date; he actually wanted to go out with me.

As Josh turned around and walked to his next class, I realized that everything had changed as much as Amy had said. But I questioned if it was just the looks and clothes that had made the change. Was that the secret to happiness in high school? Or was there something more?

I was bursting to tell Amy about my date with Josh, but I had to get through Pre-calculus and English before Amy and I met up in gym class for the final period. Being overweight and uncoordinated had made gym class feel like some sort of medieval torture, so it had always been my least favorite class. Now, for the first time in my life I was actually looking forward to gym.

By the time I got to the locker room to tell her, Amy had already heard. I wondered if Einstein had considered the rate of spreading gossip when declaring that nothing was faster than the speed of light.

"Tell me all about it," Amy said as soon as she saw me. "I want details!"

I filled her in while we got changed. I was so excited that I almost managed to not be self-conscious while changing into my gym clothes.

"Wow," Amy said when I finished. "You've had quite the day." She paused and looked me up and down. "And, to add to your list of superhuman feats for the day, you make those school-issued gym clothes look good."

Despite several attempts by well-meaning but controlling groups of parents, our school had managed to avoid being sucked into having a dress code. But for gym class we all had to wear black shorts and grey t-shirts provided by the school. I usually felt horribly exposed since the shorts always felt way too short and my legs were not what I would have called my finest features. White and flabby, I always felt like I was walking on two bratwursts with everyone staring.

I looked in the mirror, and despite what Amy had said, I was surprised by what I saw. I knew my legs were thinner, but I still couldn't think of myself that way. The legs I saw in the mirror looked like legs I had seen on other girls – normal legs.

Mrs. Herst, the gym teacher, herded us all out of the locker room and onto the gym floor. I groaned when I saw the volleyball nets set up. I was not very coordinated and had absolutely no talent in sports. I was especially dismal at volleyball. I missed the ball more often than I hit it, and I invariably ended up on a team with ultra-competitive girls who by the end of the game would start shoving me out of the way rather than watch me flub another hit.

Today was no exception. Amy was sent to another court and three of the girls on my team were on the varsity volleyball team that went to state last year.

I stuck myself in the back corner, hoping to hide for a while, but Ginger Johnson was serving and immediately identified me as the weak link. My heart started pounding as she served the ball directly at me. To my surprise, the ball seemed to move more slowly than I remembered. I positioned myself under the ball and bumped it to the front row where Anna Tupper spiked it for a side out. She turned and gave me a high five. Definitely the first time anyone had ever congratulated me for my performance in an athletic event.

Ginger must have thought it was a fluke – I certainly did – because on the next volley she hit the ball straight toward me again. But once again, I was able to get under the ball and bump it up. She tried three more times, and each time I was able to easily bump the ball up. After that I was no longer the main target. What had once seemed so difficult and complex now came naturally. I decided it must be a side effect of my enhanced vision. Since I could see the ball more clearly, I had a better idea of where it was going.

When I rotated to the front row, I noticed an even bigger change. As Ginger jumped up to spike the ball at me, I leapt to a previously unimaginable height and blocked her hit. She looked over at me with a mixture of disbelief and anger in her eyes.

On the next volley, Anna set the ball perfectly and I jumped up and spiked it past Ginger for a point. Now, that certainly wasn't because of better vision. There was more to this change than I had realized.

I pushed the worries about what the changes might mean out of my mind while I played. For the first time in my life I was having fun playing a sport. It was amazing how much more fun it was when I didn't suck horribly at it.

By the time gym was over I was both exhausted and exhilarated. Amy and I changed into real clothes and headed back to our lockers. On our way out Anna gave me a high five and said "Good game, Montgomery. You should try out for the team this year."

Amy looked at Anna and back at me, her face a mixture of disbelief and amazement. She had been playing on a different court and obviously hadn't seen what had happened in my game. Given my past experiences in volleyball, her disbelief was more than understandable.

"Good game?" she said. "What happened?"

"It's no big deal," I said. "I've gotten better at volleyball."

"And?"

I tried not to make a big deal out of it, but I couldn't stop the grin on my face. "And I may have spiked the ball at Ginger Johnson."

"You didn't!"

I shrugged and kept moving. As we walked through the halls the looks and whispers grew even more noticeable. Amy's grin grew larger and larger as we continued down the hall. She was like a gossip sponge, pulling it all in and processing what my newfound status as most discussed girl in the school meant for me.

Despite Amy's excitement, I was still uncomfortable with this much attention. I was ready to go home just to avoid the way people stared at me. Amy and I stopped briefly at our lockers and made a quick getaway to the student parking lot.

We were almost out to the car when I spied Josh approaching with Mason and Tyler. I took a deep breath, prepared for the worst. Clearly the school gossip had convinced him he'd made a mistake.

"Hey, Madison," he said.

I scanned his face for any sign of what he was thinking, but I didn't see any evidence of concern. In fact, he was giving me that smile that made my knees all wobbly.

I put on my quirky heroine face and smiled back. "Hey, Josh."

At that point, his confident smile evaporated into a shy, bashful expression.

Mason whispered something to Taylor that caused him to laugh. I didn't catch the words, but apparently Josh did because he reached over and punched Mason in the shoulder.

He turned back to me. "So, are we still on for Friday?"

I turned to Amy for help, but she was too busy studying Josh to notice. Why would he ask that? Was he trying to get out of the date? Was he embarrassed to be going out with me?

"Yeah, I think so," I said, not sure what else to say. "If you still want to, that is." In my panic, the quirky heroine had disappeared.

Josh cocked his head to the side and looked confused. Then he smiled again. "Of course. I'll pick you up at 7:00."

As the three of them walked away, Taylor muttered something that caused Mason to erupt in another a fit of laughter. Josh kicked Taylor in the rear. The three of them walked off laughing and punching each other.

Boys are weird.

We got in the car and Amy started laughing.

"What's so funny?" I asked.

"In one day you managed to wrap Josh completely around your little finger," she said. "I don't know how you did it."

Usually I trusted Amy's judgment, but this time she was totally off. "He is so not wrapped around my finger. I think he wants to call off the date. Why else would he ask if the date was still on?"

Amy lightly banged her head on the dashboard. "Madison, Madison, Madison. You are truly naïve. He was looking for an excuse to talk to you again."

"So why ask if the date was still on?"

"He's a boy. He's insecure by nature. He just wanted some reassurance, and probably to prove to Mason and Taylor that you were going out."

I heard her words, but nothing Amy said made any sense to me. "Why would he want to do that? I'm the one who should be worried about whether he wants to go out with me."

Amy buckled her seatbelt. "You're still stuck in the past," she said.

"Take a good look in the mirror. You are gorgeous. If anything, you're out of his league."

I put on my seat belt and started the car. "What are you talking about? There is no league higher than Josh."

"Woodbridge is a small pond, my dear," said Amy. "You won't be here forever. But until then, enjoy the ride. It's going to be a year we will never forget."

CHAPTER 3

A KISS LIKE NO OTHER

I was just changing into my fifth outfit in the last ten minutes when Mom knocked at my bedroom door.

"Madison?"

I glanced into the mirror, adjusting my blouse and smoothing it down. "Come in."

Mom poked her head through the door. "Josh is here," she said.

She had that goofy grin she always wore when she talked about Josh. I could tell she had the whole proud-mom thing going on. A few months ago, neither of us thought I would ever go on a date. Now I was going on a third date with Josh.

On our first two dates we had connected in a way that I hadn't thought possible. We had talked for hours, making up for the lost years since we had been friends. There had been no awkward pauses or lack of conversation. It was as if the past five years hadn't happened, and we simply picked up where we had left off.

I looked at my watch. He was early, and I hadn't even decided on an outfit yet. "Ok, stall him. I'll be down in a minute."

Mom looked at the clothes strewn around the room. "I would go with the blue one," she said, pointing at one of the blouses I had discarded on the bed. "It doesn't wash out your color." She closed the door behind her before I had a chance to react.

It doesn't wash out my color? What was that supposed to mean? As opposed to what I was wearing now? Even when she was trying to be helpful, my mom had a way of bringing out my insecurities. Not that it was difficult to do. I may have changed on the outside, but it took more than a few months to overcome a lifetime of experience.

I took a deep breath. It was time to stop obsessing. Josh was downstairs, alone with my parents, and the potential for embarrassment was growing exponentially with each moment I delayed. My dad hadn't been home the first two times Josh picked me up, so I was pretty sure he was going to make up for the lost opportunities while Josh waited.

I ignored my mom's fashion advice and threw on a beige sweater. It would have to do. I grabbed my purse, checked it for the essentials, and ran downstairs.

My dad sat on the couch next to my mom, his arms folded, doing his best to look intimidating. Physically it worked, but I knew my dad well enough to tell that this was an act.

Josh sat in the love seat across the room, looking very uncomfortable. Clearly, my dad's tough guy act was working.

A look of relief crossed his face when I walked in, and then his eyes lit up as he took a second look at me. I grinned. That was a reaction I could get used to.

I grabbed his arm and pulled him toward the door.

"Bye, Mom. Bye, Dad. I'll be home by curfew." I pulled Josh out of the house before my dad could make any parting threats. I'd been waiting five years to go out with Josh, and I didn't want it spoiled by my dad's misguided notions of proper parental protection. Earlier in the week Dad had talked about buying a shotgun, just so he could be sitting on the front porch cleaning it when Josh came to pick me up. I didn't think he would actually go to that kind of extreme, but I wasn't going to take any chances.

Josh let me into his car, a new Mustang his parents had given him for his birthday, and then climbed in himself. He was always a gentleman, opening doors and taking my arm as we walked. In a lot of ways he was an old-fashioned kind of boy. I liked that.

I settled into the leather seat as Josh put the car in gear and began driving. Now that we were away from my parents, I could relax and stop worrying about what they were going to say.

I looked over at Josh, enjoying the opportunity to watch him unobserved while he concentrated on the road. I never got tired of looking at him. He wore his sandy hair a little longer than most of the other kids at Woodbridge High, but style here in the Pacific Northwest was always a bit different from the rest of the world. Especially in a small town like Woodbridge. His brown eyes were large and dark, with long lashes that curled up, and a strong jaw-line. All of his features seemed to fit together perfectly to create the face that I could never get enough of.

He must have felt me staring at him, because he turned his head and glanced at me. "So, where do you want to eat tonight?"

I did my best to keep my expression even. This was a pet peeve of mine. He asked me out - I wanted him to plan the date. Maybe this was an unrealistic expectation born out of years of sitting at home watching romantic movies on the weekends, but I couldn't help it.

"Oh, I don't know," I said. "What sounds good to you?" And so the 'where to go' dance began. I didn't want to make a decision that he might not like, and he was completely unwilling to take the lead. Eventually we settled on a small Mexican restaurant off 3rd Street because it was near the theater where we were going to see the movie later.

The food wasn't bad; it was the closest thing to authentic Mexican food around. They used lots of fresh vegetables in their dishes, which still tasted delicious to me.

After dinner we went to the movie theater, but being opening weekend, the movie had sold out. Nothing else at the theater looked good, and I was afraid that we were going to have to go through another round of 'what do you want to do?' but Josh surprised me.

"Do you want to go to the Riverside Trail?" he asked.

I had heard plenty of stories about what went on at Riverside Trail. It was a nice paved path along the river on the east side of town, but it was also very secluded with plenty of places along the trail to find some privacy.

I hesitated. Did I want to be alone with Josh? And what was he expecting?

He must have sensed my discomfort. "Just to walk, I mean," he said, blushing. It was his cute blush that won me over - a gentleman's blush.

"Sure," I said. "Let's go."

***

The feeling I had as we pulled into the parking lot at Riverside Trail was nothing short of surreal. Was I really here – with Josh? Me? A few months ago, I would never have believed it possible.

Josh opened my door for me and held out his arm. I briefly debated taking my purse - it held the EpiPen that I kept because of a severe allergy to bee stings – but I decided the inconvenience of taking my purse outweighed the minimal odds of getting stung, and I left it in the car. I slipped my arm in his and together we strolled down the path, mostly in silence. It was a typically beautiful Northwest late summer evening. The sky was clear, and the stars visible through the gaps in the tall trees. The moon was out, not quite full, but bright enough to cast shadows as we walked. Occasionally, as the path followed the course of the river, it would turn and the moon would be reflected on the surface of the water. It was beautiful, almost breath-taking.

Several times we passed other couples walking back the other way, but for the most part we were alone.

Josh adjusted his arm, pulling me in closer. That was something I wanted to encourage. Feeling brave, I leaned in and rested my head on his shoulder as we walked. "What are you thinking about?" I asked.

"You don't want to know," he said.

"Sure I do."

He shook his head. "Nothing, really. I was just letting my mind wander. It's relaxing being with you, and I was just enjoying the moment."

I chuckled. "What a total cop out. But I do like that you feel relaxed around me." Which was partially true. Yes, I wanted him to be relaxed, but the part of me that had watched too many movies wanted him to be so nervous he could hardly make a coherent sentence. Was that too much to ask? Ok, probably. But the fact that he didn't seem at all nervous made me wonder how much he really liked me.

"What about you," he asked. "What deep and profound thoughts are you currently experiencing?"

I shook my head and wagged a finger at him. "Oh, no, the secrets of the female mind are not so easily obtained."

Josh stopped and pulled me close, putting both his arms around me. "They're not, huh? Just how are these... secrets obtained?"

"You have to earn them," I said, breathing in deep, enjoying his scent and the feel of his arms around me. I reached my arms around him and put my head on his chest. This felt good. It felt safe. I could have stayed like that for years. This was what I had been fantasizing about for the past five years.

He reached a hand up and stroked my hair. It sent shivers down my back. "Earn them, huh?" he said. "By doing what?"

"Oh, it's not difficult to earn a female's secrets," I said. I pulled back a little and smiled at him. "All you have to do is to know us so well, be so focused on our emotional needs, so invested in the relationship that you instinctively know what we are thinking, without having to be told."

Josh laughed. "Oh, is that all? And to think I thought it would be difficult." He leaned in, his face only a few inches from mine. "Am I focused enough?" he asked.

It suddenly became very hard to breathe. My heart began to pump faster as the realization of what was happening began to sink in.

He was going to kiss me.

Was I ready for this? Of course not. How could I possibly be ready for something this monumental? Wasn't he breaking some sort of unwritten dating rule by kissing me before even holding my hand? I mean, yeah, a kiss on the third date wasn't setting any speed records, but this was taking me completely by surprise.

As Josh leaned towards me, my heart began pounding in overdrive. I began to understand what people meant when they said that they felt like their heart was going to break out of their chest – mine felt like it was going for some sort of Olympic jumping record. He closed his eyes, pressed his lips to mine - and the world exploded into color.

It was like a veil had been pulled from my face and everything was suddenly clear. The colors all around me, the greens and browns of the trees, the pale yellow of the moon, the blue of Josh's shirt became intense and bright. It was as if I had never seen real colors before, only the weak shadows of them, and now I was seeing the real thing.

Thousands of sounds that had previously been inaudible flooded my ears. A hundred scents assaulted me, all jumbled together, but dominated by the glorious smell of Josh. Not the cologne he was wearing, although I could smell that too, but a scent underneath, more subtle, intoxicating, alluring.

But it was the feel of Josh's lips on mine that overwhelmed me. I closed my eyes, enjoying the sensation. It was electrifying. Exhilarating. I didn't want it to ever stop.

No sooner had I began to enjoy the kiss than Josh pulled back. I opened my eyes and saw that his face was a mask of fear, his eyes wide and horrified. "What's happening?" he said.

Completely baffled by his reaction – was I that bad of a kisser? - I looked down at myself and saw, a bright light surrounding me, enveloping me so completely that I couldn't even see the color of my clothing. I was glowing. What was wrong with me?

Seeking comfort, I grabbed for his hand. Something crunched, and he screamed, clutching at my wrist. Instinctively, I let go and pushed myself away from Josh, only to send him flying. He flew ten feet through the air, arms flailing, and smashed into a tree with a sickening thud. His limp body slid down the trunk and collapsed into a heap on the ground.

I held up my hand, horrified at what I had done. I wanted to run to him, to see if he was all right, but I didn't dare. What if I hurt him more? What if he was already dead?

I stumbled to the river and peered into the water. My reflection was choppy, but with my enhanced vision I could see that I was glowing from head to toe, a brilliant white light surrounding me.

What was happening to me?

I turned back to Josh and saw him beginning to move. He was alive! I started toward him, but he raised a hand to stop me.

"Keep away from me!" he said. He pushed himself up until he sat up with his back against the tree and cradled his crushed hand with his good one. His whole body trembled and his eyes were wide with terror.

I took a step towards him. "Josh, I –"

"Don't come any closer," he said.

"Please, Josh," I said. "I'm sorry. I don't know what's happening." I took another step toward him. I had to make this right. I couldn't stand the look of fear in his eyes.

"Go away!" he shouted. His words hurt more than a physical blow.

What was happening? How could any of this be real? He had just kissed me, how could he never want to see me again? I needed to get home, to be where things were normal.

"Go!"

I turned around and ran as fast as I could.

The trees blurred around me as I sped along the river path at a speed that shouldn't have been possible. A hundred yards flew past in the space of a breath. I raced along the path, through the parking lot, and out onto the road with hardly any effort. I felt no more tired than if I had been going for a leisurely walk.

Which I had been – before I almost killed Josh. I pushed that thought out of my mind. It was too much to process right now. I just needed to get home.

I concentrated on running and found that I could move even faster.

I sped along the back roads, at least thinking clearly enough to avoid the freeway. A glowing girl on the freeway would probably cause a massive accident and attract unwanted attention.

As I rounded a corner less than two miles from my house, I saw a car driving straight towards me. Without thinking, I pushed off and jumped. I leapt over the car, sailed twenty feet into the air, and landed lightly on the other side all without breaking stride. I heard the squeal of tires behind me, but no sound of a crash, so I continued my frantic flight until I reached home.

I collapsed in the front yard, grateful to live in a house that was isolated and surrounded by trees. As I lay there, I forced myself to relax.

Gradually my pulse slowed, my senses grew duller, and the glow faded. It was over – for now.

This was, without a doubt, the worst night of my life. I curled up into a ball. I wanted to cry, but my eyes were strangely dry. I could feel the tears there, needing to come, but blocked.

Instead of crying my body spasmed, and I began to shake uncontrollably, my teeth chattering.

I was too ashamed to even go inside, so I shivered alone on the ground. No matter how hard I tried, I could no longer keep out the memories of what had happened tonight. Over and over I relived the terrified look I had seen on Josh's face, the sound of his body hitting the tree, and his words of rejection. But I didn't cry.

What had I become?

CHAPTER 4

TALES MY BOYFRIEND TOLD

I calmed down as much as I could before entering the house. As I expected, my parents were watching TV in the living room. I could tell from their expressions as I walked in that it was obvious I was still upset.

My mom rushed over and gave me a hug. "Oh, Honey, what happened?"

That was all it took to unlock the floodgates. I sobbed into my mom's shoulder for several minutes. When I finally pulled back, my dad was gone. He must have decided this was a girl thing. He always got uncomfortable when Mom or I started crying.

"I don't want to talk about it tonight," I said. "I just want to go to bed."

Mom looked as if she were going to insist, but then she pulled me close again and squeezed me tight. "Of course. We can talk about it in the morning."

I went upstairs and got ready for bed. I took comfort in the routine, grateful for something to distract me from the memory of Josh crashing into that tree.

But when I crawled into bed, I was too wired to sleep and there was nothing left to distract me. Unwanted images from our date flooded my mind, washing out all other thoughts.

Had there ever been a worse first kiss in the entire history of dating? It was like the Hindenburg of first kisses. How could a kiss that had felt so... glorious end up with Josh smashing into a tree? That had to have been a dating first.

But the power - that was the real issue. The kiss would have been fine if I hadn't started glowing like a nuclear meltdown survivor. How was that even possible? I wasn't strong enough to hurl Josh into a tree with a simple push, but I somehow did. My brain seemed caught in an endless loop as it struggled to reconcile what I experienced with what I believed to be possible.

After several excruciating hours, my brain reached its limit, exhaustion overcame me, and I fell into a dreamless sleep.

***

The next morning was Saturday, so I was able to sleep in – sort of. No one woke me up, but I could only stay asleep for so long. Once I woke up enough to remember what had happened there was no going back to sleep.

I got up, stretched, and went to the bathroom. When I came out, my mom stood there waiting for me. She looked tired and worried. Now that I thought about it, she probably hadn't slept very well either, knowing that something had upset me like that.

She gave me a hug. "Are you ready to talk about it yet?"

I hugged her back trying to think of an answer. I couldn't tell her the full story. I hardly believed it, and I had been there. Right now, the entire thing felt more like a dream than something that actually happened.

I decided to go with the truth, but vague. "There's nothing really to talk about," I said. "Things just didn't work out between Josh and me. I don't think we'll be going out any more."

"Why not? What happened?"

I shrugged. "It's hard to explain because I don't know. That was why I was so upset. Nothing that happened last night made any sense." Boy was that the honest truth.

Mom furrowed her brow. "Well, what did he say?"

Ok, the honest-but-vague approach wasn't working. Mom wouldn't be satisfied unless there was some concrete detail to analyze. She had that determined look in her eye, like a pitbull with a piece of meat. She wasn't going to let go until she was done.

"I don't want to relive last night," I said. Still being honest. "He didn't give me an explanation, but I think he wanted to see someone else." Anyone else, was probably more accurate, but I needed to end this conversation.

Mom hugged me again. She pulled back and looked me in the eyes. "I'm so sorry. Do we need ice cream and a movie tonight?"

If there was ever a situation that called for ice cream therapy, this was it, but just the thought of too-sweet ice cream made me feel queasy.

"I'll pass on the ice cream, but a movie sounds great."

Mom shook her head. "You still can't eat ice cream? That's just awful. What about popcorn?"

"Popcorn I can do," I said.

"Good. I'll go warn your father."

I took a long shower, got dressed, and was just starting to do my hair when someone knocked at my bedroom door.

"It's Dad."

I took in a deep breath. What could Dad want? Did he want to talk already? I knew he would want to find out what happened, but I figured I had a few days before he would get involved. Then I had a horrible thought. What if he had already talked with Josh? I wouldn't put it past my dad to call him, or even worse, confront him in person to find out what had happened.

"Come in," I said.

Dad opened the door and walked in holding my purse by the strap. Why was he holding my purse? I had left it in Josh's car when we started walking along the trail. That meant...

"Dad, you didn't—"

He held up a hand. "I found this on the front porch this morning when I got the paper. I admit to being curious as to why your purse was left out on the porch, but that seems like a question for another day."

I reached for my purse, but Dad opened his arms for a hug instead. How could I resist my big teddy bear of a dad? I wrapped my arms around him and held on tight.

He bent down and kissed the top of my head. "I love you, Madison," he said. He lifted my chin so I looked him in the eyes. "And I always will, no matter what. Understand?"

I squeezed him again. "Yes, Dad. I love you too." Despite my mood and everything that had happened, I couldn't help but grin.

"Good." He smiled and handed me my purse. "I thought you might want this back." He left the room and closed the door behind him.

I sat on the bed and stared at my purse. I was glad to have it back, but the fact that Josh had left it on the porch instead of calling me or even knocking on the door was disturbing and only confirmed my fears that he would never speak to me again.

Opening the purse, I looked through it to see if everything was intact. The contents appeared to be undisturbed, which was a bit of a letdown. For a moment, I hoped that there would be a letter from Josh asking me to meet him at some prearranged rendezvous point where he would tell me it had all been a big misunderstanding and that he really loved me.

I really needed to stop watching movies.

I checked my cell phone and saw five voicemails and seventy four text messages. None of them were from Josh. Most of the texts were from Amy wanting to know if I was nervous about the date, how the date was going, and how the date went. The final texts had a more concerned tone, wondering where I was and why I hadn't responded.

I sent her a short text telling her that the date didn't go well, but that I would talk to her about it at school. I really didn't want to discuss it anymore, or even think about Josh for the rest of the day - as if that were possible.

No sooner had I set the phone down, than it buzzed from an incoming text message. I picked up the phone, hoping it was from Josh, but it was just Amy begging for details. I tossed the phone on my bed and left the room.

The rest of the weekend dragged by excruciatingly, painfully, mind-numbingly slow. If this weekend had been in a race against a little old lady with a walker, it would have been lapped. Twice. And everyone would have already gone home before it crossed the finish line.

It wasn't all bad. Mom and I did have our movie night, but to be honest I did it more for her than me. I could tell Mom was really worried about me and watching the movie together made her feel like she was helping me. Fortunately, she was in comforting mode, rather than her previous Spanish Inquisition mode, and she didn't ask me any questions.

I didn't hear from Josh the entire weekend. Not a phone call, an email, or even a text message. Nothing. Didn't he need to at least officially break up with me or something? I suppose him screaming at me to keep away could be interpreted that way, but I didn't count it because what had happened simply couldn't have happened, and so it must not have happened.

Or something like that.

***

Amy was waiting at my locker on Monday. She gave me a hug as soon as she saw me. "I'm so sorry," she said.

With the entire weekend to recover, I had regained some of my composure. I managed an attempt at a smile. "He's just a boy, right?"

Amy was quick to jump onto that bandwagon. "That's right. An emotionally stunted little boy who clearly is incapable of a meaningful relationship. In twenty years, after a series of failed relationships, he'll find himself alone and so miserable that he'll finally enter therapy and realize that breaking up with you was the beginning of his life of misery." She paused, and when she saw my bemused expression added, "And he's a jerk."

Sometimes listening to Amy felt like being on a day-time talk show. She was like a forty-five-year-old divorcee in a sixteen-year-old body. But I loved the fact that I could always count on her being on my side.

"No, he's not a jerk," I said. I couldn't help it. I still really liked him. It was my fault everything went wrong. He had wanted to kiss me. Could I blame him for not wanting to see me after I threw him against a tree and nearly killed him?

From the way Amy was bouncing on the balls of her toes, I could tell that she was dying to know what had happened. I could also tell that her self-control wouldn't last much longer. If I gave her a few details now, I could possibly prevent a barrage of incoming questions.

But what could I say? Well, Amy, after I began glowing and threw him against a tree, Josh got scared and told me he never wanted to see me again. Oh, and I ran faster than humanly possible and jumped fifty feet over a car. Do you think he was overreacting?

Yeah, that wouldn't work so well.

"Well, we talked and agreed that we should see other people," I said. That was sort of true.

I opened my locker and hung up my backpack. I took out my Physics book, closed the locker, and leaned against it.

Amy's bouncing had gotten faster. "Did he say why?" she asked.

I nodded slowly. "It just wasn't working out between us," I said. "We were too different." He was a normal human being, and I was some sort of dangerous freak. It didn't make for a compatible relationship.

Despite the fact that I had been emotionally preparing for this all weekend, a few tears began to roll down my cheeks.

Amy's bouncing stopped, and she looked horrified. "Oh, Madison, I'm so sorry. I shouldn't have been asking you about this."

I wiped the tears from my eyes, trying to keep my makeup intact. Given my luck lately, I probably looked like a deranged raccoon. "No, really. It's ok," I said. All right, that was a complete lie, but if Amy started crying I really would lose it, and I didn't want to start today off by crying in the bathroom.

Once I had my tears under control, I gave Amy a smile. "See, I'm fine. Perfectly fine."

She tilted her head and gave me a look that clearly said she didn't believe a word I said. However, she did stop asking about Josh, for which I was grateful.

Amy and I talked for a few minutes, and she filled me in on what was happening around school – I had been a bit preoccupied with Josh and hadn't been paying much attention. There was a big football game next Friday against our arch rival Riverview High; Ginger Johnson, the varsity cheerleader captain, had broken up with her college boyfriend; and two seniors had been suspended for vandalism.

We were just about to head to class when I saw the top of Josh's head over the crowd in the hallway. He hadn't yet seen me, and I caught my breath as he came closer. I grabbed Amy's arm and squeezed.

"What — oooh," she said as she first reacted to my squeeze and then saw Josh. "Do you want support or privacy?"

"Don't go," I said, almost begging. I didn't want to face Josh by myself. Already I could feel the tears welling up.

Amy put her arm around me. "Don't worry. I'm here for you."

As Josh approached, I saw his demeanor had changed. Usually he was very outgoing and greeted everyone as he walked through the halls with high fives, pats, and other rather complicated man-rituals that seemed to be different for each one of his friends. For the girls, he always flashed that beautiful, slightly crooked smile that made hearts melt.

Today, however, he walked by himself, head down, and unsmiling. He completely ignored everyone, despite several attempts to get his attention. By simply doing nothing, he caused quite a stir, and I could see the confused looks and tiny knots of conversation he left in his wake.

When he finally got close enough that I could get a good look at him, my heart dropped. He had a pronounced limp favoring his right leg, and on his left wrist and forearm he wore a full cast. I immediately flashed back to the moment I had gripped his hand in fear and heard the crunch. I had done this to him.

My first instinct was to rush toward him and see if everything was all right. I wanted to throw my arms around him, beg his forgiveness, and promise him that it would never happen again. But that look on his face was all I needed to know that it would never be all right between us again.

As he walked by, Josh looked up and met my gaze. His dull, glazed look evaporated and was replaced by one of... sadness? Concern? I couldn't tell what it was.

Our eye contact lasted no more than a few seconds before he turned away and continued limping down the hall, refusing to even acknowledge me. When he reached the boy's restroom, he looked back with one last glance, pushed his way in, and disappeared.

"Ok, Madison," Amy said. "What's going on?"

"Huh?" I was still distracted by Josh pulling a Houdini into the bathroom.

"You tell me that Josh breaks up with you, and then he comes into school looking like he's been hit by a truck. What did you do, order a mob hit on him?" She was smiling, clearly thinking it was a joke, but I couldn't bring myself to laugh.

"I... I'm not sure what happened," I said. I had a hard time concentrating. I leaned against my locker, hitting the back of my head against the door in frustration.

There wasn't much time before the bell rang, so Amy and I waded through the flow of humanity to Physics class. Not that I remembered much about that class. I spent most of the time alternating between horror at what I had done to Josh and fear about who I might hurt next.

I walked through my daily motions in a daze. Classes that had seemed so important to me only a few days ago now felt hollow and empty. How could I care about Math and History when I was some sort of time bomb, ticking away the seconds until I exploded again? It might not be today or tomorrow, but I felt certain it would happen again. I could sense the power inside me, contained for now, but waiting to come out again.

When lunch came, I sat at a table by myself. Amy was in a different lunch period, and I didn't want to sit with my newly acquired friends. They had only befriended me because of Josh, and my relationships with them felt superficial and fragile. They were nice enough, but I always felt as if I were walking on eggshells with them. Besides, sitting near Josh didn't seem like such a good idea right now.

I abandoned all pretense of eating when Josh walked in. He bought his lunch and sat down in his usual spot at his table. Our table. At least, it had been, but I highly doubted it would ever be our table again.

From across the cafeteria I could see the interrogation start as soon as he sat down. Megan Richardson and Selma Torres both looked back at me before leaning forward and speaking to Josh. When he answered, the entire table stopped talking to listen.

What was he telling them? That I was some sort of freak who almost killed him? Or was he going to be a jerk and claim he had gotten what he wanted from me and kicked me to the curb? Isn't that what boys did when they broke up with girls? Whatever he said, it caused Mason Cross and Taylor Simpson to turn and gape at me in disbelief.

My body quivered, my heart raced, and my senses sharpened. I gripped the edges of the table, afraid that I was going to start glowing and destroy the cafeteria. My hearing had sharpened to the point that I could hear the conversation at Josh's table as if I were standing next to it.

Mason shook his head. "Seriously? She broke up with you?"

Josh nodded slowly. "She said I was a great guy, but I couldn't meet her emotional needs."

"What emotional needs?" Taylor asked.

"You know," Josh said. "Um, to be understood, to focus on the relationship. That kind of stuff."

"It was only your third date and she was already talking about the relationship?" said Mason. "There's just something wrong with that."

"That's because guys have the emotional depth of a puddle on the sidewalk," said Megan. She grinned at Selma who folded her arms and nodded in agreement.

I couldn't believe what I was hearing. Why was he telling them that I broke up with him? I didn't want to break up. There was nothing I wanted less than that. Had he just assumed that I wouldn't want to go out with him again? Had I completely misread the situation? Maybe there was still a chance of getting back together.

Hope soaring inside me, I waited until Josh finished eating and got up from the lunch table. I dumped my trash and walked up behind to tap him on the shoulder. "Can we talk?" I asked.

Josh's eyes widened. He looked around as if he was nervous about who might see us talking. He gently grabbed my arm and pulled me out of the cafeteria and down the hall until we found a relatively secluded spot by the janitor's closet.

"What?" he asked.

I took a deep breath. "I heard you talking in the cafeteria," I said.

He raised his eyebrows. "From across the room?"

Ah, so he had been watching me. I shrugged. "That's not important. I just wanted to tell you that I don't want to break up. I don't understand what happened on Friday, but it scared me, and I feel afraid and alone. I need you now more than ever." I leaned in and wrapped my arms around him.

Josh didn't hug me back. After a moment I pulled away, feeling awkward. Josh looked at his feet and didn't say anything right away. "Madison, I know you don't want to break up, and neither do I, but we can't be together."

"Why not?" I asked.

Josh sighed and looked up at me with those beautiful, deep brown eyes. "You're everything I ever wanted in a girl," he said. "You're smart, beautiful, and funny." Oh, those words felt wonderful out of context. Why couldn't he just stop there before the big BUT that was clearly on its way?

"But Friday night changed everything." He lifted his arm and held up the cast. "How can we be together when in the back of my mind I'll always be wondering if something like this is going happen again?"

"Josh, I-"

"What if next time we're out in public and you end up hurting a bunch of people? Or we're at my house and you accidently break my little sister's neck?"

"I would never-"

"Never? Can you really promise me that?"

I tried to say it wouldn't happen again, but I couldn't get the words out. They would have been lies because deep down, I knew this wasn't over.

When I didn't answer, Josh lowered his arm. "That's what I thought." He sighed and used his good hand to push his hair out of his face. "I don't know what happened on Friday, and I really don't want to know. I just know I don't want to be around you when it happens again."

Crash. Burn. As Josh turned to walk away, I still had one last question.

"Why are you telling everyone that I broke up with you?"

Josh stopped, but didn't turn around. "I just figured that it might be easier for you if everyone thought you had broken up with me."

He looked back and shrugged. "I still care about you, Madison. I just can't be with you."

I turned away, not wanting to watch him leave, not wanting him to see the tears that were sure to come. Why did he have to be so – good? He wanted to make it easier on me? He should have told everyone he had gotten what he wanted from me and dumped me. Then I could have hated him. Instead his noble gesture made me care about him more than ever.

That was pain.

CHAPTER 5

FOOTBALL AND FOREST FREAKS

The next two weeks flew by in a haze of despair. For the first few days, well-intentioned friends bombarded me with a barrage of questions that were the emotional equivalent of removing my own appendix without anesthesia. Everyone assumed that since I was the one who broke up with Josh that I was fine, and it was OK to grill me for details.

I was not fine.

My responses were vague and unsatisfying, usually resulting in more questions that I didn't know how to answer. How could I explain why I supposedly broke up with Josh when all I wanted was to be with him, to feel his comforting arms around me holding me tight?

Amy wanted to know why I told her that Josh had broken up with me when he was telling everyone that I had broken up with him. I couldn't think of a good reason, so I told her it was complicated and that I didn't really understand either. I think she suspected that my revised story wasn't the entire truth, but she didn't press me on it.

After about a week the breakup became old news and curiosity began to die down. It remained fresh and painful in my mind, though. Maintaining a normal social façade was too difficult, and I became socially withdrawn. I ate alone in the cafeteria, seated at a table as far away from Josh as possible.

Amy, however, was determined to not let me ostracize myself. She made a concerted effort to force me into as many social situations as possible.

On Wednesday, when she invited me to go to the football game that weekend, I automatically declined. I didn't feel like being with friends - my heart hurt in ways I had never known possible. My emotions were too saturated, and there was no room or desire for fun. But stubborn, well-meaning Amy wouldn't take no for an answer. She used every trick in the book, including massive doses of guilt.

She cornered me at my locker Friday morning. "Please, I need you there with me," she said. "Cory Jones is going to be there, and he is this close to asking me out." She held up her finger and thumb practically touching. "If it's just you and me, we can casually sit close to him and then work our way into doing something with him and his friends after the game."

I sighed. The football game was the last place I wanted to go. Just the thought of these schemes and plans made me tired. Besides, Josh would likely be there, and the last thing I needed was to be around him right now. What if he came with another girl? I didn't think I could handle seeing that. "Amy, I –"

"Please," she said. She dropped down to her knees in the middle of the hall and actually begged. "This is my chance to get close to him without scaring him off. Besides," she had a mischievous gleam in her eye, "Ryan Jacobs will be with him."

"Stop that," I said, and I pulled her to her feet, trying not to laugh. "People are staring." That was true. Her little begging routine had drawn some very odd looks.

Who was this girl? She sure didn't seem like the Amy I had grown up with. Somehow, while I was going through my own changes this summer, she had turned into the Machiavelli of dating. This plan had layers upon layers of conniving.

Last year, I had had intermittent crushes on Ryan Jacobs during the times I had gotten tired of waiting for Josh. Using him as incentive meant Amy was going to play dirty and wouldn't quit until I gave in.

She batted her eyes in a parody of innocence. "Pretty please? I'll be your best friend."

I couldn't resist. I wasn't interested in Ryan Jacobs any more, but if I was ever going to get over Josh, I did need to get out of the house and do something. Amy's intentions were pure – mostly - even if she was going to use me to get closer to Cory. I pulled out my books and closed my locker. "Fine," I said.

Amy squealed and gave me a huge hug. "Thank you, thank you, thank you!" she said. "You won't regret this! Friday will be a night to remember!"

***

Friday night I borrowed my mom's car and picked up Amy before the game. She had gone all out with full make-up and perfectly styled hair. She wore her tan skirt - which I knew was the shortest one she owned - and a tight blouse that didn't skimp on the cleavage.

I, on the other hand, had pulled back my hair in a ponytail and worn jeans and my black sweatshirt with Woodbridge High written on it in bright orange letters.

Amy took her time assessing my appearance as she climbed in and set a canvas bag down at her feet. She didn't try to hide her disapproval.

"You look very, uh... school spirited," she said.

I glared at her. "It's a football game. And besides, you look cold." There were a few other adjectives I wanted to use, but I held my tongue.

She grinned at me. "I know. Do you think Cory will let me borrow his jacket?"

I rolled my eyes and pulled out of the driveway. Amy never did anything half-way. "What if he doesn't have a jacket?" I asked.

Amy put a hand on her chest and gave me a wounded look. "Do you think I'm an amateur?" She held up the bag at her feet. "A stadium blanket. If he's not wearing a jacket, I invite him to join me under my blanket. It's warm enough to be inviting, and small enough to require some cuddling. I've planned for all the contingencies."

I couldn't help but laugh. She was like an unstoppable force of nature. Poor Cory didn't stand a chance.

Even though we arrived a half hour before kickoff, the parking lot at school was almost completely full, and we had to park on the opposite side by the woods. I didn't like parking there, especially at night. The trees were so thick that anything could be hiding in there and you would never see it until it was too late.

Shortly after I was born, a girl had been abducted from this same parking lot and taken into the woods. They found her body the next day, but they had to check the dental records to confirm it was her. The mystery had never been solved, but even sixteen years later there were still rumors and stories about things that happened there. It was now affectionately known to the students of Woodbridge High as the "dead woods."

Amy left her blanket in the car, since it was the backup plan, and we crossed the parking lot to the ticket line. We bought our tickets and walked into the stadium.

The home stands were a sea of black and orange, our unfortunate school colors. This was our big rivalry game and everyone was there. The entire crowd, myself included, looked like Halloween had thrown up on them. Amy scowled when she saw how everyone was dressed. Her short skirt and tight blouse definitely stood out.

Never one to give up easily, Amy began scanning the crowd, looking for Cory and his friends. We found them in the right side of the bleachers. Sure enough, Cory was wearing a leather jacket. Amy dragged me up the stairs to sit a few seats away from them and one row back.

"Now we just need to wait for Cory to come to us," Amy said with confidence. We sat there for a few minutes, but Cory didn't even notice us. He and his friends were too busy talking and laughing to pay attention to anything else.

I looked at Amy and shrugged, but she didn't seem worried.

"Patience," she said. "We can't make it too obvious or we'll scare him away."

While Amy was waited for Cory to take the bait and fall into her trap, I scanned through the crowd. I couldn't help it; I'm a die-hard people watcher.

At some point while I was watching Lizzy Cole flirt with Gary Crean, Cory must have noticed Amy. By the time I looked back over, he had struck up a conversation with her. Amy winked at me and motioned to Ryan Jacobs who was sitting on the other side of Cory talking to another friend.

I shook my head vigorously. I was not at all interested in pursuing another guy.

Amy gave me another wink and then began shivering and wrapped her arms around herself. "It's so cold," she said. "I should have worn a jacket."

Like a performing animal executing what it has been trained to do, Cory removed his coat and placed it over Amy's shoulders. He sat down next to her, and she snuggled in, scooting closer to him. "Thanks, Cory," she said, flashing him a wide smile when he put his arm around her shoulder – to keep her warm, of course.

The game started and our team won the toss. By the end of the first quarter we were up 13 – 0. Comfortably encircled in Cory's arms, Amy appeared satisfied that she and Cory were together and began pulling me into the conversation, preparing to get us invited to hang out with them after the game.

I resisted her efforts and concentrated on the game. I actually liked football, and watched quite a bit of it with my dad. While I wasn't an expert, I knew enough to hold my own in a conversation with most guys.

Right before half time, Amy leaned over to me. "Why don't you go get the blanket?" she asked.

"Why do you want the blanket?" I asked. She didn't need it since she was already wearing Cory's jacket and wrapped in his arms.

"I think Ryan might be getting a little cold," she said.

A complete lie. Ryan was wearing a warm jacket and looked perfectly comfortable. I narrowed my eyes. "He's fine."

Amy gave me an exasperated sigh. "Do you want to move past Josh, or remain a self-imposed social pariah?"

"I'll move past him," I said. "I'm just not ready."

"Look, a frozen turkey is never ready unless you pull it out of the freezer," said Amy.

"Are we talking relationships or cooking?" I asked.

Amy ignored me and pressed on with her bizarre metaphor. "And you never will be ready if you don't get out of the freezer, let go, and have some fun... you big turkey." Amy reached over and gave my hand a squeeze. "You can do this." She looked over at Ryan.

"Besides, it's not like he's hard to look at. Just trust me; tonight is the night. You might never get this opportunity again."

With a groan I stood up and clomped down the bleachers. How could I tell her that I didn't want to be in a relationship because I was dangerous? What if every time I kissed a boy I ended up hurting him? I was a disaster waiting to happen.

Getting my hand stamped at the gate, I trekked out to the car. It made me a bit nervous to be out there by the woods alone, but I didn't want to face Amy's wrath if I came back without the blanket. Besides, there was a good chance I was more dangerous than anything out there.

I grabbed the blanket and began the long journey back to the stadium. How was I going to get out of this situation? I could simply turn around, get in the car, and leave. I was pretty confident Cory would make sure Amy was well taken care of. I could feign early curfew and go home right after the game. Except Amy would see right through that.

I was almost back to the stadium when I turned the corner near the concession stand and walked into my worst nightmare.

Ginger Johnson, looking excessively perky in her black and orange cheerleader outfit, stood in front of Josh, her head raised and eyes closed as he leaned forward and gently kissed her.

I stared, too stunned to move. Ginger Johnson was kissing Josh.

My Josh. My kiss.

My cheeks flushed and my heart began a sort of arrhythmic jazz beat. My senses sharpened, and I saw the kiss in perfect detail. I heard the soft sound of their lips pressing together and even smelled Ginger's perfume.

Pressure mounted inside me, and I knew it had to come out. I turned around and ran.

Within three steps my body began to glow and my speed increased dramatically. I dashed into the parking lot, moving so fast the cars I passed were little more than brightly colored blurs.

I was desperate to get away before anyone saw me, but as I scanned my options, there was only one place where I could go and hide: The dead woods.

Within seconds I was running through the forest, weaving between the trees. It should have been difficult to avoid the trees and other obstacles while running so fast, but my reflexes were so heightened that it seemed effortless.

The darkness of the forest was deep and black, but with my enhanced vision I could see everything in perfect detail. A thousand, a hundred thousand sounds vied for my attention. The smell of sodden wood and decomposing leaves pricked my senses, as did the scents of animals and running water.

I leaped over a stream as I approached, hardly even breaking my stride to do so. How far had I come? A mile? Two miles? I had been running for only a few minutes, but given the speed I was traveling, I was quickly moving far away from the school, and Amy, and my car.

When I reached a large clearing, I forced myself to stop. I dropped to my knees, not from exhaustion – I felt fine physically – but from despair and hopelessness.

What was wrong with me? How could I be doing this? - Did Josh really kiss Ginger? - I thrust one of my glowing hands into the ground. My hand slid through the earth like it was Jell-o, and my arm sunk in up to my elbow. I made a fist and the dirt oozed through my fingers. I pulled my arm out, leaving a deep hole.

I watched in amazement as the dirt fell away from my arm, unable to stick to me. – Was he over me that quickly? - My arm looked bright and pure.

I stood up and walked toward a tree with a trunk too wide to put my arms around. – Stupid boys. - I pulled my arm back and punched the trunk.

The results were spectacular.

Even though I had only used a fraction of my strength, the trunk splintered, exploding into shards. – Why did I have to see them kiss? - My fist smashed through the tree and it toppled backwards with a loud groan, severed where I had punched it.

I stared at my fist, opening and closing my hand. It was hard to believe that it belonged to me. How could I be strong enough to destroy a tree? Why didn't my fist hurt? I was frightened, but in the back of my mind a small voice wondered what else was I capable of?

As I looked at the remains of the tree, a strange feeling came to my attention. Only it wasn't really a "feeling". It was a sensation I had never experienced before. It began gradually, but soon became so strong there was no way to ignore it.

"Darkness" didn't accurately describe it, because it wasn't an absence of light, but that was the only way I could make sense of it.

It was as if I had developed some other sensory organ, and I didn't have the vocabulary to match.

From out of the trees five figures emerged. They looked vaguely human, but four of them were so thin as to be almost skeletal. They were covered with greenish brown skin that was dry and cracked, like monstrous scabs. The fifth one had an enormous abdomen, making it look like a snake that had recently fed.

Each of the creatures had an oversized, elongated head attached to a thin neck. Their gigantic mouths were filled with sharp teeth that dripped a thick yellowish fluid. The eyes on the creatures were large and sunken, and looked like glowing red coals shining in the dark.

The monsters spread out and surrounded me, low hisses and growls escaping them. Their too-thin arms ended in oversized hands that were three times as large as a human's. The fingers ended in long curved claws and had so many joints that they appeared to be rolling and unrolling.

My first instinct was to scream and run away, but it was overshadowed by a curious anger. Something about these creatures felt wrong - they had no right to exist. Their very presence offended me.

One of the creatures leapt at me, claws extended toward my face. I ducked and grabbed its neck as it sailed over me, redirecting its momentum into the hard earth and shattering its skull. Nasty black goo pooled on the ground, reeking of rot and death. The creature kicked a few times in convulsions and then lay still.

The hissing from the other four creatures grew louder. They

moved in closer, their arms outstretched, as if trying to encircle me and not let me escape. As soon as one of them came within reach, I pulled back and punched it in the chest. The results were surprisingly similar to punching the tree. My fist shattered its ribcage and sent what remained of the creature flying backwards.

From behind, the third creature wrapped its arms around my chest, squeezing me so hard that I couldn't breathe. Considering how skinny these things were, they were surprisingly strong. The creature lifted me off the ground and I flailed about, trying to escape.

While I was held helpless, a fourth creature – the fat one – slowly approached, claws extended, and yellow fluid dripping off its teeth.

Anger exploded at the thought of these creatures touching me. The glow that surrounded me grew brighter and I reached upward with my arms until I felt the creature's head. Grasping it with two hands, I pulled with all my strength. With surprising ease, the creature's head pulled free of its neck. As I brought my arms forward, I lost my grip on the head and it flew forward, directly toward the oncoming creature.

The creature dodged sideways, avoiding the flying head, which smashed on the ground. The arms around me loosened and I flung my arms wide, freeing myself from the now headless corpse.

When I turned around to find the remaining creatures, they were gone. I was left alone in the clearing with the reeking remains of the three I had killed.

I spun around several times, but I saw nothing, and the strange sensation I had before they attacked was gone.

I looked down at my glowing body and saw that it was covered with bits of bone, blood, and other fluids too repulsive to think about.

But like the dirt when I'd punched a hole in the ground, this filth didn't stick to me either. The fluids slid off without a trace, and the bits of bone disintegrated with a series of small pops until I was completely clean.

I walked over to where I had smashed the first creature into the ground. Instead of a corpse, I found a pool of black ooze, more disgusting than anything I could have imagined. The stench was like rotten cheese mixed with death... and feet.

What were these things? Monsters? Aliens? I had never heard of creatures like these.

The creatures were disturbing enough. Far more disturbing was the fact that I seemed to be connected to these creatures. My body instinctively knew how to fight them. It recognized them and acted to defend itself. I could have never destroyed those creatures so quickly on my own, not even with super speed and strength.

What had I gotten into? And how had I gotten into it?

My body began to relax. My senses dulled and the glow surrounding me subsided. I realized that I was alone in the dead woods and had no idea how many miles I needed to travel to get back to the school.

Even if I knew which direction to go, it would take me at least an hour to hike back. How was I going to explain this to Amy?

I looked around the clearing, trying to figure out which way I had come. I had just about figured it out when I once again sensed something.

This time the feeling was different. It still defied description, but that sense of darkness was absent.

Two glowing figures zipped into the clearing and came to an abrupt stop. They halted so suddenly didn't seem to have a chance to slow down. They had gone from speeding blurs to complete stillness in an instant. So much for Newton's laws of motion and that whole inertia thing.

I looked at the faces of the two figures and my breath caught. It was difficult to make out their features with the bright glow that surrounded them, but the fragmented glimpses looked beautiful, like images of Greek gods come to life.

"Where did he go?" the one on the right asked.

I opened my mouth, but my brain was too jumbled to get any words out. Who were these men? They were glowing, so did that mean they were like me? And what did they mean "he"? Did those things I fought even have a gender? It figured that something that gross would have to be male.

Unable to speak, I pointed towards the far side of the clearing where my back had been when the creatures vanished. They had to have escaped that way.

In a flash the two glowing forms were gone, leaving a bright afterimage on my retinas. Again, ignoring of those so-called laws of motion.

I watched their bright forms fade into the forest - along with any chance I might have to find out what was going on.

Realizing that I may have lost my only opportunity to discover the truth, I felt my heart begin to race. The now-familiar sense of power welled within me, waiting to be released. I took two steps and the world burst into color as I began to glow.

It was a simple thing to see the trail they had followed. Broken twigs and bent leaves that I would have never spotted before stood out like shining beacons to my hypersensitive eyes.

The trail twisted and turned, winding through the woods for what seemed only a few seconds, but had to be a couple of miles. It seemed to be heading in the general direction of the school, which, while convenient for me, was a horrible thought. I couldn't imagine the destruction those creatures could cause if they entered a stadium packed with helpless students.

My ears heard growls and the crashes from up ahead, and I slowed down so as not to drop in uninvited on a party I wasn't sure I wanted to attend.

I crouched behind a tree and looked forward. The two glowing figures had caught up with the uglies and were wreaking havoc. The skinny creature leaped toward one of the men. To my surprise (and admittedly a bit of pride) he used the same maneuver I had. He ducked down, grabbed the creature's neck, and used its own momentum to smash it into the ground, breaking open its head and spraying monster nastiness all over. Although, I was pretty sure I hadn't made that big of a mess when I had done it.

The remaining creature backed away slowly. It was much bigger around than the others and appeared to be less willing, or able, to fight. Was it pregnant? Was it full of little baby monsters waiting to come out like thousands of newly-hatched spiders? The thought made me shiver. Spiders made my skin crawl, but the image of a bunch of baby whatever-those-things-were was truly frightening.

The glowing men spread out on either side of the creature, appearing much more cautious than they had been with the other one.

In a flash they attacked, one of them grabbing the creature's legs, the other ramming a fist through its head, splattering monster brains for at least fifty feet. Ok, I had definitely made less mess when I had fought them.

What happened next was so repulsive that I almost threw up. They thrust their hands inside the creature's chest and pulled in opposite directions. With a series of pops and cracks, the monster's ribcage pulled apart, revealing a woman trapped inside. She had light, freckled skin and red hair matted down with a layer of clear jelly-slime that encompassed her. They ripped apart the rest of the creature and pulled her out.

She seemed unconscious, her body completely motionless. After a few seconds she took in a huge gasping breath, and then lay still, breathing normally, but still not conscious. One of the men reached down and gently, almost tenderly, cradled her in his arms.

Leaving the creatures to dissolve into goo, they began running again. I followed, but kept my distance. I wasn't ready to actually be a part of this yet. Unfortunately, I had a feeling that I already was.

They reached the edge of the woods at the school parking lot where a black Range Rover with tinted windows was illegally parked. They stopped at the edge and waited for a moment. Slowly, (but much faster than I had ever done it) the glow surrounding them disappeared, and they stepped out of the woods.

I moved as close to the edge of the woods as I dared given that my glowing personality was shining through at the moment. My enhanced vision gave me an excellent view.

Now that the glow had faded, I could see what those men actually looked like. Only they weren't men at all. They appeared to be roughly high-school aged. I sometimes had a hard time judging these things, but they certainly didn't look old.

One of them had blond, spiky hair and green eyes. He had high cheekbones and a strong jaw line. He didn't look as angelic as he had while glowing, but he was gorgeous by anyone's standard. There was something about his eyes and the way he held himself that gave the impression of a very mischievous boy trying hard to be good.

The other one had dark, longish hair and the bluest eyes I had ever seen – but maybe that was just an effect of my enhanced vision. His nose was slightly crooked, as if it had been broken at least once, and his features didn't quite have the flawless look of the blonde one, but there was something about him that was very striking.

The dark haired one opened the rear door of the Rover and pulled out a blanket and placed it on the back seat. The blond guy gently placed the woman on top of the blanket, and tucked it in around her. He slid into the seat next to her, and the dark haired one climbed into the driver's seat. With a roar, the engine started and the Range Rover sped out of the school parking lot.

CHAPTER 6

A VERY VISUAL CONNECTION

By the time I made it back to the stadium the game was almost over, and Woodbridge was ahead by forty nine points. It wasn't until I sat down next to Amy that I realized I didn't know where the blanket was. I had lost it at some point during my run through the forest.

Amy gave me a look, half exasperated, half annoyed, until the expression on my face must have told her something was wrong.

She leaned in and gave Cory a squeeze before slipping out from under his arm. "Give me a sec," she said. "I'll be right back."

Grabbing my arm, Amy pulled me up and took me out of the bleachers to a semi-private spot by the drinking fountain.

"What's wrong?" she asked. The annoyance was gone and replaced by a look of concern.

Where did I start? So much was wrong that I couldn't possibly explain it all. I went with the only thing I could tell her.

"Josh kissed Ginger," I said, and I bit the inside of my cheek to keep myself from crying. I could still see it clearly in my mind. Even with everything else that had happened since, that one moment was etched into my mind forever. A mental tattoo with no possibility of removal.

Amy's eyes widened. For a half second she got that excited look on her face she always got at the prospect of new gossip, but then the implication of what I said sank in and it quickly faded.

"Are you sure?"

"Believe me, I wish I weren't," I said. I looked up, trying to keep the tears back.

As always, Amy was quick to jump to my defense. "What a jerk. You just barely broke up."

I was grateful to have her on my side, so I didn't remind her that she had been pushing me to do the exact same thing. Logically, it made sense. This was high school. The odds of any relationship lasting past graduation were about the same as being struck by lightning the same day you won the lottery.

After a few minutes of silence, Amy spoke again, a big grin plastered on her face. "So, I have good news. Cory and his friends are going out after the game and invited us to come along. Want to go?"

So, her diabolical scheme to ensnare Cory had worked. I may have changed physically over the summer, but that was nothing compared to how Amy had changed. What had happened to the shy girl who wanted to come to my house and watch sappy romance movies all weekend?

"Would you hate me if I didn't go?" I asked. "I don't think I'm up to it tonight."

Amy sighed, the excitement draining out of her. "No, that's fine. I understand. I'll tell Cory that we can do something next week."

"Just because I'm not going doesn't mean you can't," I said. "Based on the amount of cuddling I saw going on tonight, I am sure Cory would be willing to find some transportation for you."

"Are you sure?" Amy asked. "Not about the transportation – I mean, clearly that wouldn't be an issue – but about my going without you." She looked skeptical. "You're not just trying to be a martyr are you?"

I grabbed Amy by the shoulders and turned her so she was facing the entrance to the bleachers. "I have no plans on being killed for any causes tonight," I said. I considered explaining that I was actually being very selfish because the prospect of going out with Cory and his friends tonight was about as enticing as being bludgeoned with a blunt object, but I decided that might hurt her feelings.

"I don't know," she said.

"Go," I said, giving her a gentle nudge towards the bleachers. "I'll be fine. I just need some time alone. I'll see you Monday."

And that was enough to finally convince her. I watched her climb back up the bleachers, and then I walked out to my car.

I unlocked the door and stood there a moment, looking into the dead woods. They had seemed creepy before, but now they looked absolutely dangerous. I was standing on the boundary of a war zone. One step forward, and I would be in the line of fire from monsters and who knows what else.

Those boys.

They had glowed like I did. I was connected to them in some way, but how? They seemed to be able to control their glowing. Did that mean it was something that could be learned? And if so, would they be able to teach me?

At that thought my fantasies began to run wild. If I had my condition under control, then Josh and I could get back together again. He had told me that he cared for me, but was worried I was dangerous, right? That kiss between him and Ginger was probably just her trying to seduce him.

I pushed away the voice in my head that pointed out that he hadn't looked as if he were putting up much of a fight.

If only I had been able to follow them.

***

On Monday the school was abuzz with elation at blowing out our rival in football. The football players wore their orange letterman's jackets with black sleeves, strutting through the halls like jack-o-lanterns brought to life.

I hadn't seen Amy again all weekend. She had texted me to say that things had gone "spectacularly well" with Cory and that he was going to give her a ride to school.

She was waiting at my locker when I got there, a big grin on her face.

I really didn't want to hear how "spectacular" her night with Cory had been, but given the fact that she had stood by me and listened to me gush when I was going out with Josh, I figured I owed her the same.

"So," I said, forcing enthusiasm into my voice. "Tell me all about it!"

"It was so much fun," Amy said. "You should have been there. We all went to the Safehouse for dinner and Cory treated it like a real date and paid for my meal."

I did my best to look interested.

Amy continued. "Then we went to Cory's house and watched a movie and played pool. They have this huge game room with a giant TV and everything. During the movie we cuddled on the couch, and he held my hand." This last part was practically squealed.

"That's great!" I said. "But, weren't you holding hands at the game?"

"No, he had his arm around me, but that didn't really count because he could have just been doing that to be nice since it was so cold."

"So at his house—"

"—there was no need anymore. All signs of affection were purely voluntary."

For the next five minutes I got the in-excruciatingly-minute-detail version of her night with Cory, and how he had volunteered to take her to school. When she finally began to run out of steam, she got a mischievous gleam in her eye and said, "Oh, and Ryan asked about you, too."

Great, just what I wanted to hear. "And you said?"

"Well, I told him that since you and Josh had broken up that you were back on the open market." She shrugged and tried to look innocent.

Amy was saved from facing the full fury of my wrath by the timely arrival of Cory.

"Can I walk you to class?" he asked.

The look on Amy's face was pure bliss as she gave me a small wave and walked off with Cory.

I watched them leave with mixed emotions: relief that I wasn't going to have to deal with my own emotional issues while listening to her tell me how perfect everything was, and sadness because I could feel the beginnings of cracks in our friendship. For so long it had just been the two of us. Now that other people were in the picture, it felt as if things had changed and we would never go back to the way things were.

I closed my locker and headed to Physics class, so wrapped up in my musings about friendship that I didn't notice Josh and Ginger until they were only a few feet away.

Hands linked, they seemed to glide down the hall in slow motion, like something out of a movie montage. Ginger wore her cheerleader outfit in celebration of the big win, and Josh had on a tan sweater that brought out the color in his deep brown eyes. The only thing missing was romantic music and sappy gazes.

Once he noticed I was there, Josh avoided looking at me, his signature smile missing. Whether this was done out of sadness, politeness, or embarrassment, I couldn't tell. Ginger, however, glared as if challenging me. As they walked past, she turned her head to follow me, staring me down.

I ignored her and walked into Physics class, sliding into my seat. Aaron Parker was already there and appeared to have been waiting for me. He immediately struck up a conversation asking me about my weekend.

Given the high levels of suckiness I'd experienced over the past few days, this was a topic I wanted to avoid like a Spice Girls reunion tour. But since saying it sucked would only make him ask me about it, I decided to go with generic and boring.

"It was all right. How was yours?"

It didn't take much to get Aaron to talk about himself. He told me all about how he had skipped the Football game and gone to a frat party in Portland, which according to his description was filled with college students and beer.

"You should have been there, it was crazy."

I would have chosen other words to describe it. Moronic was pretty high on the list. Hanging out with a bunch of judgment impaired frat boys fell pretty low on my list of fun things to do. "Yeah, not really my thing," I told him.

"Aw, come on," he said. He leaned in close and lowered his voice, as if letting me in on a big secret. "There's another party this weekend. Why don't you come with me?"

He was asking me out – in a sort of pathetic, I'm-not-taking-the-hint kind of way. Aaron was a nice enough guy, but why would he ask me to go do something I had already told him I didn't enjoy? Clearly, he didn't want to go out with me, he just wanted someone to come with him to the party. There was a difference.

"Sorry, Aaron. I'm not into that kind of thing," I said.

He shrugged. "Sure, I understand." He pulled out his notebook and began leafing through the pages.

Relieved to have that conversation over, I began checking over my Physics homework. It was pretty basic stuff, so I wasn't too worried about it, but I needed something to do to break up the awkward silence.

I didn't get off as easily as I had thought. After a few minutes Aaron said in a very casual, off-hand way, "So, do you have any plans this weekend?"

This had officially become an awkward moment. I had zero interest in going out with anyone besides Josh right now, and even if I took Josh out of the equation, Aaron was too much of a partier for my tastes. His kind of fun and mine were worlds apart.

"Yeah, I do," I said. It was a complete lie. The sad truth was that I didn't have any plans for this weekend. No doubt Amy could wrangle me a double date with Ryan Jacobs – she'd been hinting about it for the past week - but I didn't want to go out with someone just because I didn't want to spend the weekend at home. I would have felt badly about lying to Aaron, but since it wasn't any of his business, I spared myself the guilt trip and simply held my breath, hoping that he didn't ask me what I was doing, because I hadn't thought that far ahead.

At that moment, all thoughts of Aaron Parker were driven out of my head as a new student walked through the door.

I recognized him instantly. Dark hair, slightly crooked nose, and those amazingly blue eyes. His face had been etched into my mind since I first saw him at the football game.

Only now he wasn't glowing or fighting monsters.

I sat up straighter, a thrill running through me. My senses sharpened and everything around me took on a crisper look.

The dark haired boy turned me as if startled. His piercing eyes met mine. With my enhanced senses it was more than a simple look. It was like peering into his soul. Surprise and hope drifted on the surface, but deeper down lay a hidden sadness and – He broke eye contact and swept his gaze across the room as if looking for something.

I slumped, suddenly drained, as if I had just sprinted a marathon.

What had happened? For a moment I had felt... drawn to him somehow. But watching him now, he didn't appear to have felt the same. In fact, he completely ignored me and continued to look around the classroom.

After a moment he walked to Mr. Shumway's desk and held out a piece of paper. "My name's Rhys Owen. I'm a new student."

His voice had an odd sort of lilt. It sounded as if he had just the slightest trace of an accent, but I couldn't place it.

Mr. Shumway glanced at the paper and directed Rhys to an empty desk two rows up and three rows left of mine. Rhys sat down and pulled a notebook out of his backpack.

I watched him fascinated, wondering if this was fate or simply an impossibly convenient coincidence of the deus ex machina variety. Sitting mere feet away from me was the possible answer to all my questions. If anyone could explain what was happening to me and how I could control it, it would be him.

But my fantasy of learning how to control my powers was stopped short as reality came crashing back. What did I know about this guy aside from the fact that he had the same sort of powers I did? Could I trust him? Was he a good guy? For all I knew he was some sort of homicidal super-villain.

I missed most of the class, lost in thought as I contemplated Rhys' arrival and thought through what felt like every possible permutation of next steps. In the back of my mind I was vaguely aware of Mr. Shumway talking about velocity and angles, but I was not prepared when he startled me out of my thoughts by asking me to solve the problem he had written up on the chalkboard.

Once again, my senses sharpened – did it have something to do with being startled? – and I took in the problem on the chalkboard, immediately knowing the answer without having to think about it.

"Thirty two meters per second," I said. I knew it was the right answer, but I had no idea how I knew it was right. It was a new type of problem that Mr. Shumway had just introduced today, and we both knew he had called on me because I hadn't been paying attention.

But somehow, I was able take in the problem, figure out the process for solving it, do the calculations, and come up with the correct answer without any conscious effort. It was like looking at a page of text and instantly understanding everything written there without reading the individual words.

Mr. Shumway raised his eyebrows. "Very impressive, Madison. Clearly you were paying attention. Now let me walk all of you through this and show you how she got that answer."

As Mr. Shumway began working through the problem and my clarity faded, I noticed Rhys turning his head to look at me. The expression on his face wasn't one I would have expected: confusion.

When he noticed me looking back at him, Rhys turned away and began scanning the other kids in the class one by one. No, that wasn't quite right. He looked at each of the boys for several minutes, but he completely skipped over the girls.

That was strange.

When class ended, Rhys took one last glance back at me and walked out the door. By the time I left the classroom, he was lost in the crowded hallway.

I made it through history and study hall in a bit of a daze. At lunch I sat in what was quickly becoming my own private table in the corner. I tried not to look at Josh when he came in, but despite my best intentions, my eyes found excuses to watch him completely independent of my control. I was just glad that Ginger wasn't in this lunch period. I didn't think I could handle having to watch the two of them together.

I ate slowly, trying to imagine nefarious ways to keep Josh and Ginger apart. Unfortunately my ideas tended more to the desperate and pathetic rather than clever and conniving. I needed Amy for anything truly devious.

I had given up scheming and was trying to find a way to keep from watching Josh when Rhys entered the cafeteria. He was probably the one thing that could take my attention from Josh for more than a few eye blinks.

Except for the other boy who followed him in.

The blond boy from the woods walked in right behind Rhys, a mischievous grin on his face. The two boys couldn't be more different. Whereas Rhys looked straight ahead and didn't seem to notice the people in the cafeteria watching them, the blond boy looked around soaking up the attention.

Rhys headed straight for an empty table and sat down, several steps ahead of the blond boy who had slowed down and looked at the other tables as he passed. He clearly had been hoping Rhys would sit with some of the others rather than choosing an empty table. After a moment he shrugged and sat down with Rhys.

I shifted positions at my table – one of the plusses of eating by yourself – to get a better view of the boys. They sat directly across from each other, neither of them talking. Rhys was concentrating on his food. The blond boy ate at a more leisurely pace while looking around the cafeteria. Like Rhys had in Physics, the blond boy appeared to be looking for something.

Or someone.

I couldn't help wondering who they were and why they were here. I could see from the reaction of the other students in the cafeteria – Megan Richardson couldn't keep her eyes off of Rhys and Selma

Torres was definitely eyeing the blond boy - that I wasn't the only one who wondered this, but I was pretty sure my interests were different from theirs. Sure they were both incredibly good looking, but what I wanted from them had nothing to do with their looks.

Lunch ended and I made it through Pre-calculus without event. In English I found Rhys was in my class. Once again he paid little attention to the teacher and spent the entire period studying each of the boys in turn.

Well, it looked like Megan was going to be rather disappointed since it appeared that Rhys didn't have much of an interest in girls.

After English I headed to the opposite side of the school for Gym class. Amy was already changing when I got there.

"Did you see the new guys?" she asked.

"Yeah, Rhys is in two of my classes," I said. "I don't know the blonde guy's name, but he and Rhys are both in my lunch."

Amy paused and looked at me with her eyebrow raised in mock surprise. "I'm impressed, Madison," she said. "Usually you're oblivious to the social workings of good ol' Woodbridge High."

I started changing. "Noticing two boys doesn't mean I've lost my obliviousness," I said. "It's hard not to notice new people here."

"Point taken," said Amy with mock severity. "I will not question your cluelessness again."

I waited for a minute, hoping that Amy would give me all the details about them, but she kept quiet as she finished dressing.

Finally, I couldn't contain my curiosity. If they had just been regular guys I wouldn't have cared, but I really needed to find out about these two.

"So, do you know the name of the blond boy?" I hoped my tone sounded off hand and casual.

"I knew it," said Amy. "You do care!"

I shrugged. "Care is such a strong word. More like mildly curious."

"All right," said Amy. "Here's what I know. Their names are Rhys Owen and Eric Douglass. They're brothers who just moved here from somewhere out of country - I didn't find out where. They were both adopted which is why they have different last names. Their father was in the military, so they've moved around a lot, but he just retired and moved here."

We walked out of the locker rooms and into the gym. We were still on our volleyball unit for another week, so our teacher, Mrs. Herst, had the four nets already set up.

Amy leaned over and whispered. "So, which one do you like?"

I shrugged. "Neither."

The look on Amy's face was easily readable as disbelief. "How dumb do you think I am?"

She was too darn perceptive. She had clearly picked up on my interest in Rhys and Eric, but given how much I had hidden from her it was no surprise she jumped to the wrong conclusion.

Mrs. Herst blew her whistle and Amy lightly punched me in the shoulder before we lined up.

I ended up on the same team with Ginger Johnson, which was about as fun as pulling out my fingernails. I wasn't sure what I'd done to make her hate me – well, it had to be the fact that I dated Josh, but I didn't know why that bothered her - but she refused to speak directly to me and went out of her way to exclude me from the game. Several times I caught her whispering to Marcy Williams and then the two of them burst out laughing while looking at me.

I tried to ignore them, but it was difficult, and I found myself getting angry. My reaction really took me by surprise. Not long ago, people laughing at me had been a natural part of my school day. Back then it hadn't really bothered me – or I'd at least gotten used to it. Now, I had one person doing it and it was getting under my skin.

After Gym class, I hurried and changed hoping to see Rhys and Eric again before they left. I didn't consciously think through my plans, but in the back of my mind I had considered following them after school to see what I could learn.

I dashed to my locker – which was unfortunately on the other side of the school - and switched out the things I would need at home. I had to hurry if I was going to make it to the parking lot before they left.

Walking as quickly as I could, I wound my way through what now felt like labyrinthine passageways until I emerged into the sunlight. It was likely to be one of the last sunny days before the annual winter deluge.

I scoured the parking lot and spotted Eric and Rhys getting into their Range Rover.

Moving quickly I walked towards my car, my backpack shaking awkwardly as I picked up speed.

Before I could reach the car, a voice called my name. "Madison!"

I looked back and saw Amy hurrying towards me, holding up a hand as she ran.

"Wait!"

Longingly, I watched Rhys and Eric get into their SUV. I sighed and waited for Amy.

"What's going on?"

"Cory got detention today," Amy said. She looked so sad that you might have thought someone had just slaughtered a litter of puppies in front of her. "Can you give me a ride home?"

Normally I loved spending any time I could with Amy, but the timing on this was bad. Monumentally bad. Paris Hilton acting bad.

I really wanted to get in my car and follow Eric and Rhys. But this was Amy, my best friend. How could I deny her when she looked so sad?

"Sure, let's go," I said and watched as Rhys and Eric pulled out of the parking lot.

When I turned away and unlocked the car, I noticed a smirk on Amy's face. She had seen me watching them.

Great.

CHAPTER 7

IS THAT ALL YOU'VE GOT?

For the next two weeks I kept a close eye on Rhys and Eric. At first I tried to be inconspicuous, not wanting anyone to notice my special interest in them, but I eventually realized I would stand out less if I didn't try to hide the fact that I was watching them since the rest of the girls in the school seemed to be doing it rather openly.

Rhys was still quiet and constantly watched all the boys in the school. He rarely seemed to be paying attention in class, but whenever a teacher asked him a question, he knew the answer.

Eric appeared to be more social, although the two of them still ate lunch together by themselves. Several times other students had joined them for a day, but for one reason or another they never went back a second time.

Every day after gym class I rushed out in a vain attempt to follow them from school, but I consistently missed them. Usually they had already left by the time I got to the parking lot, but sometimes they appeared to be simply waiting in the hallways, watching people go by, occasionally whispering to each other. Unfortunately, I was never close enough to hear what they were saying, and that super sense heightening thing that sometimes happened to me didn't just show up on demand.

To make matters worse, the situation with Ginger Johnson had deteriorated. It took me a while to understand why she seemed to hate me so much, but I finally pieced together enough of her comments to get the big picture.

She had been dating Jed Flick, the star of our football team last year. He had gotten a full-ride scholarship to USC and dumped her less than two weeks after the school year started. Add that shame to the fact that she was going out with someone who had told everyone that I – former fat girl and geek - had broken up with him and her ego had taken quite the beating.

She seemed determined to make herself feel better by embarrassing me. I wasn't sure how making me seem like more of a loser would make it easier to accept that I had gone out with Josh, but I had a strong feeling logic wasn't a factor here.

On Friday, I went to my locker and noticed something white on the upper vent. I opened it up to see that shaving cream had been sprayed inside, covering everything.

My first reaction was humiliation, but it was quickly replaced by anger. It didn't take Stephen Hawking to figure out who did this. I slammed my locker shut and looked around, my senses heightened.

I saw Ginger all the way down the hall, walking away with Marcy

Williams and Jessica Scholl. They were several hundred feet away, but I could see them as clearly as if they were standing next to me. The trio was walking arm in arm and despite the distance I heard them laughing as Ginger tossed a can of shaving cream into the trash.

I fought the urge to drag Ginger back to my locker by the hair and rub her face in the shaving cream.

Where had that reaction come from? I wasn't a violent person. I was the opposite of violent. Pacifists pushed me around. Or at least they used to.

I turned around and slammed my fist into a locker, leaving a surprisingly deep dent. I pulled my hand back and looked at it, shocked that I hadn't broken anything.

"Whoa, what's with the Mike Tyson impression?"

Amy walked up to my locker holding hands with Cory Jones.

"Yeah, well, I kind of feel like biting a certain someone's ear." I opened my locker and showed her the damage.

Amy opened her mouth, but at first nothing came out. "Who did that? Who would be that mean? Especially to you. No offense, Madison, but you aren't prepared to get into this kind of nasty cat fight - you're too nice. Attacking you is like going hunting at the petting zoo."

"I'll go get some paper towels," Cory said, leaving Amy and me alone.

Part of me was flattered that Amy thought I was too nice for cat fights. What she didn't know was that under the nice exterior was... something – I still didn't know what – that had the ability to fight back. And right now, it wasn't that far from surfacing.

"I'll give you three guesses," I said. "And all of them had better be dating Josh."

"Ginger?" Amy paused, looking thoughtful. "Yeah, that does make sense."

"I saw her throw a can of shaving cream away just a few minutes ago."

"So are you going to tell someone?" Amy asked.

I shook my head. "I don't have any proof. It would be my word against hers." I sighed and leaned against the lockers. My anger slipped away, replaced by a sense of resigned inevitability. "What should I do?"

"Nothing," said Amy.

I looked at her quizzically. That didn't sound like my best friend. "Wait a minute. Now that I finally need your help with some scheming you suddenly start channeling Ghandi?"

Amy held up a hand and looked offended. "Please. I have not given up on scheming. But if you retaliate, you'll be playing into her hands. She wants you to fight back. She's trying to provoke you into playing a game where she is an expert and you don't even know the rules."

Cory returned with a stack of paper towels. "I pretty much cleaned out the boy's room," he said. "But don't worry, it's not like guys ever wash their hands. I think these same towels have been in there since freshman year."

"Eww," said Amy, taking a step away from Cory. "You do

though, right?"

Cory reached out and pulled Amy close. "Of course I do."

I took the towels from Cory and began cleaning off my things. After a few minutes, the warning bell rang.

"You guys better go," I said. "You're going to be late."

Amy hesitated. "Are you sure?" she asked. "I could stay and help you clean up."

At least this part of Amy hadn't changed. She only hesitated and asked if I was "sure" when she didn't want to do something, but felt guilty about not doing it. If she had really wanted to stay, getting her to leave would have required a crowbar and several burly men to pry her off.

"No, you and Cory go ahead. There's no point in all of us being late."

Amy gave me a commiserating smile and left. I spent the next ten minutes cleaning up my locker and came into Physics class well after the tardy bell.

I tried slip in as unobtrusively as possible, but it didn't work. "Miss. Montgomery, I would like to speak with you after class," said Mr. Shumway.

Not a good sign. I had been hoping he'd let it slide since I had never been tardy before.

Rhys glanced at me briefly as I came in, but it was nothing more than that – a glance. I wanted to pull him out of class and demand that he answer all my questions, but I didn't know enough about him to reveal my secret. The longer I went without my learning anything about him, the more frustrated I became. I needed to get some answers soon, before I lost control of my powers in a public place and laid waste to the mall or flattened an office building.

These weren't normal teenager problems. Normal teenagers worried about zits, popularity, dating – that sort of thing. My problems sounded like they belonged to Godzilla or the Incredible Hulk. Not exactly the role models a teenage girl wants to have.

After class was over I spoke with Mr. Shumway. I explained what had happened, and fortunately, he was very understanding. I think the fact that I had aced the last test may have given me a bit of an edge in this situation. Being smart has its perks - if not being punished when the most popular girl in school picks on you can be considered a perk.

As it turned out, the shaving cream in my locker was the high point of school that day.

My next class was American History. Class itself was fine, if not exactly an edge-of-your-seat adventure. The problem began at the end of class when I went to turn in my homework. I felt around on the tray under my desk where I had put my homework folder, but it was missing.

I immediately turned to glare at Ginger Johnson – it had to be her, who else would take it? - but she just looked at me coolly and smiled. Anger flared inside me, and I felt that familiar heightening of my senses. Why was she torturing me? She already had Josh. What more did she want? If anyone should be mad, it should be me.

But Ginger sat two desks up and one over from me, too far away to have taken my folder herself. Besides, I would have noticed if she'd come near me. Once again my mind quickened, drawing conclusions I couldn't have reached on my own. I instantly knew that Mark Smith, who sat behind me, had pulled it from under my desk while I wasn't looking and had passed it forward via Andy Brewer, Julie King, and Lauren McCrea, all of whom were friends of Ginger.

The bell rang and Ginger gave me another annoying smile as she picked up her things and pranced out of the room, leaving me to deal with the wrath of Mrs. Gardner, which involved prostrating myself, repeated self-flogging, and begging for mercy.

In the end I was able to negotiate only a half letter grade drop if I did the assignment over and turned it in tomorrow.

I left the room feeling a strange mixture of humiliation and cold fury. All I can say is that it was a good thing Ginger was nowhere in sight.

Nothing happened in study hall so I used that time to redo my history homework.

Unfortunately, my brief respite from Ginger turned out to be far too brief. At lunch, I noticed that my seat felt slippery when I sat down. I stood up and saw that someone had smeared the chair with Vaseline. The back of my pants were completely covered, and I spent most of lunch in the girls' bathroom trying to clean them off. I finally gave it up as a lost cause and called my mom to bring me a new pair.

I got through Pre-calc without any problem, but in English I didn't need Ginger's help to look like a complete idiot. As I walked in the door, I was so busy staring at Rhys that I didn't watch where I was going and banged my hip on the teacher's desk. My books spilled out of my arms and scattered across the gritty tile floor.

My senses sharpened, and I was able to catch myself and prevent a full face-plant on the floor. When I looked up, Rhys was staring at me, a puzzled look on his face.

This time I was the one who turned away. I still had vivid memories of what it was like the last time I looked in his eyes with my sharpened senses, and I wasn't sure if that was strictly one way or if he could also see into me. And the last thing I wanted was for him to see that deeply into me while I was having possibly the most humiliating day of my life.

I bent to gather my books but Rhys beat me to it. He held them out, a slight smile just faintly touching his lips. It was amazing that something as simple as a smile could transform his face. I had always thought he had been handsome, but with that smile he was beautiful. I was so transfixed that I forgot to reach out to grab the books.

"I think these are yours."

With an almost superhuman effort I ripped my gaze away from his smile and took the books. "Thanks," I managed to croak out. I dropped my head and hid behind my hair as I slunk into my seat.

Thanks? That was all I could come up with? The boy I had wanted to talk with for over two weeks finally spoke to me and "thanks" was all I could come up with? That was almost more embarrassing than dropping my books. I could live with someone thinking I was a klutz – I had been one most of my life - but the idea that he might think I was an idiot made me want to crawl under a rock and drop a mountain range or two on top of it.

I tried to listen as Mrs. Abrams discussed the themes in Heart of Darkness, but I couldn't concentrate. I honestly wanted to focus, but my attention kept wandering to Rhys. That smile was the first sign of emotion I had seen from him. It had somehow changed my perception of him.

When the bell rang, Rhys made his usual bee-line for the exit, but he did glance back at me before slipping out the door.

I made my way to the gym on a bit of a high, despite the horrible, nasty, humiliating day I had.

Amy knew something was up the moment she saw me go into the locker room.

"I know that goofy grin," she said. "Spill it."

"I don't know what you're talking about," I said. My strange obsession with Rhys wasn't something I could easily explain.

Amy gave me an exasperated look. "You know I'll find out eventually, so why don't you save us both the trouble and just tell me?"

I rolled my eyes. It can be a real pain having a hyper-perceptive best friend with no qualms about the tactics she uses if she thinks she's acting in your best interest.

"If you want to know the truth, today has been one of the worst days I can remember." While not the complete truth, it was still an absolutely true statement. I had to stick to the facts or Amy would see right through me.

Amy looked skeptical. "I'm sorry, but that was not a worst-day-ever grin. That was a Josh-makes-my-heart-go-pitter-patter grin. What happened?"

I started to fill her in on what happened during the day – excluding Rhys' smile - but Mrs. Herst was already herding us into the gym, and I didn't have time to get really explain.

The volleyball unit had ended and now we were starting basketball. Mrs. Herst had gone over the rules and basic skill drills the day before. Today we were going to actually play.

The gym was big enough to run two full-court games, so she divided us into four teams. Amy and I were on different teams. I was grateful that Ginger wasn't on my team, either. Well, I was grateful, until my team was matched up to play against hers.

Ginger was one of those ultra-athletic girls. She was a cheerleader and played volleyball, basketball, and soccer. She also was extremely competitive – didn't I know that from firsthand experience – and wasn't above playing rough to win.

Given all the nasty things she had done to me today, I suspected that things were going to get ugly. My first instinct was to fake being sick to get out of playing, but watching Ginger stare me down changed my mind. I'm not a confrontational person, however, every once in a while something happens that makes me dig in my heels and hold my ground.

Ginger had humiliated me by making me look bad in my strongest area – academics. It was time to return the favor.

Starting now.

I took the inbounds pass and dribbled the ball up the court.

Ginger immediately picked me up and guarded me. She swiped at the ball trying to steal it away, but I held on. I found an open teammate under the basket and passed it in for an easy layup.

On the way back up the court Ginger bumped me hard, knocking me several feet. She took advantage of my moment off balance and ran down the court where Marcy found her for an easy basket.

The game got rougher from there. Ginger pushed, hit, and even scratched me at every opportunity. Mrs. Herst was splitting her time monitoring the two games, and Ginger made sure to be on her best behavior while under surveillance.

But despite Ginger's dirty play, I held my own. For several minutes we battled to a draw, neither of us gaining an advantage, until Ginger pushed me from behind as I jumped for a rebound, sending me flying out of bounds.

The sound of her laughter while I picked myself off the floor was too much. I felt that pent up energy inside, waiting to explode.

I took a deep breath. If I didn't calm down, I was going to burst into... well, whatever it was that I turned into.

Closing my eyes, I breathed deeply and searched for a calming image. I tried to picture Josh, but when I closed my eyes, it was the vivid blue eyes of Rhys that I saw, layers of emotion buried inside them.

What was I doing?

I opened my eyes to get the image of Rhys out of my mind. I shouldn't be seeing him. I should see Josh. I loved Josh.

While my attempted relaxation didn't go the way I intended, it did prevent me from starting to glow.

I jumped back into the game, sped up the court, and stole the ball from Ginger from behind. I couldn't move as quickly as I had the night my powers first manifested, but this in-between stage that heightened my senses gave me some other physical advantages as well.

Before anyone realized what I had done, I ran the ball toward my basket and laid it in for an easy two points.

The next time Ginger got the ball, I swiped at it in mid-dribble, stealing it out of her hands. This time I didn't run to the basket, but I slowed down and let Ginger guard me. I gradually backed up until I was almost at half court. Ginger was breathing heavily now. She wasn't used to having to work this hard to guard someone. At the half court line, I stared Ginger in the eyes and then - without taking my eyes off her - I shot the ball. I held the follow-through as I stared down Ginger.

The ball sailed in a graceful arc and swished through the net. Play stopped for a minute as everyone took in what I had done. Then in an explosion of sound, my teammates cheered and hugged me. Ginger shook her head and took the inbounds pass.

For the next fifteen minutes I put on a display of basketball skills that not even an NBA pro could have duplicated. I stole the passes, made half court shots, and blocked the ball with ease. The only thing I didn't do was dunk, mostly because I thought that might be pushing the line and generate questions I couldn't answer.

On the final possession, Ginger had the ball in front of the basket and kept backing into me, trying to push me out of the way. My increased strength was too much for her, and the harder she tried, the more frustrated she got.

"Come on Ginger," I said, egging her on. "I thought you were supposed to be good at this. Is that all you've got?"

In what I was pretty sure was a first, Ginger actually growled at me. "No, that's not all I've got," she said. "I've got Josh. He told me that he really dumped you." And with that she bumped me as hard as she could to create some space, and then shot the ball while falling backwards.

I leaped into the air, Ginger's words still ringing in my ears, and swatted the ball as hard as I could, blocking her shot.

The ball smashed into the side of Ginger's head and knocked her to the floor. She slid several feet and lay there, unmoving.

A piercing whistle split the air. Mrs. Herst ran over to check on Ginger.

"Someone go get the nurse," she said.

What had I done? Horrible thoughts ran through my head: Concussion - Broken neck – Paralyzed – Dead.

I stood alone while everyone crowded around Ginger's inert form. After a few minutes she opened her eyes and tried to sit up, but Mrs. Herst made her stay on her back.

"How did this happen?" Mrs. Herst asked.

Marcy Williams spoke up. "I saw what happened, Mrs. Herst. Madison hit Ginger in the head with an elbow on purpose. I think she has some jealousy issues." She smiled at Mrs. Herst, and then glared at me.

"All right everyone, hit the locker room," said Mrs. Herst. "Ginger will be fine, but I still want the nurse to check her out." She turned toward me and put her hands on her hips. "Madison, I want to speak with you for a moment."

"What Marcy said isn't true, Mrs. Herst," I said, after everyone had left for the locker room. "I blocked her shot, and the ball accidentally hit her in the head. That's all." Of course, the fact that I had increased speed, strength, and reflexes made the "accident" part a bit harder to defend.

The truth was, I had wanted to hurt her. For that one instant after she mentioned Josh, I had wanted to make her suffer for what she had done. For the shaving cream, the stolen homework, the Vaseline on my seat, and most of all, for taking away Josh.

Only I hadn't wanted it to be like this. I didn't mean to physically hurt her, I had just wanted to humiliate her the way she had humiliated me – by beating her at what she takes pride in.

The school nurse arrived, knelt down next to Ginger, and began asking questions.

Mrs. Herst grabbed my arm and pulled me out of Ginger's earshot. "Madison, I saw you and Ginger going at each other all during class."

It took quite a bit of self-control on my part not to drop my mouth open in shock. "Then why didn't you stop it?" I asked.

"To be perfectly honest," Mrs. Herst said, "you seemed to be holding your own just fine. Ginger is a very talented athlete. Frankly,

I thought it was good for her to face a bit of a challenge on the court."

"But-"

"But that didn't give you the right to hurt her, Madison."

"I told you, I didn't hit her with my elbow-"

"I've seen how you've changed Madison. I've watched you lose weight and I've see your natural athletic talent shine through. I also saw how you played today, Madison, and I know that whatever happened to Ginger was not an accident."

My mind raced, looking for a way to justify or defend myself, but I didn't try very hard. She was right. It wasn't an accident.

"So, with that in mind, I am going to give you detention for committing a flagrant foul."

I hung my head, wishing that I hadn't pulled my hair back in a ponytail so I could hide behind it. I looked over at Ginger, who was being helped to her feet by the school nurse.

"Fine," I said and headed back into the locker room.

Amy immediately pelted me with a dozen questions, but since half the girls in the locker room were watching us, I told her I didn't want to talk about it right now. She looked offended, but didn't press the issue.

When Ginger came in, all the attention switched to her. Sympathetic girls surrounded her to ask if she was all right. The way she was being treated, you would think she had been wounded while pulling small children out of a burning orphanage in the middle of an earthquake.

No, I wasn't proud of what I'd done, but seeing everyone fawn over Ginger was more than I could handle. I quickly yanked on my clothes and picked up my detention slip from Mrs. Herst. It was my first one, and I really didn't know what the process was.

Luckily, Amy had a bit of a rebellious streak and while not exactly intimate with the detention process, was at least fairly well-acquainted. She explained where I should go, and in exchange I told her everything that happened – the shaving cream (she already knew about that), the missing homework, and the Vaseline.

When I finished, Amy was properly outraged for me. "She did all that stuff to you and now everyone is treating her like a martyr? That's like feeling bad for a serial killer because he got rope burn tying his victim up."

"Wow, serial killer comparisons? Don't hold back, Amy. Tell me how you really feel."

"Oh, don't get me started on the inferiority complex that will plague her through her troubled teenage years and ultimately prevent her from developing any lasting connections with another human being, dooming her to a life of solitude and twenty three cats."

That was my Amy.

I went to my locker and took out my books. If I had to sit through detention, at least I could get some homework done.

I gave my detention slip to Mrs. Abrams in Room 114, who had detention duty today. She raised her eyebrows when she saw me come in, but didn't say anything. I was too embarrassed to even talk, so I sat down in the corner closest to the door, ready to make a quick getaway after I'd done my time.

Detention turned out to be rather anti-climatic. I thought it would be filled with dangerous looking people who carved their initials on the desk while the teacher either fell asleep or read a magazine, completely ignoring us. That's what I get for letting my parents show me old John Hughes movies.

Our detention only had two other people in it and none of us spoke the entire time. Once I realized that neither Judd Nelson nor Eric Stoltz was going to show up, I focused on my homework, and by the time detention was over, I had finished my History reading.

I walked out of Room 114 feeling strangely disillusioned. It hadn't been the horrible seventh circle of hell that I had imagined. Having experienced it, I could now see why the threat of detention didn't seem to phase some people.

The halls were relatively empty, and echoed hollowly with the sound of my footsteps as I made my way out of the school. I walked out the front doors and crossed the lot to where I had parked. I climbed in my car and was about to start it up when I noticed someone behind me in the rear view mirror. I turned to get a better look and immediately turned back, my pulse quickening.

Rhys stopped suddenly and looked around, grabbing Eric's arm to get his attention. Clearly he was searching for something, but what? They both looked around, peering into the few cars left in the parking lot. Eric walked past me and gave me a wink as he continued his search.

After a few minutes, they held a whispered conversation that was too soft for even my enhanced senses to hear. Then they climbed into their Range Rover and pulled out.

This was it. This was the moment I had been waiting for. After weeks of frustration, I was finally going to find out more about them.

I let them drive past me and waited until they were about to turn out of the parking lot before I pulled out. I wanted to follow them, but I didn't want them to notice me.

The problem was, I had never learned how to follow someone without attracting attention. That hadn't been covered that in Driver's Ed. Clearly a serious flaw in the driver's education system, and a skill that would be much more useful than watching those scare-tactic movies with footage of real accidents.

Despite my lack of "tailing" skills, I was able to at least keep the Rover in sight as I drove. I had some close calls when the boys got farther away than I had planned or turned onto a street that I didn't notice until I was almost past it, but thanks to my enhanced abilities, I managed to make the turn anyway. There were definite perks to having these powers.

We wound through the main part of town and into the Heights, a ritzy area with a lot of big houses. There were fewer turnoffs here, so I let them get farther ahead.

Most of the houses in the Heights were better described as mansions, with gated driveways, and enormous manicured lawns. Because of the large yards, the houses were spread very far apart.

After traveling a few miles up the road, the Range Rover turned into a gated driveway. Rhys reached out and punched in a code. The gate opened, and they drove up the driveway.

The house was enormous. It was three stories tall with the rustic appearance of a massive mountain cabin. Made of dark wood, it had many large peaks and gables with enormous windows.

I drove past at a crawl, taking in everything that I could. Eric and Rhys got out of the vehicle and walked into the house. Rhys seemed much more relaxed than he had been at school. I even saw him laugh at something Eric said.

They walked into the house without using any keys. It had been left unlocked, I noted. If further reconnaissance became necessary, things like that were good to know.

When I was past the house, I parked my car to the side of the road and walked back. The gate blocked car access, but the fence around the property was made of long rails and was easy enough to squeeze through.

I scurried up the lawn, feeling exposed until I stopped at a large artificial waterfall that had been built into the landscape. It was a perfect place to hide and observe.

I spent the next fifteen minutes watching the house and everyone I could see there. Through the windows I saw three other people. The first was an Asian man with dark skin and dark hair, somewhere in his mid-thirties. The second was a redheaded girl in her early twenties, and the third was a large man with dark hair and dark skin – I couldn't place his nationality, Samoan? - who was built like a professional football player.

And that was the extent of the useful information I could get from that far away. Part of me wanted to move closer and try to learn more, but now that I knew where they lived, I could come always come back later.

I ran back to my car and started it up. The road was too narrow to make a u-turn, so I drove forward looking for a driveway I could turn around in.

As I drove, a wave of heat came over me and I began sweating profusely. A few hundred feet farther, nausea caused my stomach to roil. In addition to the physical symptoms, I felt that indescribable sense of darkness come over me, but a thousand times more powerful than it had been in the woods.

Unable to continue driving, I swerved to the side of the road and slammed on the brakes. I tried to open the door, but I was too late and vomited all over my lap and the steering wheel. I fumbled with the door handle and finally shoved it open.

Gasping, I pulled myself out of the car, sucking in fresh air. I tried to stay upright, but my legs were too weak. I teetered and fell to my knees. With another painful wave of nausea, I emptied the remaining contents of my stomach onto the ground.

The heat had become unbearable. Sweat poured off my face in streaming rivulets. Exhausted, I lifted my head and found myself surrounded by hundreds of the creatures I had fought in the woods.

An army.

Behind them, like a demented general directing his troops, stood a reptilian monster the size of a bull elephant. It lifted its head on a long snake-like neck and roared.

The creatures charged.

Cold fear drifted through my body. I was going to die.

Then I began to glow.

CHAPTER 8

FIGHTING WITH THE BIG BOYS

Power exploded through me as my body began to glow. My senses burst into life, making everything more vivid and real. Hundreds of the creatures I had fought in the woods swarmed towards me. An unavoidable tidal wave of death. Their slimy grey skin glistened in the sunlight, and I had a horrible suspicion that they were covered in some sort of mucus – or at least close enough to not make a difference in the grossness factor.

One of them broke away from the pack and reached me before the others. I really didn't want to touch it, but I wanted to stay alive. I met its charge with my fist, landing a punch on its head.

The upper half of the creature exploded, spraying the area – including me, eew! – with black slime. I had no time to react to the carnage and pushed the voice in my head screaming "Gross, gross, gross, gross!" into the far corner of my mind. I had to focus on staying alive.

Four more creatures attacked me at once. I caught one as it

leaped and I pivoted, using its own momentum to swing it around and back into a second creature. I then ducked under a third as it leapt. The fourth one hit me from behind, knocking me to the ground.

I rolled to my back, bringing my legs up just in time to ward off the creature as it pounced on me. I sent it flying with my feet, and it crashed into the crowd of onrushing monsters.

I leapt to my feet in time to fight off five more creatures. Those were followed by more and more in a seemingly endless parade of horror. Time passed in a blur as I fought for survival. I lost track of my surroundings as I continued my repetition of destruction. Punch, kick, throw - repeat.

Just as it had been in the dead woods, my body seemed familiar with these creatures. I instinctively knew where they were vulnerable. My muscles contracted before my conscious mind registered a threat. I was fighting by pure instinct, and it was the only thing keeping me alive.

But it was a losing battle. There were too many of them. For every creature I killed, three more seemed to move in to take its place. I slaughtered the first dozen without too much difficulty since the frontrunners had been spread out. Now that the main surge had arrived, I was completely surrounded and fighting a dozen at a time.

Slowly, inevitably, they began to wear me down. That unknown survival instinct kept me fighting, but I couldn't last much longer. Physically, I was fine. My body felt as if it could last forever. But the feeling of darkness that accompanied them began to multiply. I had recovered from the initial onslaught in the car, but now that they surrounded me, I could feel the darkness holding me, slowing me, gradually overwhelming me. My senses dulled, and my thoughts became clouded.

It was only a matter of time until I would no longer be able to fight.

Faintly, through the suffocating blackness, I felt something else.

Rhys and Eric.

I recognized the feeling from the dead woods. But they weren't alone. Two others came with them. Their features were obscured by the glow, but I recognized them from the house - the Asian man and the large man who had looked like a football player. They charged, four glowing beings rushing into the hoard of monsters, killing and destroying everything in their paths.

I didn't know if it was psychological or what, but with their arrival I felt the darkness dissipate, no more substantial than cobwebs in the path of a speeding truck.

My strength returned, even multiplied. Invigorated, I stood and lifted a pile of monsters on top of me. I flung out my arms, sending creatures - and bits of creatures - flying.

The elephantine monster, seeing the arrival of the four glowing beings, arched its long neck and roared. Somehow, I knew this creature was different from the others, and not just in size. It had an aura of intelligence, of purpose. That bellow was not an expression of fear or anger, but one of defiance.

Rhys accepted the challenge and rushed at the monster, knocking it onto its back and into my mom's car. The Jetta's roof crumpled like a wad of aluminum foil. Great, if these creatures didn't kill me, my parents would. The creature roared furiously and regained its feet, kicking the car and knocking it upside down. It bared its teeth and swung its serpentine neck in deadly arcs.

Rhys punched the creature in the head, whipping its neck around. He leaped onto the creature's back and wrapped two crushing arms around its throat, squeezing hard.

"Get Mallika!" he yelled. "Now!" The Asian man dashed towards the house.

Eric stood back to back with the football player guy encircled by dozens of the creatures. The football player guy yelled and made horrible faces as he fought, bugging out his eyes and sticking out his tongue. As I watched, he smashed two of the skinnier creatures together, sending out a spray of black ooze that coated him and Eric. I made a mental note not to try that move, or for that matter to even get close to him while fighting.

Eric, in contrast, fought with a sort of minimalist grace. Every move seemed calculated to generate the most destruction with the least required effort. He struck with precision, spraying far less ooze than the football player did, but he must have been puncturing the creatures at vital points because once he hit them, they fell to the ground and turned to goo. Curiously, he was smiling. I saw his lips moving, almost as if he were singing or chanting to himself as he fought.

I continued my battle, finding it easier now that there were others to take some of the focus off me. Not that I found this as enjoyable as Eric apparently did — what kind of lunatic liked this? — but I no longer felt overwhelmed.

The Asian man returned carrying an older woman in his arms. Dark, wrinkled skin hung limp on a frail body, and her head was covered with long, steel-gray hair tied back in a braid. This must be Mallika.

With her arrival, the large creature let out three short, almost bark-like, roars. The remaining creatures abandoned their positions and rushed to its defense. A dozen of them leaped at Rhys, forcing him to release his choke-hold on the large creature's neck and knocking him to the ground.

With a sort of reverse flash — everything got dark for an instant — the elephant-monster disappeared. The temperature immediately dropped, and our remaining opponents began to scatter.

"Don't let them escape," said Eric. "Spread out and stop them."

The Asian man set Mallika on her feet while the rest of us spread out in an attempt to prevent the creatures from escaping.

Several dozen of the creatures remained. We battled, and this time, my attention was drawn to the Asian man. He moved with a ridiculously swift, fluid motion, never directly confronting his opponents, but rather turning them aside, changing their momentum, and throwing them — into the air, onto the ground, or into each other - as they attacked.

But it was Rhys who drew everyone's attention in the end. He pulled out a small white disk and with a flick of his wrist it unrolled into a sword-like weapon with a series of small clicks. It was dull white and seemed to be made out of dozens of pieces of bone joined together. When only two dozen enemies were left, we all stepped back to watch Rhys in a dance of perfect death.

His bone sword blurred around him as he swung it, slicing through creatures with such ease that at first I wasn't sure that he had really connected. The sword seemed to pass through bone and muscle without resistance. But when the creatures fell to the ground with limbs and heads severed, it quickly became clear that each stroke was inflicting devastating damage.

As I watched, I always seemed to lag a step behind. By the time I looked at one of the creatures, it was already falling apart, and I never saw the blow that killed it. Clearly Rhys was a master with this weapon. He fought the way an eagle flew or a cheetah ran, with natural and deadly grace.

He killed the last three creatures with a single stroke, beheading two and slicing through the chest of the third.

And then it was over. A moment of silence followed, almost overwhelming in contrast to the mêlée that had just taken place.

Eric broke the silence with a whoop and the big football-player-looking-guy let out a series of rhythmic shouts, beating his chest. Rhys said nothing and wiped his bone sword on the grass. With another flick, it rolled up and he pocketed it.

The Asian man walked towards me, arms held up in what was clearly meant to be a non-threatening posture. However, it had the opposite effect. His obvious efforts to make me feel comfortable put me on edge. It felt like a trap.

"Stop," I said. My voice sounded strange in my own ears, like it belonged to someone else. "Don't come any closer." I crouched slightly, prepared to run. Not that I was sure it would do any good. They all seemed to have the same powers as me and a much better idea of how to use them. I wasn't a match for the four of them.

The Asian man halted and put his arms down. "We aren't going to hurt you," he said.

Hearing him voice my concern only made me more nervous. I took a step back.

Eric walked up to the Asian man and put a hand on his shoulder. "Let me take this," he whispered into his ear. The Asian man took a few steps back.

"I can hear you," I said. They were only about twenty yards away. I had heard whispered conversations at far greater distances. They had the same powers as I did, surely they should know this.

Eric closed his eyes for a second and his glow faded away. Without the bright light surrounding him, I could see his features clearly. "What makes you think I didn't want you to overhear me?" he asked.

"Because you whispered it."

Eric flashed a mischievous grin. "Ah, but what if I only wanted you to think I didn't want you to overhear me?" he asked in a very solemn voice.

Was he being serious? "What are you talking about?"

He shrugged. "Well, you seemed so suspicious, I thought it might be disappointing if you found out that we were just trying to talk to you and didn't have any diabolical plans."

I let out a laugh. The way he said it made my fears sound ridiculous. I stiffened. That was probably what they wanted me to think.

Ok, now I was just being paranoid.

"I have an idea," said Eric. He turned around to face the others. "Guys, turn off the 'zerk. It's time for a bit of de-escalation."

One by one, each of them stopped glowing. Within seconds I was the only one still – what had Eric called it? – 'zerking? What a bizarre word.

The old woman walked forward until she stood next to Eric. Now that I was no longer fighting for my life, I could take a good look at her.

My first impressions of old age had been correct. I couldn't guess at her age because after about sixty everyone just looks old to me. She had dark skin and wore a beautifully decorated yellow skirt that extended to her ankles. A long piece of cloth wound around her waist with the end draped over her shoulder.

"My name is Mallika," she said. Despite her wrinkled appearance, her voice still sounded young. It had a musical tone and a hint of an Indian accent. "We are all on the same side. I would invite you to relax and release your hold on your Berserker powers so we can all speak with clear minds."

What was she talking about? Berserker powers? Clear minds? My mind was more clear when I had my powers. Still, there was something about her that made me want to trust her.

I took a deep breath. "I can't," I said. "I don't know how to turn it off."

Mallika smiled sympathetically. "Of course you do not, child. After so long we tend to forget what it is like for one just discovering his powers." She motioned to Rhys. "Perhaps you could instruct him?"

Him? Did she think I was a boy? I looked down at myself. With the bright glow surrounding me, I supposed it was somewhat difficult to tell.

Rhys straightened up and walked to Mallika's side. "A Berserker's power is all about energy. To end the berserking, you need to relax. All of us have developed body control that allows us to relax and turn off the energy on demand. For you, the simplest thing to do would be to breathe deeply and regularly. Push out your stomach as you breathe in and relax as you breathe out."

Breathing was the secret to controlling my powers? I supposed it made sense. The other times I had stopped glowing it had happened after I had started to calm down.

But could I trust them? That was the bigger question. I had only seen Rhys and Eric before, the others were complete strangers to me. Although they had helped me fight the creatures. Didn't that count for something?

It couldn't hurt to give it a try – weren't those famous last words? I pushed my natural distrust away and began breathing deeply, counting slowly to four for each breath.

"It's easier if you close your eyes and imagine yourself someplace peaceful and safe," said Rhys. "But I understand if you don't feel comfortable doing that right now."

I continued breathing, trying to relax, but the excitement of the battle and the pressure to do this with everyone watching made it extremely difficult. And to be honest, I was hyper-aware of Rhys watching me, which was not relaxing in the slightest.

Gradually, the breathing seemed to have an effect, and my body began to relax. Towards the end, I even closed my eyes and discovered that Rhys was right about it being easier. Without the visual stimulus to distract me, my heart rate slowed down and my hands and arms began to feel warm and somewhat heavy.

As my body relaxed, my senses dulled and I felt the power fade. I was my old self once again.

I don't know what I was expecting to see when I opened my eyes. Perhaps some smiles congratulating me for stopping the glow, or even the rush of bodies moving in for the kill. I didn't think that was likely, but it wouldn't have surprised me.

What I hadn't expected was the look of shock and fear that dominated their faces.

The Asian man had dropped into a crouch and appeared ready to spring at me. The football player guy clenched and released his massive hands as if he wanted to crush something. Rhys had pulled out his bone sword, and stood in an offensive posture, apparently ready to slice me in half. Mallika looked thoughtful, but there was a strong sense of worry in her expression, as if she were watching a dangerous animal that could attack at any minute.

Even Eric had lost his standard-issue sardonic smile, but only for a moment. It was back so quickly I wasn't sure if I had just imagined the lapse.

"This isn't possible," said Rhys, never taking his eyes from me. He had such beautiful eyes that it almost physically hurt to have them looking at me with such malice. "Do the Binder records speak of anything like this?"

Mallika looked up while she thought for a moment. "Nothing that I have read indicates that this could be possible," she said.

"Ok, enough with the cryptic talk," I said. "Which of the thousands of 'impossible' things are you referring to? The fact that we can all glow and have freakish strength? The hundreds of nasty turn-into-goo creatures we just fought? Or maybe that dinosaur thing with the long neck that trashed my mom's car? Because, let me tell you, all of those seem equally impossible to me."

Eric's grin widened as I spoke, and he looked at Mallika with a raised eyebrow, clearly waiting for her response. The rest of them did not seem to find the situation amusing. If anything, the serious expressions on Rhys' and Mallika's faces deepened.

"No one is trying to be cryptic," said Rhys.

"Then will someone please tell me why you're all looking at me like I'm the family dog who just went rabid?"

"Because you are a girl," said Mallika.

CHAPTER 9

FINALLY, AN EXPLANATION

B ecause I'm a girl?" I repeated. They were freaking out because I was a girl? Seriously? Hadn't they been able to tell that before?

"There are no female Berserkers," said Eric. He walked over and stood close to me – a little too close for my comfort - facing the others. "Which I've always felt was a monumental injustice. Hanging out with the guys is fine, but I always thought the lack of girls was a major flaw in the whole Berserker infrastructure." His mischievous grin widened as he spoke.

Rhys rolled his eyes. "There are plenty of girls-"

"Not in the ways that count," said Eric, interrupting Rhys. "I would think you of all people should understand."

There was a tense moment as Rhys and Eric stared at each other, an unspoken argument raging between them.

The Asian man broke the silence. "Perhaps we should consider whether this conversation might not be better served in the house."

The Football Player guy nodded. "I'm with Shing," he said. "Let's go back to the house and talk through this. Osadyn might come back with reinforcements."

"I'm going to need help," said Mallika. "I don't get around the way I used to."

Without hesitation, Rhys strode over and effortlessly lifted her in his arms. In an instant he started glowing again. Then with a flash, he was gone and running through the trees toward the house. Shing and the Football Player guy – I really needed to learn his name because Football Player guy is pretty big mouthful – turned on their glow and followed them, leaving Eric and me alone.

"Can you 'zerk on demand?" he asked.

"You mean with the glowing and destroying things?"

Eric nodded. "Well, yes, I suppose. Definitely the glowing, but not so much with the destroying right now. Just running."

"Yeah, I'm not so good at separating the glowing from the destroying." I shrugged. "But I don't know how to get it started. It just happens."

"Then in the interests of my not having to walk all the way back to the house, how about if I give you a lift?"

Without waiting for a reply, he scooped me up the same way Rhys had picked up Mallika and turned on the glow. Within seconds, we were hurtling toward the trees at a speed that felt like certain death. Instinctively, I closed my eyes, threw my arms around Eric's neck, and held on as tightly as I could.

After what couldn't have been any more than a few seconds, Eric stopped.

"Ok, let go," said a hoarse whisper.

I opened my eyes expecting to see the house, but instead we were somewhere in the middle of the woods. My vision and other senses were heightened, and without looking down I knew that I was glowing.

Eric looked pained, his face red, my arms clearly choking him. Apparently, during the few seconds since he started running, I had 'zerked, and my squeeze had gone from tight to head-popping. I released my death grip, and he gently set me down.

He bent over and rubbed his neck and throat for a moment, then stood up, looking very serious. "Well, that was an experience I don't think I'll soon forget." His lips twitched as if trying to hide a smile. "Shall we run then?"

Eric sprinted off, and I followed just a few heartbeats behind. We sped through the woods, changing directions to run around obstacles and trees with ease.

This was the first time that I had run while 'zerking without being half out of my mind. Without horrifying emotional trauma to ruin the fun it was exhilarating.

Keeping pace with Eric wasn't a problem. If anything, he had trouble keeping up with me. We reached an open area and Eric looked over at me. He smiled and sped up. Taking it as a challenge, I ran faster, not only keeping up with Eric, but actually passing him. I could tell from the surprised look on his face that he wasn't going easy on me.

We reached the house in less than a minute. The others hadn't even stopped 'zerking yet. Clearly we had made up some time on them during the run.

It took me a while to stop glowing – unzerk? – and then Mallika led us all inside the house. If the outside of the house looked like a supersized cabin, the inside looked even more so. A massive stone fireplace dominated the living room, and the entire house was full of overstuffed leather chairs and wooden furniture.

A woman with curly auburn hair stood in the living room, hands on her hips, clearly upset. She looked maybe twenty or so, with determined green eyes blazing in a face dusted with freckles. I had seen that girl before. Only the last time I had seen her she was covered in slime and being ripped out of a monster's body.

"And where did you lot run off to in such a hurry?" she demanded. Her voice was angry, and I had to concentrate to understand her thick Scottish accent.

"Easy, Kara," said Eric. "There was an emergency and we didn't have time to explain."

If her eyes had blazed before, Eric's comment made them practically burst into full-on flames. The girl looked ready to spontaneously combust.

"No time to explain?" Her voice grew louder. "Sure, I'm just a Binder, I can't break trucks with my bare hands, so what do you need me for?" She threw up her hands and turned her back on Eric.

Eric reached out to put a hand on her shoulder. "Osadyn was there," he said. "It really wasn't much of a party." He turned her around to face him. "I promise."

For a moment Kara looked appeased. She let out a huge sigh. "Fine, I understand."

Then she saw me and gave Eric a look of panic, her hands flying up to cover to her mouth.

Eric looked back at me and shrugged. "Don't worry Kara," he said. "She's one of us."

If Eric had thought that would soothe her, he couldn't have been more wrong. Kara burst into tears and threw her arms around Eric's neck, mumbling into his shoulder.

Laughing, Eric disentangled himself from her arms. "None of the Binders died," he said. "She's the new Berserker."

Kara's expression showed an odd mixture of relief and curiosity. "Berserker? But..."

Mallika crossed the room and embraced Kara. "We know, Kara. We were all surprised."

Kara stared at me, her face unreadable. I stared back as blandly as possible, trying to hide all the emotions – fear, exhaustion, annoyance, curiosity, and a big dash of holy-crap-what-have-I-gotten-myself-into. After a moment her face softened, and she gave me a sisterly hug. I cringed as she touched me, thinking about the monster slime that had been on her, but I forced myself not to pull away. The slime had obviously been cleaned off.

"Oh, you poor thing," she said. "This must be terrifying for you." She guided me to a large couch with a brown leather ottoman in front of it. She sat down and motioned for me to join her.

I didn't really want to sit down next to her and not just for the slime. Emotionally she seemed about as stable as someone standing on a floor covered in greased marbles during a particularly violent earthquake – but I didn't really see any other choice. I collapsed into the soft leather, which after all the recent fighting felt surprisingly good. I hadn't realized how exhausted my body was.

Mallika, Eric, Rhys, and Football Player Guy all sat down in the loveseat and other chairs in the living room. Only Shing remained standing.

He looked from person to person before addressing me. "It appears that the Berserkers are well-represented here," he said, with a slight bow.

What was I supposed to say to that? He looked at me as if expecting some sort of response. "Uh, yes," I said. Shing didn't move. He seemed to be waiting for more. "Definitely represented." I glanced around looking for help from the others.

Surprisingly, it was Kara who came to my rescue. "That's right, Shing," she said. "There are plenty of Berserkers here. Perhaps your time might be equally well used elsewhere."

Eric groaned. "Kara, don't tell me he's got you talking in circles now too." He winked at me, a wicked gleam in his eye. "I just barely figured out how to understand your accent. If you start talking like Shing, I'm going to have to hire an interpreter."

Kara grabbed one of the pillows and threw it at Eric's head. He easily caught it and instead of throwing it back, simply set it down on his lap.

Shing meanwhile bowed to me, his face a mask of deadly seriousness. "You are in capable hands," he said and left the room. I stared after Shing, not knowing what to make of him. Why had he wanted to leave? Had I somehow offended him?

"Don't mind, Shing," said Eric. "He was just looking for an excuse to go meditate."

Oh yeah, that cleared everything up.

"Shing likes to meditate after using his Berserker powers," explained Rhys. "He says it helps restore his balance."

I nodded as if I understood, but I was missing too much information to make sense of it. I knew what the individual words meant, but it felt like everyone was speaking a foreign language.

"So, is someone going to tell me what's going on here?" asked Kara. "Is she really a Berserker?"

Rhys held up a hand. "Hold on Kara," he said. "I think we owe our guest an explanation first." He paused. "In all the excitement, we never introduced ourselves." He crossed the room and held out his hand. "My name is Rhys."

I shook his hand. "I already knew that." I pointed at Eric. "His name is Eric. Or at least that's the name he went by at school."

Eric and Rhys exchanged looks. "Clearly our undercover skills need some work," said Rhys. "We were trying to be inconspicuous."

I let out a laugh. With all the tension I had been feeling, the release of laughter felt wonderful. The idea of the two of them being inconspicuous at Woodbridge High was ludicrous. "In a town like this, it's not possible for two new guys to be inconspicuous, especially if they're cute." Did I just say that out loud? Cute? It was all I could do to not clap my hands over my mouth in horror, but that would have just made it worse. Instead I stiffened and hoped no one noticed my neon-glow blush. It was a long shot, but sometimes irrationality was my only defense.

Rhys didn't seem to think much about the comment, but as soon as the word "cute" came out of my mouth, I saw that twinkle in Eric's eyes.

"Well, normally that's not a problem when Rhys works alone," he said. "I blame myself, really." He let out a dramatic sigh. "This isn't the first time my good looks have caused me problems."

Football Player guy groaned loudly and rolled his eyes.

"Was it your looks or your arrogance that caused the problems?" asked Mallika.

I wasn't sure what to make of Mallika. Her comment sounded like a joke, but she looked so serious and proper.

Eric apparently took it as a joke. "Both really," he said. "But is it arrogance if it's true?"

Kara threw another pillow at him. This time he didn't even bother to dodge. It bounced off his head and landed near the Football Player guy. He picked up the pillow and handed it back to Kara.

Up close he was even larger than I had thought. He was easily one of the biggest men I had ever seen in person – larger than even my dad, and that was saying a lot. He stood a full head taller than everyone else and his shoulders were about the width of a city bus. He was the kind of guy you wouldn't want to get stuck next to in an airplane. At least he wasn't falling asleep and drooling on my shoulder.

"We haven't been introduced yet," he said in what sounded like an Australian accent. He shook my hand, his massive fingers completely enfolding mine. I felt like a toddler shaking hands with someone wearing a baseball glove. "My name is Aata."

"Ata?" I said, unsure I had heard correctly. It was not a name I had heard before. Maybe just calling him Football Player guy would be easier.

"Close. Aata. You repeat the 'ah' sound twice – Ah Ah Ta."

"Okay," I said slowly. "Aata. I'm Madison. Madison Montgomery."

"Good to meet you," said Aata. He grinned showing large white teeth. On someone that big a smile could have been frightening. But for Aata, it transformed his face from that of a massive scary man, to that of a goofy boy in a body much too large for him. In some ways, it reminded me of Eric's grins.

Aata released my hand and returned to his seat.

Eric cleared his throat. "You probably would like an explanation about who we are and what's been happening to you."

I nodded and sat up straighter. I was going to finally get the answers I had been looking for since that day back at the DMV last summer.

"I'm sure you would," Mallika said. "But I think it best if I explained." She looked at Eric. "I believe after the last time Eric helped orient a new Berserker, we all agreed that he was perhaps not the ideal choice for this assignment."

Eric put on an exaggerated wounded expression. "What-"

Mallika interrupted him. "It took almost a full year to help Pierce sort out the facts from fiction in your 'enhanced' version of the Berserker story. You wouldn't want to inflict that on this poor girl, would you?"

Eric opened his mouth as if to protest, and then burst out laughing. When he finally stopped he said, "All right. You tell the story. I obviously wouldn't have been able to keep a straight face anyway."

I made a mental note to disbelieve anything Eric said without getting confirmation from other sources.

"While the ultimate origins of the Berserkers are clouded in the past," Mallika said, "we do know that they have existed for many thousands of years. They are guardians and warriors, protecting the world from a danger it does not even know exists."

Talk about a cryptic beginning. A torrent of questions washed over me, threatening to burst out and spill into the room. I took in several deep breaths, doing my best to push the questions away and focus on what Mallika was telling me.

"Somehow, we don't know how," said Mallika, "six beings from another dimension – or possibly six separate dimensions - came to earth. The legends surrounding their arrival are not very detailed and I suspect have changed so much over the centuries that they actually contain very little truth.

"What we do know is that these six beings possess immense

power and an insatiable appetite for destruction. Five of them are called the lesser Havocs. You saw one of them today - Osadyn."

Immediately I knew she was referring to the large reptilian creature Rhys had fought. I nodded.

"The other Havocs are of similar power, although each one has unique abilities. Fortunately, all but Osadyn have been bound and are powerless... for now."

"What do you mean bound?" I asked. "Are they tied up somewhere or in some sort of gross monster prison?"

Aata let out a snort of laughter. When I looked over, he grinned at me, and I couldn't help smiling back.

Mallika held up a hand to silence him, not taking her eyes off of me.

"In a way, you have the right of it," she said. "For each of these creatures, there exists one Berserker and one Binder. Rhys is Osadyn's Berserker, and I am his Binder. Only his blood and my power can imprison Osadyn, no other Berserker or Binder could do it. Once a Havoc has been bound, it becomes insubstantial and powerless, tethered to the location of the binding. A bound Havoc has been pushed out of phase with our world so that, although it still exists, it is unable to be seen by mortals or affect anything in the physical plane."

"Why haven't you bound Osadyn?" I asked. "If the Havocs are that bad, why let any of them be free?"

"It's not that simple," said Rhys, fixing me with his deep blue eyes. Immediately, I felt my breath catch, the beginnings of my senses sharpening. Remembering what I had seen when I had looked into those eyes before, I turned away. The thought of peering that deeply into his soul felt like a violation. It had been an accident before. I wouldn't do it on purpose now.

"It's extremely difficult to bind a Havoc," continued Rhys. "The hardest part is keeping it from running away when it senses its Berserker and Binder together. You saw how Osadyn fled when Shing brought Mallika to the fight. They know which Binder and Berserker can affect them and don't stay around long when there is danger of being bound."

"What were those other creatures with it - the ones that turned to goo?"

"They are called Bringers," said Mallika. "They are minions summoned by the Havocs to do their bidding. They use them as warriors and slaves. They are called Bringers because they are particularly suited to capturing Berserkers or Binders. They have the ability to swallow a person whole and bring them to the Havoc they serve."

"Trust me, it's not a pleasant experience," said Kara. I remembered seeing her unconscious and covered in slime as Rhys and Eric ripped the Bringer apart to free her. Yeah, that didn't look fun.

I took a deep breath. Even though Rhys and Mallika were doing all the talking, I felt exhausted. The mental effort to absorb and accept all this was draining.

Concern in his eyes, Rhys looked at me appraisingly. "Are you all right?" he asked. "This can wait if it's too much for you right now."

I shook my head. "No. I've had enough time in the dark. I want answers."

With a quick glance toward Rhys, Mallika continued. "Those Berserkers here - Rhys, Eric, Shing, Aata, and you -" she said, gesturing at me, "are all connected to one of the lesser Havocs. One Binder to bind a Havoc, one Berserker to protect the blood and defend the binding.

"But there are seven other Berserkers as well. These seven are all bound to the sixth creature - Verenix, whom we call the Corrupter." An involuntary shudder ran through the room at the mention of Verenix's name – an unspoken tension that hadn't been there when Mallika talked about the Havocs.

"These seven are not connected one to one, like you five are to the Havocs. The Corrupter is so powerful that it requires the strength of seven Berserkers and Binders to bind it. To free the corrupter would require the blood of all seven of the other Berserkers at the same time – not an easy task, I assure you. One of the Berserkers remains in hiding at any given time, and all of the seven are never together in the same place under any circumstances."

My mind worked furiously to process what Mallika was telling me – and what she was not telling me. These security measures were impressive, but they wouldn't be necessary if there wasn't a danger of someone trying to free the Corrupter.

"But who would want to free the Corrupter?" I asked.

A small frown pulled down the corners of Mallika's mouth. She didn't seem to like my question. After a moment's hesitation, she sighed. "There are those who think they can control these creatures," she said slowly. She seemed cautious and appeared to be carefully weighing her words. "They are under the mistaken delusion that if they can free the Corrupter, or any of the five Havocs, they will be able to harness its abilities. They are desperate people willing to do anything for power."

Silence fell over the room. From the introspective expressions it seemed clear those present had all had dealings with these "desperate people", and they weren't the fluffy kitten kind of experiences.

Rhys spoke next. "That's what we do, Mallika, but she needs to know how all this affects her." He gave her a meaningful look, clearly trying to communicate something without using words. A sick sort of feeling crawled into my stomach. Whatever Rhys was hinting about, I was pretty sure it wasn't going to be good news. With my luck it would turn out that Berserkers fed on puppies or turned into monsters after dark.

"What is it?" I asked, looking from Mallika to Rhys. "Whatever it is that you're not telling me, I would rather know than not know. Unless not knowing will somehow change things?"

"It will not," said Mallika.

"Then I want to know."

Eric laughed, a sound completely out of place among all the serious looks. "Oh, get on with it and tell her all ready," he said. "You're all making it worse by dragging it out."

Both Mallika and Rhys glared at Eric, who threw up his hands and walked out of the room, mumbling to himself.

"You have no doubt noticed certain changes in your body, since you came into your powers," Mallika said. "The enhanced senses, strength, and balance you experience while in the Berserker state are quite noticeable, but they are only the beginning."

I nodded, trying not to let my impatience show. I resisted the urge to tell her to get on with it because I figured that would only make this process longer.

"You also..." she trailed off, peering at me intensely. "Given the fact that you're a girl we don't even know if the same rules apply to you. The powers of a Berserker in a girl could manifest in a completely different way."

My tension must have been obvious because Kara looked at me and said, "Please, Mallika, can't you see you're torturing the poor girl? Just spit it out and let's get this over with."

I wanted to hug Kara.

Mallika nodded, and then leaned her head back and closed her eyes for a long moment. "Keep in mind that what I tell you is true of all Berserkers as far as we know. For you, things may be different.

"Aside from the powers and abilities you have – some of which you still do not know – there is one other physical change that your body goes through as you become a Berserker. You age differently – more slowly. Thirty years from now, I will most assuredly be dead, while you and the other Berserkers will have aged only a single year."

I let out a sigh of relief. That was the big secret – that I would age slower? Talk about an anti-climax.

"Is that it?" I asked. "You were worried about telling me that I would age more slowly?"

"It sounds cool at first," said Aata. "But once everyone you know starts aging and you don't, it becomes less fun. How do you explain to people at your twentieth high-school reunion why you look exactly the same as you did when you graduated?"

"It pulls you out of society," said Mallika. "Out of the world of mortality. You have a few more years before anyone starts to notice, but eventually you will have to give up your family and friends."

I was going to look like I was sixteen for the next thirty years? It would take me – let's see, five times thirty - one hundred and fifty years to even look like a twenty-one-year-old? How could I give up my family and friends? What did they expect me to do – just pick up and leave? Aata was right, this wasn't sounding as fun as it seemed at first.

Eric returned. "I see by the chipper looks that you told her about the aging. Don't worry, Madison. It's not as bad as they all make it seem." For a moment, I saw a faraway look in Eric's eyes as he spoke. A look that told me there was some old pain there. Pain he was trying to hide, or forget. But just as quickly as it appeared, it vanished, replaced by that mischievous gleam. "Being a Berserker is a lot of fun if you just let go and enjoy the ride," he said.

"But why me?" I asked. "Why now? What did I do to get these powers?"

"For the why, well, no one knows how people are chosen," said Mallika. "As far as we can see, there are no factors that all Berserkers have in common. Not genetics, not personality, nor any kind of physical characteristic aside from being male. Now throw in you being a girl and the puzzle becomes even more complicated.

"As for why now, that is a bit easier, although not pleasant." She threw a meaningful look at Eric, who gave an exaggerated sigh and walked back out of the room. "A new Berserker appears every time an old one dies. Berserkers live for an extremely long time – in fact there is no record of any of them dying of old age - but they do die."

"Desperate people?" I asked. If they didn't die of old age, that meant they had to be killed, and given the Berserker powers I had seen, that wasn't likely to be an accident.

"Sometimes," Mallika said. "Although standard weapons have very little effect on a Berserker. Most of the time they are killed by the Havoc they are trying to bind, or a swarm of Bringers, like you faced today."

"So I became a Berserker because the one before me was killed?"

"That's a stark way of putting it, but accurate. Juan, the Berserker you are replacing, was captured by Osadyn. The binding can only be broken with the spilled blood of a living Berserker. Rather than letting Osadyn use his blood to break the binding for Pravicus – the Havoc his blood bound – he killed himself, rendering his blood useless."

There was a moment of silence as we all contemplated Mallika's words. I slumped back in the chair, feeling nauseated. While I believed what I was being told – it's hard to disbelieve after so much evidence – it was difficult to comprehend what all this meant. Until my Berserker powers surfaced, my biggest problems had been social ostracism at school and occasional fights with my parents. They had seemed like big deals at the time, but my new reality made them feel rather insignificant. I couldn't imagine being in a situation where I had to give up my life to save the world. Could I do it? Was I that brave?

"After the death of a Berserker," Mallika said, "a new Berserker appears somewhere in the world. Unfortunately, we have no way of identifying the new Berserker until he berserks for the first time. Once that happens, the other Berserkers can sense the new one. We then search for the Berserker, hoping to find him, or her I suppose, before anyone or anything else does."

Rhys spoke up. "That's why we came to your school. We could sense you in the general area, but we had a difficult time tracking you down. Since new Berserkers are generally between fourteen and eighteen, we figured the best way to find you would be to infiltrate the high school."

"So, I'm a Berserker," I said. "Whether I like it or not, monsters will be after me - some human, some not – wanting to spill my blood to free a Havoc. Am I missing anything?"

Aata pulled a quarter out of his pocket. "She sounds as gloomy as you about all this, Rhys." He threw the coin up into the air. It came within inches of the vaulted ceiling and then plummeted back down. Aata looked directly at me and held out a hand to the side. Without taking his eyes off me, he caught the coin between his thumb and forefinger. He grinned at my look of amazement. "I know there are a lot of risks, and it sounds kind of bad when you think about it too much, but being a Berserker is a lot of fun, too." He winked at me. "Don't worry, Eric and I will show you the fun parts of being a Berserker."

Kara groaned. "You know, Madison, I think having a girl Berserker might be just what these boys need. Dilute a bit of the overflowing testosterone."

"Testosterone?" cried Aata in disbelief. "How about the estrogen flood we're forced to deal with every day?"

Back and forth it went for several minutes as Aata bantered with Kara about the quirks of men and women. Rhys kept silent through all this, and I took the opportunity to surreptitiously watch him. He intrigued me. Yes, he was pleasant to look at – no denying that – but it was more than that. When I looked at him I felt like I was seeing just the smooth surface of a very deep pool.

My cheeks turned red when Rhys glanced over at me and caught me in mid-stare. I turned away, pretending to listen to Aata and Kara. I watched them, but saw nothing. My mind was focused on Rhys and on resisting the temptation to check if he was still looking at me.

Finally, Mallika said: "That is enough discussion of gender differences. There is one more very important fact to reveal to Madison."

The conversation skidded to a halt, and all eyes focused on Mallika. Despite everything we had gone through, she still sat upright with perfect posture, giving the impression of a queen on a throne.

"Osadyn." The silence somehow grew deeper as Mallika spoke

that name. It seemed to bring a palpable weight with it. Weight and fear.

"There have been many theories over the years about the nature of the five Havocs. For many centuries they were thought to be merely animals – powerful, but lacking intelligence. We no longer believe that to be true. They raise armies, set ambushes, and even select specific targets. They think, they plan, and they are focused.

"You, Madison, are the Berserker whose blood binds Pravicus. Over the last twenty years, there have been five different Berserkers in the same position. That is unheard of in our world – Berserkers generally live for hundreds of years, if not longer. We can only attribute it to the fact that, for some unknown reason, Osadyn wants very badly to free Pravicus.

"That means you, Madison, are in serious danger. You are too new to the Berserker world to understand just how serious today's attack was. All the histories indicate that the Havocs rarely attack directly, preferring to work through others in the shadows, and they never attack Berserkers.

"But that is no longer reality. We've witnessed a change in Osadyn's behavior over the past twenty years, and we've concluded that Osadyn has begun focusing his efforts on the easiest target - the new Berserker. We used to be the hunters, but now we are being hunted."

"You mean I'm being hunted," I said. "Osadyn's not after the rest of you, just me, right?"

Mallika slowly nodded. "That is correct."

I looked around the room, but no one met my eyes. The atmosphere had changed from one of comfortable banter to wary silence, and it obviously had to do with Osadyn coming after me.

"What's going on?" I asked. No one answered. "What aren't you telling me?"

"We can't do it," said Rhys, his head down and staring at the floor. "Not to a girl."

"Can't do what?" I demanded. No one answered. "Can't do what?" I repeated significantly louder.

"Use you as bait," said Eric. He leaned against the door frame, his arms folded, looking grim. When had he walked back in?

"Bait?"

"Bait," Eric said. All eyes turned to him, even Mallika's. "Normally, we try to hunt down any unbound Havoc. But it's a bit like hunting a rabbit on foot - a really ugly, dangerous rabbit that could turn and rip out your throat at any minute. Havocs usually run from us. They know we're there to bind them, and they don't make it easy for us. Now Osadyn has begun hunting the Berserker whose blood binds Pravicus. From a tactical perspective, since we know he wants to slaughter you and drain your blood to free Pravicus – oh all of you stop looking at me like that, it's the truth isn't it? – we have the unique opportunity to set a trap."

There was an immediate uproar as everyone started talking at once. Rhys stood up and began shouting at Eric while Kara placed herself between them, trying to calm them down. Mallika and Aata joined the fray, and the room soon became so loud that it was

146

impossible to hear myself think, let alone make out what everyone was saying.

"Stop!" I yelled, my hands clenched into fists.

The silence that followed felt wonderful. I closed my eyes and took a deep breath, thinking things through.

Bait. Images of worms on hooks and buckets of chopped fish flashed through my mind. Not pleasant thoughts. Bait helps to capture animals, but it doesn't often survive the process. Was I prepared for that?

What was the alternative?

Run? For how long?

Like it or not, I was a Berserker. There was nothing I could do to change that. Osadyn had chosen me as his target and even if I ran, he'd eventually catch me. Did I want to be bait in a trap or spend my life running?

When I opened my eyes, everyone's attention was fixed on me. Mallika's gaze was particularly piercing, but I turned away from her and looked directly at Eric as I spoke. "I'll do it."

CHAPTER 10

LIES, EXCUSES, AND SURPRISES

Once again the room erupted into chaos. I hated listening to arguments. More than that, I hated people arguing about me. I groaned, wishing there were something hard to bang my head against.

Kara seemed to sense my distress. She walked over and whispered in my ear, "You'd think at their age they would have better manners than this." She gave my hand a squeeze and let out a piercing whistle just a few decibels shy of a jet engine taking off.

"You should all be ashamed of yourselves," she said and put a protective arm around me. "Can't you see your squawking and growling is upsetting the poor girl?"

All eyes turned to me, and I felt the heat of embarrassment color my cheeks. What Kara said was true, but it made me feel like a toddler listening to her parents fight.

"I appreciate your concern," I said to Rhys, as he was the one who seemed most opposed to putting me in any kind of danger. "But the fact that I'm a girl doesn't change anything. Osadyn is still hunting me. I still have powers. No matter what we do, I'll still be a target. If Osadyn is going to come after me, I would rather fight when and where we choose."

Rhys opened his mouth to speak, but Mallika put a hand on his arm. "Let's not discuss this right now," she said. "I think Madison has more than enough to think about for today. We can talk this over when we've had a chance to cool down and think through the, ah, additional facts that have come to light." She looked at her watch. "Besides, it's getting late and I imagine that Madison's parents might get worried if she doesn't come home soon."

I checked my watch and saw that it was already 5:30. Where had the time gone? I guess time flies when you find out evil creatures want to spill your blood. Not that I really wanted to go home right then. Going home meant explaining to my mom how her car had gone from a compact to a sub-compact. Not something I was looking forward to.

"I'll take her," said Eric. He grabbed my hand and started to pull me towards the door, but stopped when Rhys blocked his path.

"Can I talk now?" asked Rhys in a rather dry tone. He looked from person to person until he had everyone's attention. "Regardless of what we eventually decide regarding Osadyn, the fact remains that Madison is in danger, and should have someone guarding her - at least until she is better trained in her powers. We've already seen that Osadyn is going to actively seek her out."

"Agreed," said Mallika. "You and Eric can watch her during

school since you already have a pretense to be there. Shing and Aata can take the overnight shifts."

Overnight shifts? I didn't like the sound of this. Being under twenty-four hour guard sounded more like prison than protection. I was about to protest when my mind flashed back to Osadyn, massive and powerful, directing hundreds of those creatures towards me.

Maybe protection wasn't such a bad idea.

While they worked out the logistical details, Eric took my arm and pulled me out of the house.

Once outside, he took a deep breath and stretched. "Ah, it feels good to finally be out of there."

He let me into the Range Rover and even opened my door for me. It felt strangely formal, almost like we were on a date, rather than being relative strangers thrown together by magic and monsters.

"Where to?" he asked. "Do you need anything from your car, or do you just want me to take you home?"

I sighed. I didn't really want to go back to the car. That would force me to confront the situation, and how I was going to explain things to my mother? Unfortunately, my backpack and purse were in the car, and I would definitely need them.

I blew out a breath. "The car."

"The car it is," he said. We drove back to the remnants of Mom's Jetta. It looked even worse than I had remembered it - battered and dented like a discarded child's toy.

The doors were so warped that I couldn't get them open. How was I going to get my things out of the car?

Eric saw my distress and stepped in to help.

"One of the real advantages of being a Berserker," Eric said, "is the fact that you never need the Jaws of Life." He 'zerked and ripped the roof off the car with his bare hands.

"And is this something you need to do often?" I asked.

Eric winked at me. "More often than you'd think."

We salvaged what we could from the car, which was basically my personal belongings. The more I looked at the damage, the more I dreaded having to tell my parents about the car. What excuse could I possibly come up with to explain this? A car crash wouldn't work since there was no way I could have gotten out of the car alive, let alone without a scratch.

"Let's go," I said, once I had everything worth taking. "I need to get home and figure out how I'm going to explain this to my mom."

Eric laughed as he helped me load my things into the Range Rover. "Don't worry," he said. "I'll take care of everything."

"You'll take care of everything?" I asked. "And how are you going to do that?"

"You'll see."

We pulled into the driveway and Eric escorted me out of the car. He insisted on carrying everything, despite my objections.

"Honestly, I'm perfectly capable of carrying my own backpack," I said.

"So am I," he said, and we walked up to the front door.

I took a deep breath before going inside. This wasn't going to be pleasant.

Mom was in the kitchen making dinner. A delicious aroma of garlic bread and alfredo sauce filled the house.

I looked over at Eric and for an instant saw an expression of wistfulness infused into his features, as though he were coming home after a long trip. There was a sort of sadness there, hidden behind the smile.

"Madison, is that you?" called Mom.

"Yeah, it's me," I said.

"Oh, good," she said. "It was getting late, and I hadn't heard from you. Your dad's out running an errand and dinner will be ready any minute." She walked out of the kitchen drying her hands on a dishtowel and stopped when she saw Eric. "Oh, you have a, um, friend." She looked meaningfully at me.

Leave it to my mom to think that any boy I brought home would be some sort of romantic interest. "Relax, Mom," I said. "Eric is a friend from school who gave me a ride home. He was just leaving."

Eric strode forward and shook my mom's hand. "A pleasure to meet you, Mrs. Montgomery," he said. "My name is Eric Douglass."

Mom looked slightly nonplussed. "Nice to meet you too, Eric." She turned to me. "Perhaps you can explain to me why you needed a ride home when you took my car to school?"

I still didn't have a convincing story to explain what had happened. Car accident? Falling meteor? Outbreak of bubonic plague?

"It was my fault," said Eric, before I could speak.

"Your fault?" I asked.

Eric put on a very serious expression. "Yes, my fault. You see, my uncle is a rare and exotic animal dealer. And no, he doesn't deal with any of the legally questionable animals like some do who give the whole industry a bad name. Anyway, he recently came into possession of a rare albino moose."

I glared at Eric. What was he getting at? Was he trying to get me grounded for life?

"An albino moose?" said Mom, a confused look on her face.

"Yes, a moose," continued Eric. "My uncle was shipping it by truck from Canada down to California where he has a buyer. Well, you see, I have a particular fondness for moose, so my uncle thought it would be a treat for me to see this rare specimen. We arranged to meet in the school parking lot where there would be enough room to let the moose stretch its legs."

Pausing for a moment, Eric put his arm around my shoulders. I felt a shiver of excitement and that familiar feeling of my senses heightening.

Eric turned to me, a look of slight panic in his eyes. For a full second, he stared at me before turning back to look at my mom.

"Well, everything went fine at first," he said. "We brought the moose out and let it walk around for a bit. Then it saw your car."

Mom raised an eyebrow and began twisting the dishtowel in her hands.

"I've since found out that this is a perfectly natural moose reaction," Eric said, "but the moose apparently mistook your car for a rival male and attacked."

"A moose attacked my car?"

Eric nodded solemnly. "It was very thorough. A fully grown moose like this one can weigh up to eighteen hundred pounds. I'm afraid there isn't much left of your car."

The towel in Mom's hands was twisted so tightly that it had folded in on itself and formed a sort of ball. "My car is totaled?"

"Yes, but don't worry, my Uncle takes full responsibility for this unfortunate incident and his insurance will cover everything. We've already had the car towed away, and I will have a brand new car waiting for you in the driveway tomorrow morning before school."

Mom looked thoughtful as she processed Eric's ridiculous story. There was no way she was going to buy this. I would have been better off telling her I had been hit by a drunk driver or something that might have at least generated a bit of sympathy for me.

Finally, Mom smiled. "Well, Eric," she said, "I'm glad to hear your uncle is willing to make this right."

"You're not mad?" I asked.

Mom let the towel untwist, and flipped it over her shoulder. "Why bother? It wasn't anyone's fault, really. Well, it wasn't a very smart idea to let a fully grown moose walk in a parking lot, but no one could have predicted it would attack a car." She turned and walked back into the kitchen.

Once we were alone, I grabbed Eric and pulled him towards the front door, away from the kitchen and where my mom couldn't overhear. "What were you thinking?" I hissed.

Eric just shrugged and gave me that annoyingly smug grin. "Since we couldn't tell her the truth," he said, "we might as well have fun with the story. Besides, I've found that the more ridiculous the story, the more likely people are to believe it – to a point at least. They think you couldn't possibly make something like that up."

"What about the part about your uncle's insurance and having a new car in the driveway tomorrow? How are we – no wait, hold that - how am I going to explain things in the morning when there's no car here?"

But Eric didn't seem to be the least bit concerned. "Oh, I'm sure you'll think of something," he said. And with a wink he slipped out the front door, leaving me alone to deal with the fallout of his lies.

I walked into the kitchen, prepared to face the inquisition now that Eric was gone, but to my surprise Mom didn't seem too worried about the car. She was more interested in finding out whether I had been in any danger from the moose.

At dinner that night, Dad also seemed more concerned about my safety than the fact that the car had been totaled. All in all they were taking the news much better than I had thought. When I mentioned that, Dad shrugged.

"I guess it means we love you, or something," he said with a wry smile. He reached across the table and gave my hand a squeeze.

Before I went to bed that night, I thought about the day's events: Ginger's repeated sabotage, the basketball game, detention, being attacked by Osadyn and his minions, and finally discovering I was a Berserker.

Had all that been today?

I was pretty sure that time must have somehow lengthened to cram an extra dozen hours into the day, because it didn't seem possible for so much to happen in such a short amount of time. And given all the strange stuff that had happened to me lately, the idea of time lengthening didn't seem quite as impossible as it once would have.

I had expected to be awake for several hours thinking through everything, but instead, I fell asleep as soon as my head hit the pillow.

The next morning I woke up to my alarm, a feeling of dread surrounding me. I got ready for the day on autopilot, wracking my brains trying to think of a way to explain why there wasn't a new car in the driveway. By the time I was dressed and ready to go, I still hadn't come up with an answer.

Serious stares greeted me as I entered the kitchen. Obviously, my parents had been outside and seen the empty driveway. My mind raced, looking to some sort of inspiration, but I had nothing.

"Good morning, Madison," said Dad. His voice sounded strange. It was that over-enunciation thing he did when he was angry and trying to remain calm. "There is a package for you on the counter."

A small package wrapped in bright red paper sat on the island on top of a card in a matching envelope.

I opened the card first. It was from Eric.

Dear Madison,

I hope you didn't get into too much trouble for my reckless actions last night. I couldn't find a Jetta exactly like the one that was totaled, so I had to improvise. I hope that this will be an acceptable replacement.

Sincerely, proverbially, sophomorically and many other adverbs,

Eric

Inside the box was a set of keys with a Mercedes symbol on them. I looked up at my dad, finally understanding the strange tension I had been feeling.

"It's in the driveway," he said.

I walked outside and saw it gleaming in the morning light. The sleek metallic gray body rode low to the ground, a predator ready to hunt down its quarry. I had no idea what kind of car it was, except that it was a Mercedes and that meant it was expensive.

A lot more expensive than Mom's Jetta.

"You know you can't accept this," Dad said.

No surprise there. I loved my Father, but I also knew he was a very practical man, and an expensive sports car like this was a huge waste of money in his opinion.

I didn't know for sure how much money we had, but I was pretty sure from some oblique comments Mom had made in the past that Dad was loaded from some sort of inheritance. The "consulting job" he claimed to have was more of a hobby than an occupation.

Of course, you would never know Dad was wealthy from the way we lived. Everything we owned practically screamed middle class, and my parents wouldn't dream of spoiling me by buying me my own car – no matter what tactic I tried. Mom let me co-opt her car most of the time, but they had both made it very clear that it was hers, not mine, and that usage was based solely on their capricious whims and could be revoked at any time.

So, given my parents' attitude towards excess and wasted money, Eric couldn't have picked a worse car to replace my mom's Jetta with.

I examined the car more closely. I had seen other Mercedes before, but I did not recognize this one. When I attempted to open the door, instead of pulling out like a normal car door, it lifted diagonally into the air, like the wing of a large metallic bug.

Standing in the driveway, I wasn't sure if I wanted to laugh or cry. In a few short months, my life had been turned completely upside down: I had strange super powers like something out of a comic book, giant monsters wanted my blood, and now Eric had given my mom an obscenely expensive car.

Could my life get any stranger?

"Who is this Eric person, anyway?" Dad asked. "I haven't heard you talk about him before."

"He's a new kid who just moved into the Height's area with his family. His brother is in some of my classes."

Dad was immediately suspicious. "When a guy spends that much money to impress a girl – especially in high school – you know he has ulterior motives."

I instinctively wanted to defend Eric, but I didn't for two reasons. First, if you didn't know Eric and I were Berserkers and a monster had crushed my car, it did seem strange for him to give me such a nice car. And second, even given that we were Berserkers and a monster had crushed my car, it still seemed strange. I didn't know much about cars, but this one looked like it might have cost more than our house. Why give me such an expensive car to replace the Jetta?

I spent most of breakfast arguing with my parents about the car. They were united in their opinion that we could not accept it, and there was no budging them on that point. I would have had better luck trying to get them to let me tattoo a swastika across my forehead.

After some masterful negotiating on my part, however, I did manage to convince them to let me drive it to school and give it back to Eric.

When I eased into the driver's seat, I noted with relief that it was an automatic, not a stick. I had spent some time in my dad's truck, learning the basics of a manual transmission, but I had never gotten very good at it. The last thing I wanted was to wreck this car while trying to return it.

Even though was an automatic, it was still extremely difficult to drive. The lightest touch on the gas pedal sent the car roaring forwards and triggered an automatic slam-on-the-breaks reaction. As a consequence, the first few blocks of the drive were punctuated by multiple loud squeals from both the car and myself.

To make things even more nerve wracking, after several minutes I noticed that someone in a large black truck was following me. The windows were tinted, so I couldn't tell who it was. I recalled Mallika's warning about desperate people who wanted to free and control the Havocs.

As I started to panic, I felt my senses sharpening and my reflexes quickening, a sensation that I was now starting to think of as "pre-zerking". It gave me some of the physical powers, but I didn't start glowing and destroying things.

In my pre-zerking state, I no longer felt out of control in this car. I pressed on the gas and was immediately slammed into my seat as the car leapt forward.

I took a quick right, sped forward, darted left, trying to lose the truck. After several minutes of this, I could no longer see the truck behind me. I doubled back towards the school and headed there as quickly as the car would take me, breaking most traffic laws in the process.

When I pulled into the student parking lot, Eric and Rhys were waiting next to their Range Rover. I parked next to them and got out, glad to have their company.

Glancing over my shoulder, I spoke before either of them had a chance to say anything. "There's someone following me," I said, "in a big black truck with tinted windows."

"You mean that one?" asked Eric, pointing at the truck pulling into the school parking lot.

It was the same truck. How had it followed me here?

"Don't worry," said Rhys. "It's just Aata. He had the assignment to watch you last night and to make sure you got to school safely.

Aata pulled up next to us and rolled down his window. He shook his head. "You drive like a maniac," he said and then laughed. "Nice job. If I hadn't felt you 'zerking, I wouldn't have been able to follow you."

Eric looked at me quizzically. "You 'zerked in the car?" he asked. "How did you manage to avoid destroying it?"

I blushed, partly from Aata's compliment, but partly because Eric remembered me telling him that I tended to destroy things while 'zerking.

"I didn't 'zerk," I said. "I don't know what you call it, but it was that sort of pre-zerk where you feel your reflexes sharpen, but you don't fully 'zerk and glow and destroy buildings – or cars. What do you guys call it?"

"Impossible," said Eric. "Or at least that's what I would have called it before we had a girl Berserker." He exchanged a significant look with Rhys. "'Zerking doesn't work like that for us - it's an all or nothing deal. I've never heard of any other Berserker who has experienced that, but I think it's becoming clear that the rules have changed. We are going to have to question everything since the old rules don't seem to apply to you."

They wanted to ask me more about my pre-zerking, but the Mercedes had attracted a crowd of admirers and any pretense at privacy was shot. Aata drove back to the Berserker house, while Eric, Rhys, and I walked into school.

On the way in the door I handed the keys to Eric. He looked at them for a moment and then tried to hand them back to me. "What's this for?"

"I can't accept the car," I said. "My parents insist I give it back."

Eric seemed genuinely surprised. "But I was just replacing the car that had been destroyed. Your mom seemed fine with the idea."

I didn't make any motion to take the keys back. "Yeah, that was before she knew you were going to replace her Jetta with a Mercedes. My dad now thinks you have ulterior motives, and insists that I give it back."

Eric raised one eyebrow. "Ulterior motives? I like the sound of that." He tossed the keys up in the air, caught them in his hand and pocketed them. "He's right. I did have some ulterior motives. I figured we were going to be spending quite a bit of time together as you get trained, and I thought this might provide a bit of a diversion during the off hours."

I stopped in front of my locker. "Sorry, no diversions for me, apparently. Can we just arrange to get the Jetta replaced and then call it good?"

Eric gave me a deep bow. "Whatever you desire. Your wish is my command." He paused for a moment. "Or at least one piece of information I'll consider before doing whatever I feel like."

Since Rhys was in my first period class, he walked me to Physics. Eric accompanied us part-way, and once we reached the hallway that led to his first class, he reluctantly left.

After Physics, Rhys escorted me to History class. After History, Eric was waiting to take me to Study Hall. After Study Hall both of them escorted me to lunch. The whole thing seemed a bit weird. It was almost like they were in some kind of competition to see who could walk me to the most classes.

The three of us sat together at lunch. They joined me at my old table, rather than sitting at the more central location they had occupied before.

"Your table gives us more privacy," explained Rhys. "We only sat out in that one so we could have a better view of the students while looking for the new Berserker." The look on Eric's face indicated that he disagreed with Rhys, but he didn't object to the seating arrangements – not out loud at least.

During lunch it quickly became clear that Rhys and Eric had wildly different agendas for the conversation. Rhys wanted to make specific plans on how we were going to keep me safe and perhaps work out a schedule for protection, whereas Eric felt that the whole danger thing was blown out of proportion and that we should just relax and get to know each other.

I, however, wanted to know more about being a Berserker, so I began asking carefully targeted questions.

"What's it like being a Berserker?" I asked.

My question must have taken them by surprise, because for a moment no one answered. Eric recovered first. "Long stretches of boredom punctuated by exciting events."

"It's a duty," said Rhys. "There are some things that I love about being a Berserker, but it requires a lot of sacrifice."

"Like what?" I asked.

"Like family and friends," said Rhys. "Your social and communal identity. You give up being part of a larger group of people who share the same values, ideals, common experiences and memories." Rhys reached out and put a hand on top of mine. My heart skipped a beat and it became extremely difficult to pay attention to anything but the warmth of his skin on mine. "Being a Berserker isolates you from the rest of the world. You can interact with individuals, but you can never get close. Getting close risks people discovering who we are and what we are guarding, and that puts everyone involved in danger."

Eric's eyes narrowed as he saw Rhys' hand on mine. He set down his sandwich and turned his chair to face me. "This is where Rhys and I have a fundamental disagreement about life. He can't let go of what he's given up and start to enjoy life again." Rhys started to protest, but Eric cut him off with a gesture. "Yes, there is sacrifice. I too had to give up my loved ones... eventually. But being a Berserker means doing things that other people can only dream of - strength, speed, endurance, and extended life. I've traveled all over the world, Madison. I've climbed to the top of Mount Everest and gone diving in the deepest ocean trenches. These are all things I would have never experienced if I hadn't become a Berserker."

"And my point is that we have no one to share our experiences with," said Rhys. He had released my hand while Eric was talking and was now staring into his milk carton. He seemed far away, as if he weren't really with us. "The joy of life is not in the experience itself, but sharing that experience with those you love. When those you love are dead, all that remains are those you are bound to by duty."

And so it went on for the rest of lunch, the two of them arguing back and forth, and I got the impression that this wasn't the first time they'd had this discussion. The interesting thing was that they really had the same basic premise – being a Berserker was a huge sacrifice – but their reactions to it were different.

As for me, listening to them completely jumbled my emotions. I felt as though I been thrown off a cliff and was plummeting downward with no idea what was below me or when the ride was going to stop. All I knew was that it would have to stop eventually, and I was afraid it would end with a very messy splat.

After lunch Eric and Rhys escorted me to Precalc, neither of them seeming to want to let the other one be alone with me. Eric in particular seemed to be vying for my attention. He placed himself between Rhys and me whenever possible, and was very adept at focusing the conversation between the two of us, excluding Rhys.

After that brief moment when he held my hand, Rhys had avoided physical contact. It must have simply been a comforting gesture without any significance beyond that. This theory was supported by the fact that he didn't compete with Eric for my attention. He simply stayed by us while Eric directed the conversation.

When Gym finally came around, I was glad to be away from the two of them. I really liked being with each of them individually, but this whole situation was getting strange. The tension between them was putting me on edge.

Amy had already changed by the time I entered the locker room. She had an excited look on her face, as if barely contained gossip was about to break forth in a torrent of who-likes-who and did-you-see-what-she-was-wearing.

"So," she said. "Are the rumors true?"

I opened my locker. "You're going to have to get a bit more specific than that, Amy," I said.

Amy put her hands on her hips. "Don't play coy with me, Madison. Come on, is it true that Eric and Rhys have been walking you to classes?"

Just what I needed, more people talking about me. Didn't anyone have a life of their own around here?

Instead of answering right away, I pulled my clothes out of my gym bag. I needed to be careful. Amy was way too perceptive and she had already picked up on my interest in them earlier.

"Come on," said Amy, leaning against the lockers. "You're killing me!"

I sighed. "Yes, they walked me to my classes."

Amy began bouncing in excitement. "And?"

"There's no 'and'," I said. "We're just friends."

Amy narrowed her eyes. "Madison, it's me. Come on."

"You're reaching, Amy." I continued changing.

Amy grilled me for the next five minutes, trying to ferret out a confession of undying love for Rhys or Eric, or both. When the tough-girl approach didn't work, she switched tactics and tried pouting and guilt. No matter what I said, she wouldn't believe that I wasn't hiding a secret relationship.

I was relieved when class started, and Amy and I were separated. We had more basketball on the agenda, and thankfully Mrs. Herst made sure that Ginger and I were on separate courts. Ginger was sporting a large, strangely-patterned bruise on her forehead, but didn't appear to be suffering any complications from yesterday's basketball game.

Given recent events, I thought she would be nastier than ever, but it didn't seem to be playing out that way. She had completely ignored me all day, which I considered a huge improvement. I did catch her glaring at me a few times during class, but she appeared to be more wary of me than vengeful. Apparently yesterday had made more of an impression than just the one on her forehead.

After gym class, Amy resumed her inquisition right where she had left off. There was no hope of calling her off until she got what she wanted. She followed me to my locker, unwilling to accept that I wasn't concealing crucial information.

She was actually right: I was holding back information, but not the kind she was expecting, or that I could tell her.

While I was pulling my things out of my locker, Rhys approached and hovered a short distance away, apparently unwilling to interrupt my conversation with Amy. She noticed him before I did and subtly signaled me, closely watching my reaction.

I carefully kept any sign of giddy excitement off of my face, which wasn't actually that difficult. Yes, Rhys and Eric were cute – cuter than Josh, even – but they didn't give me the same giddy, brain-melting paralysis that Josh did. It just wasn't the same kind of relationship. I pushed away the thought of Rhys putting his hand on mine during lunch.

It was completely different.

Amy motioned for me to go talk with Rhys, so I waved him over.

"Rhys, this is my good friend, Amy. Amy, Rhys."

Perhaps I didn't get brain-melting paralysis around Rhys and Eric, but Amy did. She looked at Rhys with this strange simpering look on her face, giving off helpless-maiden-waiting-to-be-rescued vibes. Amy? My Machiavelli of relationships and all things dating related?

Rhys had clearly picked up on the vibes and looked distinctly uncomfortable. "Uh, nice to meet you," he said.

Amy didn't appear to have heard. She continued to stare adoringly at him, a lovesick puppy looking for a home. I nudged her with my elbow, jarring her back to her senses. She blushed a crimson red, a shade of color I hadn't ever seen on her before.

"Yeah, very nice to meet you," she mumbled. "I'll see you later, Madison," she said and practically ran down the hall.

What had gotten into her? If I didn't know that she was still smitten with Cory I would have thought she was interested in Rhys.

"Do you get that sort of reaction a lot?" I asked.

Rhys shook his head. "Eric's the ladies man."

"Speaking of which,' I said, "where is he?" I hadn't seen him since Precalc.

Rhys shrugged. "I'm not sure. But knowing Eric he won't be far."

We walked through the hallways without any sign of him. We didn't spot him until we reached the parking lot.

The Mercedes was gone. In its place was a gleaming blue Jetta identical to the one Osadyn had crushed. Eric lounged lazily on the hood, tying to appear nonchalant – but he looked over at us too many times for me to buy his cool act.

I laughed and ran over to him. "How did you get the car so quickly?"

"I have some connections," he said, and hopped to the ground. "No big deal."

"Maybe not to you, but this will save me hours of parental guilt lectures." I gave him a big hug.

By this time Rhys had caught up. His expression was hard to read – a strange mixture of happiness and fury. He was smiling, but it was a tight, not-so-happy smile. The smile of a person pretending – badly, I might add – to be happy. Clearly he was upset at what Eric had done.

"What's wrong?" I asked.

"Nothing," he said. When I looked into his eyes, I no longer saw anything below the surface. The deep pools I had gazed into had become shallow puddles, cutting me off from his thoughts.

"Come on, Madison," said Eric, opening the driver's side door for me. "Let's test it out."

I slid into the driver's seat and Eric into the front passenger seat. Rhys didn't move. He remained where he was, his hands thrust into his pockets. His conflicted expression had given way to a more serious, contemplative look.

"Aren't you coming?" I asked.

"No," he said. Then with an obvious effort he produced a genuine smile. The kind of smile that I could stare at for hours. "You two have fun." He turned to Eric. "I'll see you back at the house."

Eric waved as we pulled out of the parking lot. "Tell Kara not to wait up for me," he yelled out the window.

Pulling onto the street, I picked a direction and started driving. The car was in perfect working order, but it lacked the acceleration power of the Mercedes. It was brand new and still had that new car smell, something that my mom's Jetta had lost some time ago. "Where to," I asked?

"Let's go to your house," Eric said. "I want to make sure this car is acceptable to your parents."

"Really?" I said. "My house?" That wasn't exactly what I had planned on doing, but it made a twisted sort of sense, and would probably spare me the Spanish Inquisition later.

When we pulled into the driveway, my dad's truck was there.

"It looks like my dad's home," I said.

"Good," said Eric. "I want to meet him."

I hesitated. "I'm not so sure if that's such a good idea," I said. "He already thinks you have some nefarious plan to seduce me."

Eric got out of the car and came around to open my door. "Your father sounds like a smart man," he said. "I wouldn't trust me, either."

I was about to ask him what that comment was supposed to mean, but he was already walking to the front door. I hurried to catch up - there was no way I was going to let him meet my dad without some backup. Considering the way Dad treated Josh, who had given him no reason not to like him, I could only imagine what he might do to a boy he didn't like.

We slipped inside. I heard the faint sound of a keyboard clicking.

Dad must be in his office. I dumped my things by the door and walked down the entry hall.

"Madison is that you?" Dad's voice called.

"Yeah, it's me," I said. I hesitated. It still wasn't too late. Dad didn't know Eric was there. I could easily smuggle him out of the house without anyone knowing he had come.

Eric seemed to know exactly what I was thinking. He rolled his eyes, then grabbed my hand, and pulled me towards Dad's office. Clearly there was no way he was going to leave without meeting my parents.

Dad sat behind a large desk that dominated the office. He was an amateur photographer, and framed photos he had taken decorated the walls. Mom had made her influence felt by insisting on putting up curtains and some decorative knickknacks.

He didn't look up as we came in, his attention focused on his computer screen.

"Hey, Dad," I said. "This is Eric."

"Hello, Eric," Dad said. He glanced at Eric, then back to the computer screen, and then immediately back at Eric, this time his eyes wide. They stayed wide for a second, then narrowed with fury. He shoved himself away from the computer and stood up.

"You," he said, pointing at Eric. It sounded like an accusation. "Get away from my daughter!"

Eric took a step back, all pretense of coolness gone, his mouth literally hung open in an expression of shock. For the first time since I had met him, Eric appeared to be completely flustered.

"Scottie?" he said, the word barely squeaking out of his throat, "is that you?"

CHAPTER 11

REVISIONIST HISTORY LESSONS

W ho was Scottie? My dad's name was Bruce. What was going on here?

"You know each other?" I asked.

I might as well have kept my mouth shut for all the good it did. Dad and Eric were locked in an epic staring match - neither of them responding to anything.

When Dad finally spoke, it was with barely controlled anger. "What are you doing with my daughter?"

Eric's eyes flicked over to me, then back to Dad. "Madison's your daughter? The one you had before..." he trailed off as Dad held up a hand.

"Don't say another word," Dad said. He walked over to the office door and held it open for me. "Madison, I need a moment alone with Eric."

"No." My voice sounded much calmer than I felt. "I don't know what's going on here, but I'm not going to leave until I find out."

I had been prepared to watch Dad explode. Instead he seemed to deflate and lose a bit of his anger. "Please, Madison," he said. "I promise you this is nothing you want to be a part of."

"It's too late for that," said Eric.

A look of dawning comprehension crossed Dad's face, followed by an expression of horror. "A Binder?" he asked.

How did Dad know about Binders? And if he did know, why would he be so upset that I was one?

Eric shook his head, looking uncomfortable. "She's a Berserker, Scottie."

Dad's eyes narrowed and he clenched his fists. "That's not funny." He looked on the verge of attacking, and while my dad was a very large man, he was no match for Eric's Berserker powers.

"I know it seems impossible," said Eric. "But it's true, Scottie. I've seen her 'zerk myself."

The strength seemed to leave Dad's legs and he slid down the wall, sinking to the floor. I'd never seen my dad like this before. It was as if Eric had told him that I had terminal cancer and had only a few weeks to live.

Without looking up he asked, "Are you sure?" His voice sounded dead and hollow.

"Yes."

"Which Havoc?"

"Pravicus."

Dad nodded as if expecting this. "So all those years of running and hiding were for nothing," he said. "It's all come full circle."

This had gone on long enough. "Will someone please tell me what's going on here? Dad, how do you know about all this?"

Dad got to his feet, his initial shock past. He took a deep breath before speaking. "Because I was a Berserker."

My initial reaction was to laugh. Dad? A Berserker? Ridiculous. How could someone like my dad possibly be a Berserker? He was way too boring – a dad, not a Berserker. Besides, it didn't fit in with what I had been told. Once you were a Berserker, you were one until you died – and that might be hundreds of years later. It wasn't like you could just quit and drop out.

Could you?

I walked over to Dad's chair and sat down. "It sounds like you both have a story to tell me." I crossed my legs and folded my arms. "Let's hear it."

Eric threw up his hands and stepped backwards. "It's not my story to tell," he said.

Dad ran his hands through his hair, causing it to stand up awkwardly and giving him a rumpled, tired look. "Where do I even begin? This isn't a story I ever rehearsed, thinking I would tell you one day, Madison." He blew out a breath. "I suppose it begins with your mother – your birth mother."

I immediately perked up. I loved hearing about my birth mom, but Dad rarely mentioned her. When I was younger, I used to pester Dad with questions about her, but I stopped when I realized how much the memories hurt him. Even now I could see the pain was still there.

"What does Mom have to do with any of this?" I asked.

"Your mother was a Binder," said Dad.

Now it was my turn to be surprised beyond words. I stared incredulously at Dad, but he didn't seem to notice.

"She and I met twenty-five years ago," he continued. "My old Binder had passed away from natural causes and your mom had become the new Binder. We found her in a small town in the south of France, an innocent girl who had never left the country. It took a while to convince her of her abilities, but when she finally understood, she committed to the cause with all her heart.

"Over the next few years we traveled all over the world. I'd had many Binders before, but none like Monique."

If I hadn't been sitting down, my legs would have given out. Everything that Dad was telling me about my mom was completely different from what I thought I had known.

He'd always said that he and Mom had met in college in an art class and fallen in love at first sight. She was from Cincinnati, not France, and her name was Heather, not Monique.

Tears welled up as I realized that I actually knew nothing about my mother. Everything I thought I had known was a lie.

The tears falling down my cheeks made Dad stop his story. For a moment he looked surprised, then confused, and finally he rushed over and swept me up in a hug.

"Oh, Madison," he said. "I didn't want to lie to you about your mom, but I was trying to protect you. You know I wouldn't ever deliberately hurt you, don't you?" He pulled back and looked anxiously into my eyes – which were still leaking tears.

I jerked back and turned away from him. "You lied to me, Dad. How could you lie to me about my own mother?"

Eric spoke up from the corner. "Yeah, I uh, have a surprise bar mitzvah I need to go to," he said. "I'll see you in school tomorrow, Madison." He exited the room and closed the door to the study behind him.

"I had my reasons, Madison," said Dad's voice from behind me.

"Really?" Anger flared up in me. "You had reasons to tell me lies and make me think I actually knew anything about my mother?"

Dad was quiet for a moment. When he spoke again there was a tightness in his voice, as if he were trying very hard to keep his emotions in check.

"When Monique left her village and realized what the world had to offer, she was like a bird spreading its wings. She had a childlike innocence that was unlike anyone I had ever met.

"Despite the rules, despite every piece of common sense that was in me, I fell in love with her. An uncontrollable head-over heels love. I felt that I had found my soul mate - my other half. Rationally, I knew it couldn't work. She would age normally, grow older, and die, all while I aged only a few years.

"But we were in love and all reasons to stay away from each other felt too intellectual, too far removed from our emotions for us to listen to them. We finally embraced irrationality and got married, accepting the challenges that lay ahead of us.

"For two glorious years we lived as husband and wife – Berserker and Binder. We traveled the world, exploring its wonders together.

"When I found out Monique was pregnant, I was ecstatic. I'd always wanted to be a father, but being a Berserker, I didn't see how it could ever happen. Physically, I knew I had the capability to father a child. I just never thought I would have the opportunity to raise a child – to be a father."

I turned around. Seeing Dad triggered more tears. He took an uncertain step towards me, obviously wanting to make things better, but I held up a hand to keep him away. I was still too upset to want his comfort.

"Then what happened?" I asked.

Dad paused and looked me in the eyes. "Then you were born," he said. "And you were the most perfect little girl I had ever seen." He smiled, lost in memory. "You had both of us wrapped around your little finger. Your mother refused to put you in a crib to sleep. She held you in her arms every night. You were her life and breath."

As if I wasn't crying enough, hearing about how much my mom had cared for me turned it up a dozen or so notches. I put my face in my hands and sobbed.

"When you were less than a year old, I was called to help fight Osadyn in North Carolina. We battled in a wet field near some power lines. During the fight, Osadyn knocked down a power pole and the live wires hit the wet ground, electrocuting me and stopping my heart. I died."

I lifted my head and saw Dad staring out the window, a faraway look on his face.

"You died?" I asked. "But, you're..."

He let out a small chuckle. "Alive? I am now, but the jolt stopped my heart and for almost ten minutes, I was dead. Shing and Rhys carried me to the nearest hospital, where the doctors and nurses were able restart my heart. But by then it was too late."

"Too late?" I asked. "Too late for what?"

"Too late to save your mother," he said. "When I died, she died, too."

"What do you mean?"

Dad blinked and came out of his reverie. "You do know about the connection between a Berserker and a Binder, don't you?"

"Yeah, I think so. For each Havoc there's a Berserker and Binder. The Berserker's blood is used to bind or free the Havoc and the Binder uses her power to perform the actual binding."

"All true," said Dad, "but there's much more to it than that, Madison. A Berserker lives for hundreds of years and can have many Binders during that time, but a Binder is irrevocably linked to her Berserker." He took a deep breath. "When a Berserker dies, the bond is snapped and the backlash kills his Binder."

The full consequence of what he said hit me. "When you died, it killed mom?"

"Yes." Dad turned away from me, his shoulders slumping. "It's my fault your mother died."

I watched Dad, conflicting emotions running through me. I was still angry that he had lied to me, but I also felt saddened by the burden of guilt he had obviously been carrying for all these years. I didn't know what to say, so I kept silent and let Dad keep talking.

"When the doctors revived me, I was no longer a Berserker – someone else had those powers. I was just a normal man with a little girl to raise and protect. The reality of death hit home for me, and I was afraid to lose you too, so I took you and distanced myself from the Berserker world. I moved, changed my name, and cut off all contact with my past life. I wanted you to have a normal life, not one filled with monsters and the heartache of seeing your loved ones killed.

"I moved here to get a fresh start and to forget the past." He gave a choked laugh. "So much for that plan."

Like a trickle of water rolling down an icicle, I felt my cold anger start to thaw. It wasn't gone, and it wouldn't be for a long time, but right then I knew I would eventually forgive Dad for lying to me.

"I met Mom – your new mom – shortly after moving here, but the pain was still too new, too fresh for me to get involved in a relationship. You were my focus. I had plenty of money, so I spent the next few years trying to be both Mom and Dad to make up for what you'd lost.

"She stuck around – she always told me she knew persistence would pay off – until I was ready to love again. I worried that I was betraying your mother, but I knew she would have wanted me to remarry, to find someone to be the mother to you that she couldn't be. And she has, Madison. I hope you know that. Mom loves you just as much as if she gave birth to you herself."

"I know, Dad," I said, smiling through the tears.

"And that brings us to now," said Dad. "You're really a Berserker?"

I shrugged. "Well, I glow at inconvenient times and destroy things. Does that count?"

Dad looked thoughtful – thoughtful and scared. "You do know that this is the first time there has ever been a female Berserker?"

"So I've heard."

"It doesn't make any sense," Dad said. "This isn't the first time a Binder and Berserker have had a child. There have been several others, but none ever inherited powers before. Gaining powers isn't supposed to be genetic."

I felt a little... something in the back of my mind as we spoke. A nagging feeling, vaguely familiar, but still too weak for me to really process. I half-listened as Dad discussed the impossibility of me inheriting powers and that everyone was certain that Berserker powers were not genetically passed on.

The feeling grew stronger until I finally recognized it. "Bringers," I said.

Dad immediately stopped talking. "What did you say?"

Panic welled up within me and I felt my senses sharpen to pre-zerk state. "Bringers," I said. "Several of them and they're coming this way."

"Are you sure?" Dad's voice was thick with tension.

I nodded. "At least four or five... I think. Maybe more. I'm not entirely sure."

"Come on." Dad walked out of his office, and straight to the utility closet off of the laundry room. He opened the door, fiddled with something in the dimness and a door-sized hole opened in the wall. I blinked, taken aback.

"You have a secret passage in our house?" I asked. I was completely flabbergasted. This kind of thing didn't happen in my boring house. "What, does it lead to the bat-cave, or something?"

"Hardly," Dad said, and he disappeared through the hole. "Come on."

The door opened to a steep staircase leading beneath the foundation of the house. The temperature dropped noticeably as we descended.

When I reached the bottom of the stairs, I found myself in a large room, twenty feet across with a high ceiling. It reminded me of a martial arts dojo. A large square of mats dominated the center of the room, with weights and other exercise equipment neatly arrayed along the perimeter. Paintings and photographs of people I didn't know covered the walls. Several large swords – and other weapons I didn't recognize – were mounted on the wall.

Dad crossed the room to a small glass case sitting on a stand. He fumbled with a latch and pulled out a circular disk, about the size of a fist. He held it in his hand, a mixture of fear and joy written across his face.

I had seen one of those disks before – when Rhys had fought the Bringers.

With a flick of his wrist the sword unrolled with a series of clicks until extended to its full four-foot length. Dad swung it around mes in some fancy maneuvers, showing me that he clearly knew how to use it.

"Stay here," he said. "This is set up to be a safe room. I'll lock you in while I take care of the Bringers."

"Are you serious?" I asked. "I'm the Berserker, remember? You should be staying here while I take care of them."

Dad got that stubborn look on his face - his eyes narrowing and his jaw sticking out. "You're too young to be fighting Bringers," he said. "I've fought them before, and I know how to kill them."

When Dad got like this he was impossible. He sometimes had a hard time remembering that I wasn't a three-year-old kid playing with matches. For better or worse, I was a Berserker, and I was just starting to understand how important that was.

"You're not leaving me here, and you're not fighting the Bringers alone," I said. "You're not a Berserker anymore." I turned around and walked to the bottom of the staircase before looking back. I could feel the Bringers nearby. We only had a few minutes before they arrived. "Are you coming?"

Without waiting for his answer, I started up the stairs. My pace quickly accelerated from a walk to a run. My blood pumped in anticipation and I felt myself on the edge of a true berserking. I struggled to hold it off until I'd left the house – so I wouldn't accidentally destroy it on my way out.

A warm breeze blew against my face as I strode onto the lawn. It was not typical Washington weather this late in the fall, and it was significantly warmer than it had been when I had come home.

Dad joined me on the lawn, his face a mask of determined concentration. He held the sword at the ready while scanning the trees around us.

I pointed to the trees to the north of the house. "There."

As if waiting for me to announce them, a dozen Bringers burst into the open, their skeletal frames and oversized heads just as disturbing as they had been in the dead woods.

Everything about the Bringers came into sharp focus as I fully 'zerked. Even from across the yard I could see their sharp teeth dripping saliva, hear the clicking of their bones as they ran, and smell the rotten stink of death about them. Power flowed through me, sharp and exhilarating. I felt – alive. Had I ever noticed that before?

I only had time to register Dad's stunned expression, as he saw me glowing for the first time, before the Bringers attacked. I met the first one head on, intending to snap its neck, but it twisted at the last moment accidentally impaling itself on my outstretched arm. Black goo splattered everywhere – great.

I wanted to wipe myself off, but there wasn't time. I would just have to trust my Berserker glow to fry the goop off.

Glancing over at Dad, I saw him thrust his sword through a Bringer's mouth and out the back of its skull. Without hesitating he pulled the blade free and moved on to another, slicing at its neck, but narrowly missing.

The next Bringer tried to tackle my legs. I leaped up and landed with a crack on its back before flipping into the air to land between two Bringers and smash their heads together.

"Look out! They're trying to flank you," Dad yelled.

I twisted around and threw a Bringer into the group, knocking several over, but a Bringer I hadn't noticed latched on to me from behind, wrapping its arms and legs around my waist, pinning my arms to my sides. Hot, rotten breath flooded over me as the Bringer extended its jaws to try and swallow me. I dropped low and threw out my arms, breaking its grip. I reached behind and grabbed the Bringer, throwing it against the ground so hard it turned to goo.

"Be careful, Madison," Dad yelled from across the yard. "Don't let them get behind you like that."

"Can we critique my nasty-monster fighting skills later?" I said. "I'm kind of busy."

Three more Bringers rushed towards. I dropped into a crouch to meet them.

"Don't stay stationary," Dad cautioned, fending off two Bringers. "Circle around the outside and attack from behind."

Was he really going to keep this up for the entire fight? The play-by-play critique was going to get old in a hurry.

"Enough with the in-game commentary," I said. "I need to concentrate."

Dad started to say something, but one of the Bringers had tackled him to the ground and was now opening its jaws wide in an apparent attempt to swallow him whole.

"Dad!"

There were only four Bringers left – three attacking me and the one that now had Dad halfway down its throat. I grabbed a Bringer and swung it around, throwing it into the other two before rushing towards Dad. Before I'd taken more than three steps, a Bringer dived for my ankle. I fell to the ground in a heap.

I kicked the Bringer hard on the top of the head, and its skull broke with a sickening crunch. I rolled backwards and stood up. By this time all that I could see of Dad were his feet. The growing mass inside the Bringer jerked and moved, but Dad wasn't strong enough to break out. I had to end this before the Bringer could finish swallowing Dad and run.

I picked up Dad's bone sword and faced the remaining two Bringers. I had no idea how to use the sword, but I hoped it would be more effective than pounding them with my bare hands. I rushed forward swinging the sword wildly. When I had watched Rhys use his sword it was a deadly dance of grace and precision. My approach was more like the Hokey Pokey done by preschoolers.

Fortunately, my wild and chaotic attack seemed to work. I connected with a Bringer's rib cage, nearly slicing it in half. It toppled and fell dead to the ground.

The second Bringer grabbed my arm, trying to force the sword out of my hand. I twisted around, pulling the Bringer off balance and yanking my arm free. I rammed the sword through the back of its head and out through the front. It collapsed and immediately began turning into goo.

By this time Dad had been completely swallowed by the remaining Bringer. The Bringer, however, was struggling with Dad's bulk. It had gotten to its feet, but Dad's thrashing seemed to knock it off balance.

Coming up from behind, I reached over the Bringer's head and grabbed its upper jaw, pulling it towards me. Unbelievably, the mouth simply widened the harder I pulled. There was too much give for me to stop it this way. Switching tactics, I twisted the top jaw sideways, with much better results. Bones cracked and the Bringer squirmed. With a final exertion, I was able to rip the top of the Bringers head off and it flopped to the ground, thrashing about.

As I looked at the thrashing Bringer, trying to decide how to best get Dad out, a hand thrust out of the Bringer's neck like some undead creature rising from the grave.

Remembering what I had seen Rhys and Eric do, I dropped to my knees and thrust a hand into the Bringer's ribcage. With a series of snaps, I broke the ribs apart, exposing Dad. He spluttered and coughed, but once I had made an opening, he was able to pull himself the rest of the way out.

I was so relieved that I instinctively reached out to hug him, but stopped when I realized I was still glowing and would most likely crush him with an overly enthusiastic hug. Plus, he was covered from head to toe in what looked an awful lot like snot.

The sound of a revving car engine caught my attention. Rhys' and Eric's Range Rover hurtled up the driveway, tires squealing. Before it had even stopped, Rhys, Aata, and Shing had jumped out, eyes searching for enemies to fight. Only seconds behind them, Eric, Kara and Mallika climbed out.

"Well, it looks like we missed all the fun," said Eric. He saw Dad trying to wipe the Bringer snot off himself and his face split into a mischievous grin. "Or maybe we're just in time for it."

I'd never seen Dad embarrassed before, but today seemed to be a day of firsts. He stopped wiping and pulled himself up to his full height, clearly trying to regain his dignity.

For a moment, there was an uncomfortable silence. But it didn't last long.

"Scottie!" Aata ran across the yard and, ignoring the slime covering my dad, picked him up in a big bear hug. "Good to see you, mate!" He set Dad down and looked at him quizzically. "But I must say, you've gotten quite a bit older since the last time I saw you."

Dad gave a rueful smile. "Never one to mince words, were you, Aata?"

Shing came forward next. He couldn't have been more different from Aata. He stood before Dad and gave a formal bow. "It is good to see you alive and well, my friend."

"It is good to see you as well, Shing," Dad said, bowing in reply. "It pleases me that we meet again."

Rhys approached somewhat cautiously. He almost looked embarrassed as he stood before my dad.

"Hello, Scottie," he said.

"Hello, Rhys." The two of them stared at each other, their faces completely stripped of emotion. There was clearly some history here that I was unaware of. Their expressions were so frozen it was like watching a piece of stone facing a cement wall.

There's no telling how long they might have stayed like that if Eric hadn't stepped between them. He faced Dad and threw his arms out wide.

"I know we've already had our little reunion, but... come here, Scottie!" He gave Dad a big bear hug, like Aata had. "Did you miss me?"

Dad gave Eric a cool look, but this time I could see a hint of a smile. "Do you want the truth?"

Eric shrugged. "Not really. Truth is highly overrated. I've had enough truth to last me three lifetimes. These days, I prefer a good socially-acceptable lie to the less-pleasant alternatives." He glanced around at the others. "Don't you?"

"Clearly some things have stayed the same," Dad said.

The small talk continued as Dad greeted Kara and Mallika. He had never met Kara, but clearly knew Mallika well.

After a few minutes there was a lull in the conversation. "We have a lot to talk about, Scottie," Mallika said. "It might be better if we did it out of the open."

We all went inside and sat in the living room. We waited while Dad quickly cleaned off and changed clothes. I sat on the couch next to Dad. Eric squeezed into the seat on my other side, even though there really wasn't enough room. He grinned at me and put his arm on the back of the couch so it was practically around my shoulders, but quickly pulled it back when Dad fixed him with a glare. Braver men than Eric had been quelled into submission by that look.

Mallika didn't waste any time getting down to business.

"Osadyn is in the area," she said.

Dad turned to face Rhys, who looked very uncomfortable. He

stared at the ground, not meeting my dad's gaze.

"Then why are you all here?" Dad asked. "Shouldn't you be out trying to bind him?'"

"The rules of the game have changed since you were a Berserker," said Mallika. She met Dad's gaze and held it, looking calm and confident.

Undiluted skepticism colored Dad's expression. "What could have possibly changed so much that you would sense a Havoc nearby, but instead pursuing it you just let it wander around killing innocent people?"

"Because we know what it wants," said Eric.

"And what's that?" asked Dad.

Before Eric could answer, Rhys stood up. "I can't be a part of this," he said, and stormed out of the room.

Dad watched him leave. "Why do I have a feeling I'm not going to like what you're about to tell me?"

It was time for me to jump in. Dad didn't often get angry, but when he did, it was like a force of nature unleashed. I couldn't let Eric take the brunt of that.

"It wants me," I said.

The anger drained out of Dad's expression, and his face turned gray and colorless. I suppose that was better than explosive anger. Still, it made me feel bad for springing that kind of news on him like that.

"It wants you?"

"It wants to free Pravicus," corrected Eric. "Madison is just a means to that end."

Dad glowered at Eric. So much for shifting Dad's anger away from him. Was Eric some sort of masochist to egg him on like that?

Eric didn't back down. "We need her, Scottie. For some reason Osadyn is desperate to free Pravicus and has been targeting Pravicus' Berserker. Since you, we've had four different Berserkers in that position die. You know how rare that is. Osadyn's been on the run for a hundred and fifty years, and we've never been able to catch him.

"But now we know what he wants and can finally set up a battle on our own terms. This is our first real chance to hold all the Havocs bound at the same time in over a thousand years, Scottie. You know how important that is. I understand you want to protect Madison, but this is bigger than her. It's bigger than any of us."

"So what you're telling me," Dad said in a deadly calm voice, "is that you want to use my only daughter - my untrained, brand-new-Berserker daughter - as bait to lure Osadyn into a trap."

Mallika broke in. "Scottie, it's not quite that black and white."

Dad stood up. "That's where I differ from all of you. This is my daughter's life we're talking about. It absolutely is that black and white. There is nothing I won't do to protect her and right now that means putting her into hiding immediately." He looked at his watch. "We still have time to get her on a plane to Europe tonight."

This was going to be ugly, but unless I wanted to be hiding for the rest of my life, I had to stop him. I reached up and pulled on his shirt sleeve. "I'm not going," I said. "I'm staying here."

"Oh, no, you're not," Dad said. "You have no idea what you're up against."

I stood up. "I know perfectly well what I am up against," I said. "I've already battled him." Which wasn't really the truth, if not exactly a lie. I had fought the Bringers and other creatures he sent for me, just not Osadyn himself.

Dad looked shocked. "Not going to happen, Madison. You're too young and inexperienced. End of discussion."

It was time to change tactics. Facing Dad head-on was rarely the right way to get him to change his mind - when an unstoppable force pushes against an immovable object, the outcome is never pleasant. Besides, I had sixteen years of experience in dealing with Dad. In this situation, I needed to appeal to his better nature.

"Dad, Eric is right. This is about more than just us. Osadyn is out there, and we have a unique chance to bind him. Running away won't change the fact that I'm a Berserker and my blood can free Pravicus. You taught me that I need to stand up for what I think is right. Well, this is right, and you know it."

"Madison, I-"

"Or was all that talk about 'honor' and 'choosing the right even in the face of adversity' just talk?"

Dad looked startled. Clearly I had him off balance. "You're taking things out of context, Madison. That was about peer pressure, not foolishly throwing away your life on something so dangerous that it has no chance of succeeding."

I shook my head and stood up, facing my dad. "It's the same principle." I concentrated on the feelings I had before I 'zerked. If I could 'zerk now, that might be enough to remind him that I was a Berserker, not a helpless little girl.

I felt the prezerk - just a bit more...

"I know this is hard for you," I said, "but it's the right thing to do." Almost there. "I'm more than just Madison. I'm a Berserker, Dad, and like it or not, I have a responsibility to the world." Slowly, I began to glow. I pulled myself up to my full height and even rose on my toes to add to the effect.

This time Dad didn't deflate, but his eyes lost that hard look. I hoped that meant he was ready to compromise.

He turned to Mallika and asked, "When are you going to do it?"

I breathed a sigh of relief and let go of my 'zerk. I was finally starting to get the hang of it.

"December 21st," Mallika said. "Winter Solstice and a full moon coincide this year. The odds will be stacked in our favor."

"Good," Dad said. "I want her prepared. Training every day, and I want her bonded to her weapon as quickly as possible."

Just when I thought I finally understood everything, they start spouting off new things that don't make sense. Why did it matter if it was Winter Solstice and a full moon? And I had never even heard of bonding to a weapon. What was that all about?

Eric and Mallika exchanged glances and nodded. "Agreed," said Mallika. She gave Dad a sympathetic smile. "I know this isn't easy, Scottie," she said. "Please know Madison will have around-the-clock protection until it is time."

Dad nodded. He reached out a hand and gave mine a gentle

squeeze. I squeezed it back.

"Thanks, Dad."

"I'm still not sure I'm doing you any favors," he said. "There's a good chance that I may look back at this moment as my biggest regret. But you are a Berserker, and I can't deny your right to decide."

Rhys stormed into the house, closely followed by Aata. "I can't believe you're going along with this," he said to my dad. "How can you let them do this?"

Dad took a deep breath. "It's her decision," he said. "I made life and death decisions when I was a new Berserker. How can I tell her she can't?"

"I don't like this," said Rhys. "It's not worth the risk."

I left them to argue about how much danger was appropriate for me and walked outside. Evening was fast approaching, but the air was still surprisingly warm for October. I closed my eyes and felt the soft breezes blow around me, caressing my skin and lifting my hair. I sat down on the bench on our front porch and listened to the frogs and crickets beginning their nightly battle of the bands to see who was louder.

After a moment I heard the front door open, and Eric sat beside me on the bench. I didn't say anything, waiting for a witty remark about sitting alone outside my own house while it's full of people, but it never came.

"It's not that I don't care," he said. "Because I do. Very much."

Not quite the remark I had been expecting, but he wouldn't be Eric if he played by anyone else's rules. He seemed to thrive on doing the unexpected.

"Care about what?"

"About what happens to you," he said. There was no trace of humor or that sardonic smile. This looked like genuine open emotion, something I had seen very little of from Eric.

"Why would I think that?" I asked. "You've bent over backwards to help me."

Eric shrugged. "Rhys thinks that because I want you to have the choice to fight Osadyn that I am recklessly endangering your life. Which – as he has pointed out several times tonight – is not something you do to people you care about. Therefore, since I am letting you endanger yourself, ergo, quid pro quo, and E Pluribus Unum, I must not care about you." He shook his head. "The man argues like a mafia lawyer – every word is designed as a trap."

I laughed. "Don't worry, Eric. I know you care. You care more about my freedom to choose than about the outcomes of my choices."

He winked at me. "Well, you do seem to have plenty of hyper-protective people surrounding you. If I let them have their way, you'd never have any fun."

I was about to reply when I heard the sound of tires on the driveway and saw Mom get out of Mrs. Phillip's car, back from the gym. I stood up and stuck my head in the door.

"Hey Dad," I yelled down the hall. "Does mom know about us, you know, the whole Berserker thing?" I asked.

Dad looked out from the living room and shook his head. "No, why?"

"Because she's home."

CHAPTER 12

A ROOM FULL OF BONES

Allll eyes turned to Dad.

"Into the back yard," he said. As everyone began moving toward the door, he pulled Mallika aside and said, "Can you cast a haze for us?"

She nodded and waited with Dad and me at the front door. I wasn't sure what a "haze" was, but I wasn't going to miss seeing it. Eric tried to stay with us, but Mallika shooed him into the yard with the rest. He left, but clearly not willingly.

Mom did a double take when she saw Dad, Mallika, and me standing near the front door waiting for her. I could almost see her trying to puzzle out why a strange, old Indian lady was in our house.

Before she could say anything, Mallika turned the palms of her hands upwards. A light blue mist flowed out of them, swirled around my mom, and then suddenly constricted, sinking into her skin and disappearing.

Mom made no sign that she had felt or seen anything unusual.

Her expression relaxed, though, as if she no longer wondered why Mallika was there.

"I had a great workout," she said to Dad.

"That's fantastic," Dad said, visibly relaxing. "I have a few people here I would like you to meet. Madison, can you please get your friends?"

I walked out to the back yard and called them all in. Within minutes we were all gathered in the living room, and Dad introduced each of the Berserkers and Binders in turn, along with the fact that they had powers.

"For the next several months they are going to be helping Madison learn to use her own powers, okay? They are helping her and she has our permission to go with them any time of day or night."

Eric looked over at me and grinned. Clearly he had ideas on how to take Dad up on his offer.

Dad looked at Mallika and nodded.

She stepped forward and clapped her hands together in front of Mom's face. Blue light flashed around Mom and then disappeared.

Mom blinked a few times. "I'm going to go shower and change," she said, and without asking any questions or even acknowledging that she had a house full of Berserkers, went upstairs.

Dad, Mallika and I stayed where we were, while the others wandered back out into the yard again.

"Please tell me she isn't permanently like that," I said.

Mallika put a hand on my shoulder. "Don't worry, Madison. Your mother will be fine in a few minutes. However, you will find with regard to our work, she will be strangely forgetful and unconcerned."

"What was that you did to her?"

"It is called a haze. It is part of the powers of a Binder. We have the ability to isolate pieces of knowledge in a person's mind. She knows all about us now, but that knowledge is disconnected from her conscious thought processes. When she tries to concentrate on us, or on topics that have to do with us, she will find herself quickly distracted and unable to complete her thoughts."

Dad put his arm around me. "Don't worry, Madison. I've seen this done hundreds of times. Mom will be fine by the time she gets out of the shower."

I gave Dad a hug. "That haze would have been nice to have after Josh saw me berserk. Maybe I would still have a boyfriend."

Dad stiffened. He and Mallika looked at each other and then back at me. "Josh saw you berserk?" Dad asked.

"Yeah, remember my last date with Josh when I came home so upset? It was the first time I'd ever 'zerked, and I was so scared that I accidentally sent him flying into a tree."

"Has he told anyone else?" asked Mallika.

"Not that I know of."

Neither of them said anything for a moment. "We should probably cast a haze on him just for safety's sake," said Dad. "But we have other pressing issues to deal with for now. Let us know if he becomes a problem."

I nodded. The idea of having Josh forget all about my Berserker powers was very enticing. With that knowledge gone, would he want me back? I imagined us together, walking down the halls at school while Ginger glared furiously from a distance. But that thought wasn't as exciting to me as it would have been a few weeks ago.

I tuned back into reality when I heard Dad ask Mallika, "Have you had any luck finding Madison's Binder?"

Mallika seemed slightly uncomfortable at this question. "No," she said slowly. "We've found nothing. I have three of the remaining seven Berserkers out looking and three more on standby. It's never been this hard to locate a new Binder before. The search is even more difficult because we don't know whether the Binder will be male or female." She seemed to be studying me intensely as she spoke.

We joined the others outside, and Mallika announced that it was time to leave.

"I am sure Madison and Scottie have plenty to discuss tonight."

Talk about an understatement.

That night after dinner, Dad and I spent some time alone. I'd had a chance to think through things, and I had a lot of questions – about him, not just my biological Mom.

Dad had turned on a football game in the living room, and Mom sat at the kitchen table doing some on-line shopping with her laptop.

"Why do they call you Scottie?" I asked. The question had been bothering me all evening and it seemed like a safe one to start out with. "I thought your name was Bruce?"

"My name is Bruce," he said. "Scottie is a nickname one of the previous Berserkers gave me because I was from Scotland."

"Scotland? You mean you're not from Ohio?" I began to realize that I probably knew just as little about my dad's real history as I did about my mom's.

"When you live as long as a Berserker does," Dad said, "you have to tell lies about yourself - even to those you love. You can't just be one person because people start to ask questions once you hit forty and you still look like you're seventeen. It gets even more difficult when you've lived so long that you should be dead. Do you understand?"

I did understand – intellectually, if not emotionally - it was just hard to realize how many supposed facts were actually fabrications. How did Dad manage to keep it all straight?

"So, how old are you?" I asked.

Dad shrugged. "It's depends on what you mean. Old enough. I was born in 1615. Given that Berserkers age around one year for every thirty years of life, and that I stopped being a Berserker around sixteen years ago, that puts me somewhere between forty-five and forty-six years old."

I did some quick calculations. He might be forty-six physically, but he had lived for almost four hundred years. Before the American Revolution, before the French Revolution. He had lived through all the world wars, and through some of the greatest events in history. It hurt my head to think about all the things he had lived through.

As we talked, I learned that Dad had grown up a farmer in Scotland. He had discovered he was a Berserker when defending his home from a rival clan - which I thought was a much more convenient time to discover the powers of a Berserker than during your first kiss. He had routed the attackers all by himself and been treated as a hero when others heard of the deed. But the next time he fought, he wasn't alone. When he began to glow, his clan members thought he was an evil spirit. They wanted him gone. No one dared to attempt to kill him, but they ostracized him and made it clear he was no longer welcome. Even his own family refused to speak to him. They moved out of the house, leaving him alone.

Hurt at his treatment, Dad decided to leave. He spent the following years wandering through Europe, surviving on what he could earn doing odd jobs for villagers. He specialized in helping farmers clear trees from their land. He could simply rip them up from the ground, clearing more space in an hour than a team of men could do in a week.

Because he had been traveling, it was extremely difficult for the Berserkers to catch up to him, especially given the limited transportation methods in those days. But eventually the Berserkers found him and for the first time he realized he was not alone.

"Shing was the one who explained to me who I was and what I was a part of." Dad rubbed his chin for a moment, thinking. "All the others who came with him have died since then. I don't know what has happened with the seven who bind Verenix, but Shing may be the oldest living Berserker now. If he's not, he is close to it."

Shing was something of a puzzle to me. He didn't seem to really fit in with the others. "How old is he?" I asked.

"I'm not quite sure of the exact dates, but I think he's around seven hundred to seven fifty. Something like that."

This information, thrown out by my dad as casually as if he was telling me the price of gas, was disorienting. It was going to take me a while to absorb this new version of my dad - the one who was a four hundred year old ex-Berserker.

I couldn't help myself; I began to laugh. The absurdity of it all was too much. The past few days had been a shock, and my emotions were too close to the surface right now - they somehow had to come out. It was either laugh or cry.

At first it was just a chuckle, but soon I was laughing so hard that tears streamed down my cheeks. I leaned over and lay on Dad's lap, unable to stop laughing. After a few minutes, the spasms of laughter began to subside and were replaced by gasping sobs.

Dad said nothing and simply brushed my hair out of my face while I released all the emotions that I had bottled up about what I had learned, and more importantly, unlearned – about my mom, about my dad, and about who I was.

***

The next day, Rhys and Eric picked me up for school. This time they were not in the Range Rover, but came in the Mercedes Eric had tried to give me.

I invited them in while I gathered the last of my things. Dad came over and they started talking.

"Are you sure she can't have the car?" Eric asked. "I mean, now that you know who gave it to her?"

Dad fixed Eric with a piercing look. "Especially, now that I know who gave it to her," he said. His face was a rock-hard mask of suspicion and parental disapproval, but it didn't remain like that for long. His mouth quirked and eventually broke into a smile. "You never did anything halfway, did you Eric?"

"I'm sorry to report that, well, I haven't changed a bit since I last saw you."

Rhys rolled his eyes at this exchange. He didn't say much, but I had the feeling that it wasn't from lack of anything to say. He had a quiet depth about him that made me intensely curious. If we ever got a chance to be alone I would have to find out more about him.

"We need to help her choose a weapon today," Dad said. "I want to get her trained and bonded as quickly as possible. She's going to need all the practice she can get before Winter Solstice."

"Agreed," Rhys said.

"Bring her back here after school," Dad said. "We can use my practice room to show her the options."

What was with the excessive bossiness? He seemed less like my dad and more like a drill sergeant. Not to mention that he was making decisions for me without my input.

"Hello?" I said. I raised my hand and waved it around. "I'm right here, you know."

Dad's confused look changed to one of dawning comprehension. "Sorry, Madison," he said and gave me a hug. "Old patterns of behavior return when around old friends. I guess I over-did it. How about after school you come back with Rhys and Eric so we can show you some weapons?"

I kissed Dad on the cheek. "Sounds great. Thanks."

School flew by in the blink of an eye. Surprisingly, I was able to concentrate on my classes and temporarily push away all the confusion and fear. Ginger seemed to have recovered from her fear of me and was back to her nasty self again. But the past few days had changed me. I no longer cared what she thought. The taunts she threw at me seemed childish, and I wondered how she thought I could even care.

When that didn't work, she began to position herself in strategic locations talking with Josh. When she saw me coming, she would grab him and kiss him with all the force she could muster. It was like watching a starfish attack an abalone. I could see Josh struggling to get air, but she would hold him until I had a good long look and had walked past.

A few weeks ago that kind of stunt would have had me in the bathroom in tears, but not any longer. Berserkers might age more slowly physically, but I felt as though my emotional aging had accelerated. High school antics and popularity contests now seemed childish.

Maybe it was the weight of responsibility that made me feel this way, or maybe it was because I had faced death and come out ahead, not once, but several times. But with everything I had learned since becoming a Berserker – about my mom, my dad, and even about myself - dealing with Ginger's taunting didn't seem like such a big deal anymore.

At lunch, Eric and Rhys explained what it means to bond to a weapon and why I needed to do it.

"Berserkers are immune to any man-made weapon," Eric said. "A sword, a gun, anything that was built."

"So, we're pretty much invulnerable," I said.

"Not even close. We can be killed by anything that is alive or was once living. That's why most Berserkers choose weapons made of bone."

"Why would I ever want to kill a Berserker?"

Rhys started to speak, but then stopped. He looked at Eric who shrugged.

"There's a reason we're called Berserkers," Rhys said slowly.

Why was he hesitating? I leaned forward in my seat.

"When a Berserker 'zerks, he channels some of his more... basic animal nature. The surges of anger and hate that accompany a 'zerk can become overwhelming when you're battling for your life."

Anger and hate? What was he talking about? I had never felt anything like that. Sure, it took a strong emotion to get the 'zerking started, but for me that emotion was usually fear or sadness. Anger and hate had never been part of it.

"Don't worry," Rhys added. "Those feelings are perfectly natural. We all experience them. During your training, we'll teach you how to control those feelings – to channel them into your power. But every once in a while a Berserker gets lost in the emotional rush. They sort of go feral and can't come out of the 'zerking. They start attacking everything around them, both enemies and friends."

I set my fork down and looked at both Rhys and Eric for any sign that this was some sort of joke, but even Eric looked serious, which was a rare occurrence.

The terror that was welling up in me must have been visible on my face, because Eric hit Rhys on the shoulder. "Look what you did," he said. "She's going to be terrified of 'zerking now." He gave me a comforting smile. "Don't worry. Berserkers rarely go feral. There are only a few recorded cases throughout all of Berserker history."

I looked at Rhys for confirmation and he nodded. "It's true. No one's really sure what causes it, but when it does happen, few forces on earth can stop an uncontrolled Berserker. We all take an oath that if it happens, we will do everything we can to prevent the Berserker from killing innocents - even if that means killing the Berserker."

For several minutes none of us spoke, each of us lost in our own thoughts. I tried to imagine what it would be like to see one of the Berserkers go feral. Would I be able to kill a friend?

"Have either of you ever seen it happen?"

"Let's talk about something else," said Rhys. "There are other reasons why we use bone for our weapons."

I opened my mouth to say that I didn't want to change the topic, but Eric gave a little shake of his head and I bit my tongue. "Like what?" I asked.

"Bone enables Berserkers to bond to their weapons. Because bone was once alive, it allows the Berserker to imbue it with some of his essence."

"Let me get this straight," I said. "I'm going to put some of myself into some dead bones? That's what you guys are talking about with this bonding thing?"

"Ah, Madison, you have such a refreshing way of stating the facts," said Eric with a wink.

Rhys shook his head. "It's not just some old bones," he said. "For one thing, it only works with certain creatures, and for another, you have to do it very soon after you cut off the bones you need."

"Think of it this way," said Eric. "Imagine you accidentally cut off your finger. It can be reattached hours later and still function like it always did. The principle is the same – only it's with something else's bones rather than your own."

"Ok, now this has gone from just gross, to extraordinarily creepy," I said. "I'm going to cut off some creature's arm or leg and then attach it to me?"

"Not like that," Eric said. "Not physically. But it will be attached to you – a sort of spiritual alignment as opposed to an actual physical connection. It will feel perfectly natural to use. More like an extension of your arm than something you are holding."

"Once bonded, it will feel like you've been using the weapon for your entire life, rather than for just a few minutes," said Rhys. "You will still need to learn the moves and proper form, but trust me, it will make defending yourself much easier. That's why your dad wants you to get bonded as quickly as possible. As a new Berserker, you need all the advantages you can get."

***

When we got home from school, Dad was waiting for us out on the porch. Mom had gone out and we had the house to ourselves.

Dad took us through the entrance in the utility closet and into the training room.

"I know Mom has a haze on her," he said, "but I would rather not take any chances in case she comes home early."

Laid out on a table near the edge of the mats were four bone weapons. One was a long thin pole, devoid of decorations; one was a short club; another was the circular disc used by Rhys and my dad; and the final weapon was a pair of matching bone swords crossed on top of each other forming an X.

"I figured these four were our best options," said Dad. "There are others, but we need to stick with the ones for which we have an experienced trainer on hand." He picked up the short club. Rather than being a rounded stick, the club head was a six-inch-wide flat piece of bone that was tapered on each side almost like a blade. "This is the Berserker version of a Mere," he said. "A Maori war club." He handed me the club. It was surprisingly heavy. "Notice how it narrows to a rounded edge? This club is meant to inflict a lot of damage at a very short range."

I stepped onto the mat and swung the club around. It looked like it would really hurt if it connected, but it was heavy and awkward. I supposed if I was 'zerking the weight wouldn't be a problem, but what about carrying it around in between times? I handed it back to Dad, who returned it to the table.

"Aata uses the mere and would be able to train you on its proper use," he said.

"Yeah, that's a tough one to figure out," said Eric. "Swing it around and hit things."

"You don't approve?" said Dad.

Eric shrugged. "I just think it would be a poor choice for Madison. It's too heavy to carry around – half the time Aata doesn't use it because we're attacked unexpectedly and he doesn't have it with him. Plus, its range is so short that she'd be in danger before she even had time to use it."

Dad nodded. "All valid points," he said. "Let's pull out something you might have less objection to." He picked up the long thin pole. "The short staff."

I took the staff and walked onto the mats. The pole felt light and smooth in my hands. Theoretically, I knew how this should work. I gripped it in both hands and swung it in several arcs.

"The advantage of this is that it is light and portable," said Dad. "It hardly looks like a weapon once it has been collapsed down." He took the staff back and pressed something. There was a small click and then Dad was able to collapse it into a section about six inches long – easily small enough to fit into a purse or a jacket pocket. "Eric uses the staff," said Dad, "when he bothers to use a weapon at all."

Eric shrugged. "What can I say? I prefer the natural approach."

He pulled a collapsed staff from his pocket and quickly extended it. He walked onto the mat and began a complicated pattern of thrusts and slashed that soon had my head spinning.

"Obviously," Dad said, "Eric is our resident staff expert and would train you should you choose to go that route."

Next, Dad handed me the pair of swords. The blades were about two feet long and curved into hooks on the ends. The hilts themselves were rounded, but the hand guards surrounding the hilts were half moons of bone filed into points.

"These are Tiger Hook swords," he said. "Go on, give them a try."

I held a sword in each hand and began swinging them. They felt even more awkward than the Mere club. I was sure any second I was going to accidentally impale myself.

Rhys stepped forward. "These are probably the most deadly of all the weapons here," he said, "but they are also the most difficult to learn." He reached out and took the swords from me. "Let me show you what it looks like, so you can give them a fair evaluation."

A sword in each hand, Rhys began swinging in slow arcs, gradually increasing in speed. In his hands, they became deadly weapons with multiple ways of attacking and stabbing an opponent. At one point, he even used the hooks at the end of the blades to attach them together, creating a weapon with a much longer reach.

While beautiful to watch - it didn't hurt that it was Rhys doing the demonstration – I just couldn't see myself ever being coordinated enough to use two blades at once and not hurt myself. Even with enhanced Berserker speed and agility, it looked too complicated.

When Rhys was done, Dad put the twin swords back. "As good as Rhys is with the Tiger Hook swords," said Dad, "Shing is the expert and would be the one to train you."

Finally, he pulled out the round disc. He pressed a button and the disc unrolled into a four foot long sword. This was the first time I had been able to really examine one of these up close. The other times I had seen one had been during battle and I hadn't really gotten a good look.

Dad handed me the sword. "This is called a varé."

The varé appeared to be made from dozens of tiny bones, all attached through a series of pins. The base of the sword was hollow and tapered into a thin point at the top. This allowed the sword to be rolled up into the compact disc. The butt of the sword curved in, forming a smooth bone handle.

I took the sword and began to swing it around. It was lighter than the Tiger Hook swords or the Mere club. While it wasn't exactly graceful, the varé did feel less awkward.

Dad showed me the release mechanism, and the sword immediately rolled itself into a small disc in my hand - a definite advantage.

I set the varé down on the table. It was time to choose.

The Mere and the Tiger Hook swords were definitely out, so I moved them aside, leaving the staff and varé lying next to each other on the table. The staff had a longer range, but it just didn't feel as deadly to me as the varé. I had seen Rhys use the varé and I knew firsthand what kind of damage it could do. Plus, I felt a stronger emotional attachment to the varé since I knew it was the weapon my dad had used.

I picked up the varé. "This one," I said.

Dad smiled. I could tell he was pleased with my pick.

Eric was another matter.

He wasn't exactly frowning, but there was no longer any trace of a smile and he stared at the floor.

"What's wrong?" I asked.

He shrugged. "Nothing," he said. "I think I need some air. I'll meet you guys upstairs when you're done."

As Eric ascended the stairs I looked back at Dad and Rhys. "Did I do something wrong?" I asked.

Dad shook his head. "No, you didn't do anything wrong. Eric's just not used to dealing with disappointment."

"Disappointment?"

"You didn't pick his weapon," said Rhys. "I think he had been hoping to be your trainer."

"Oh." I hadn't really considered it that way. Now I felt bad, almost like I had rejected him – which was not my intention at all. I just liked the varé better than the staff. It was nothing personal. "So, who is going to be training me with the varé?" I asked.

"I'll give you some instruction on basic techniques," said Dad. "But you really need a Berserker who is also bonded to his weapon to fully train you, so that means Rhys will be working with you."

Rhys smiled and blushed slightly. It was amazing how a simple smile could transform his face from merely handsome to breathtakingly beautiful.

If picking the varé meant seeing more of that, then I definitely had made the right choice.

***

Once I had selected my weapon, Dad went out of town for a week. Apparently the varé is made from the arm of a nasty demon-like creature called a drall, and they're rather hard to find. Dad and Shing went off searching for one while I was stuck in high school under the protective custody of Rhys and Eric.

Eric continued to view my choice in weaponry as a personal rejection. He didn't say anything directly about it, but he was distant and moody for a few days. At first I felt guilty and tried to be extra nice, but after awhile I realized he was milking the situation for all the attention he could get – so I quit playing his game. After that he got over it and went back to being his usual mischievous self.

I guess being stuck in high school when you have already been through it is excruciatingly boring. I quickly discovered that a bored Eric is an Eric who starts looking for ways to cause trouble. Fortunately he usually channeled this impulse in healthy ways - like tormenting Ginger. I guess he figured that after everything she'd done to me, she was fair game.

Some of his more elaborate pranks required quite a bit of planning, not to mention money. He completely filled her car with

Styrofoam peanuts, then had it wrapped in extra strong shrink wrap; he hired a locksmith to change the combination lock on her locker; he even arranged for a professional comedian to heckle her during cheerleading practice.

All of which, of course, she blamed on me. She tried several times to get back at me, but Eric always seemed to be two steps ahead. He twisted each of Ginger's pranks so they backfired on her.

Each day before gym class, Amy updated me on the latest school opinion poll regarding my relationship with Eric and Rhys. It seemed that around two-thirds of the school thought I was dating Eric, the other third voted for Rhys, and the entire female population insisted that I ought to make up my mind so one of the two would go back on the open market.

When I got home from school on Friday, I saw Dad's truck in the driveway. Rhys and I rushed into the house. Eric came too, but he didn't seem to be in a hurry.

Dad looked tired and scruffy, like he hadn't slept the entire week – or bothered with basic hygiene rituals for that matter. He smelled like old sweat and campfires.

"Well?" I asked. "Did you find one?"

"I did," said Dad. He stretched his arms and yawned. "You and Rhys should get to bed early tonight. The three of us leave tomorrow morning."

CHAPTER 13

BONDING IN UNEXPECTED WAYS

W e got up before the sun to reach the airport by seven o'clock. Once we checked in, Dad handed me my boarding pass. I looked at the destination – Salt Lake City, Utah.

"We're going to Salt Lake City?" I asked. I guess I hadn't expected the creature to be living in a city.

"That we are," said Dad, but he didn't elaborate. He was strangely tight-lipped about this whole trip, only telling me bits and pieces of where we were going and what we were going to do. I quickly got annoyed with his evasiveness and, once we were through airport security, I went to talk to Rhys.

"So, what was it like when you fought a drall?" I asked. "Did you go to Salt Lake or someplace else?" I figured whatever reason Dad had for being evasive, he had probably already co-opted Rhys, so I was going to have to get my information without directly asking about what we were going to do.

"It was a long time ago," said Rhys. He looked over at Dad, who was walking a little bit ahead of us, still clearly within hearing distance.

I gently grabbed his arm and slowed my pace until Dad was farther ahead.

"Ok," I said. "What's going on? Neither of you will tell me anything about what we are going to actually do. Why the secrecy?"

Rhys looked down at my arm, now intertwined with his. Self-conscious, I let go. "Sorry," I mumbled.

He let out a sigh. "I don't know what's going on," he said. "Your Dad asked me to not tell you where we are going or what we will do there. He seemed to think you would get stressed and start obsessing. He said you would do better dealing with the unknown right now than worrying about what's coming."

"I'm the Berserker," I said. "Not him. Why are letting him boss you around?"

"He may have lost this powers," said Rhys, "But I've spent over a hundred years with him, and I trust his judgment. I'm just along as a safety measure. Your dad's in charge of this expedition."

I hadn't thought about the fact that Rhys and Dad had known each other for that long. Over a hundred years? That was longer than most people would ever live. It was hard to think of them as being that old. Well, maybe not so hard for Dad. He had always seemed old to me, so it wasn't much of a stretch to think of him as being really old. But Rhys? How could someone who looked my age be... how old was he? I had never had asked. Hopefully, he and I would have some time together on this trip so I could ask him all my questions.

Clearly right now wasn't a good time, since they both seemed determined to keep me in the dark. Fine, if they didn't want to talk, I could play that game too.

All during the flight, I kept silent and didn't ask any more questions. I kept silent as Dad rented a large SUV and we began driving south. Since it was early November, I had brought my heaviest jacket, but I quickly discovered that it was much colder in Utah than in Washington – emphasis on the much.

As we drove, the landscape slowly changed from a large city surrounded by mountains, to small cities surrounded by mountains, and finally gave way to wilderness full of beautiful red rock formations. Having lived in Washington my whole life, I found the dry rocky landscape completely different and strangely beautiful. It almost felt like I was on a different planet.

After three hours of driving I couldn't keep silent any more.

"Dad, will you please tell me what's going on?" I asked. "This is driving me nuts."

"Sure," he said, a sickly sweet cheerful note in his voice. "I was going to tell you once we landed, but you seemed to be enjoying the silence, and I didn't want to disturb you."

I opened my mouth to reply, but then I saw Dad's huge smile in the rearview mirror. Instead of talking, I reached over the seat and punched him on the shoulder.

"You are such a... dad!"

Both he and Rhys burst out laughing, which made me feel like a petulant five-year-old. And that didn't exactly help my mood. I folded my arms and slumped back into my seat, staring out the window. "Fine," I said. "What's the plan?"

"I found a drall living in a place called Goblin Valley. We'll be there in another hour and half or so. I've rented us a hotel room and loaded it with supplies. We'll pick up the gear and check out before going to our campsite."

"Campsite?" I asked. "We're going camping? What is it, like thirty degrees outside? Why can't we keep the room and sleep there?"

Dad gave Rhys a significant look. "It will be cold tonight," he said.

"Ok, I said. What's going on? What was that look all about?"

"It's nothing," said Dad. "I'd just warned Rhys that you probably wouldn't be too thrilled about the prospect of camping in such cold weather. That's why we didn't want to tell you until we got closer."

I took a deep breath. I wasn't sure what bothered me more, the fact that we were going to be camping in the freezing weather or the fact that Dad seemed to think I would throw some sort of hissy fit about it.

I was not going to throw a fit. But that didn't mean I wouldn't try to talk them out of the whole camping thing.

"So, why are we not staying in the hotel room you already have?" I asked. A perfectly reasonable question, and I even said it calmly – sort of.

Dad chuckled. I wanted to hit him again.

"We're about to cut off a drall's arm and take it with us," Dad said. "It's rather large and not the kind of thing you can easily sneak into a hotel room. Besides, we have to prepare the arm for the bonding. It's a rather messy process."

I had no answer for that. Prepare the arm? That didn't sound good.

We reached the hotel – a small but nicely-kept place. Inside the room, Dad had left all sorts of camping gear. There were heavy winter coats for all of us, sleeping bags rated to below zero, and sturdy tents. Maybe it wouldn't be so bad.

In addition to the usual equipment, there was a large black pot – more of a cauldron, really – that looked like something out of a story about witches.

"Do I even want to know what that's for?" I asked.

Dad shrugged and tried to pick up the pot. He managed to get it a few inches off the floor before dropping it. "Rhys, can you give me a hand?" he asked. "It took both Shing and I to get this in here."

"Hold on, Dad," I said. I closed my eyes and concentrated. I visualized myself in situations when I had berserked before. Slowly, my senses heightened and I felt power flood into me. I stopped before a full berserking, leaving myself in the pre-zerk state.

I walked over to cauldron and easily picked it up. I smiled at Dad, who looked shocked. "Are we putting this in the SUV?" I asked.

He nodded.

I grinned and carried it out.

As I approached the room, I overheard Dad and Rhys talking together. I caught the tail end of the conversation.

"I know it's not a normal Berserker power," said Rhys. "There's nothing normal about this situation."

My return put an end to their discussion and the three of us worked quickly to get all the gear out to the vehicle. Dad watched me more closely than usual while we worked. Clearly, the fact that my powers were different unsettled him.

Once packed, we drove out to the campsite and set up the tents. It wasn't a commercial campsite – not in the regulated and divided into areas with running water and electricity kind of definition. This was just a relatively flat piece of land not too far from the back side of Goblin Valley, but completely off the main roads and very isolated. This location was clearly about privacy, not comfort.

Dad and Rhys suspended the black cauldron two feet above the ground on a cross post supported by two metal forks. I gave my best evil witch cackle and recited the witches' lines from Macbeth, but Dad and Rhys didn't seem to find it as amusing as I did.

My heavy coat was puffy and surprisingly warm. Dad had also outfitted me with warm gloves, a hat, and fur-lined boots. It was all sort of cute in an outdoorsy way. Not the kind of thing I would want on a date, but it worked well for wilderness use.

Rhys and Dad both wore down-filled coats with fur-lined hoods and looked like Eskimos transplanted from the north. As the sun began to set, the temperature plummeted. My clothing kept me mostly warm, but my face grew cold and my nose began to feel like it was frozen.

Dinner consisted of cold sandwiches and chips, along with some granola bars. I had been hoping for something warm, but Dad and

Rhys said that lighting a fire might attract unwanted attention, and didn't want to light one until it was absolutely necessary.

By six o'clock the sun had set and Dad turned to Rhys. "It's time," he said. "I'm going to go in and make sure the drall is still there. Stay here with Madison and I'll come back as quickly as I can." He gave me a hug and a kiss on the cheek and left.

I sat on a half buried log next to Rhys and for the first ten minutes neither of us spoke. We sat together listening to the nocturnal noises around us.

I wanted to ask Rhys about who he was, where he came from, and all the things I never got a chance to ask him with Eric around, but now that we were alone it felt too awkward, and I didn't know how to start.

Fortunately, Rhys broke the silence.

"Your father is a good man," he said. A strange way to start a conversation, but at least we were talking.

I nodded. "He is. How long have you known each other?"

"He was my first contact in the Berserker world, around a hundred and sixty years ago. He helped me understand that there were others like me, and that my Berserker powers were neither a curse, nor evil."

"How old are you?" I asked, unable to help myself.

Rhys smiled. "That's something I haven't thought about in a long time. Let's see... this year I'm one hundred and seventy eight. Does it bother you that I'm so old?"

What was that supposed to mean? Age didn't matter for friends. It would only be an issue if he wanted to be more than friends.

"Would it help if I told you that physically I'm only twenty years old?"

His eyes were fixed on mine. I felt my breathing tighten. I looked away. This wasn't the kind of conversation I was ready to have right now.

"Tell me about when you met my dad," I said. "What was it like for you to find out you were a Berserker?"

Rhys' face went rigid. Clearly I had hit a nerve, or several hundred of them.

"I'm sorry," I said. "You don't have to answer that if you don't want to. It's just that back at the airport when you said you had known my dad for over a hundred years, I realized that I really don't know anything about you. Aside from the fact that you're a Berserker."

Rhys leaned his head back and stared up at the sky. He took a deep breath and let it out slowly.

"I... don't normally talk about myself," he said. "But you're right, I should be more open." He paused for several moments before continuing. "I grew up in a small fishing village in Wales called Aberaeron off the coast of Cardiganshire. My father owned a fishing boat, and I was learning the trade from him. I had recently turned fifteen, and Dad and I were out fishing when a sudden storm took us by surprise. The wind howled and huge waves tossed our little boat like a toy.

"One particularly hard wave threw my father into the mast,

knocking him unconscious. Before I could get to him, a second wave washed him overboard and into the thrashing ocean. I reached out and was able to grab onto his wrist, but I wasn't strong enough to pull him in.

"That's when I felt the change come over me. Everything became clear, and I suddenly had the strength to pull my father back onto the boat. It wasn't until I had hauled him on board that I realized I was glowing. I rode out the storm holding myself and my unconscious father in the boat, wanting to pray to God to let us live, but afraid to try because I had turned into some sort of demon and wasn't worthy.

"I told no one about what had happened to me, not even my fiancé Anwyn."

It was all I could do to not stop the story right there and ask a million questions. Rhys had been engaged - at age 15? That was a year younger than I was now. I know things were different back then, but... wow.

"My powers manifested a handful of other times after that, but I always felt it coming on and fled before anyone saw me. Anwyn knew something was wrong, but how could I tell her I had become a demon?" He looked away from me, but he continued talking. "I loved her more than life itself. We had grown up together and we had both known we would marry for as long as either of us could remember. I spent the next six months in my own private hell, torn because of the love I felt for her. I couldn't imagine my life without her, but how could I let the woman I love marry a monster — a demon?

"Three months before the wedding, Scottie arrived and told me about my powers. At first I didn't believe him. How could I believe that I was a protector of the world? How could I be chosen to defend the world from evil creatures when it was obvious that I was a demon myself?

"But Scottie was persuasive, and over the next few weeks I came to believe. Once I began to believe, he tried to convince me to come with him – to leave everything I had ever known and join the Berserker cause. But I couldn't abandon Anwyn. No cause was great enough for me to leave her."

Rhys stood and began to pace. "It was then that Scottie told me about the way Berserkers aged. That I would stay young while Anwyn grew old and died. I told him I didn't care about that. I would love her no matter what. I would stay with her and take care of her until the day she died.

"But Scottie explained that I wasn't looking at the big picture. Sure I could have a few years with her, ten maybe, before people started noticing that I hadn't aged - before Anwyn noticed. 'How will they react?' he asked me. I wanted to deny what he was saying, but my own reactions to my power were proof enough. Sooner or later, people would conclude that witchcraft or dark magic was keeping me young. Perhaps they would even accuse me of selling my soul to the devil. Eventually, even Anwyn would come to believe I was evil.

"It was the thought of the pain and suffering I would put Anwyn through if I stayed that helped me make my decision. I would go with Scottie, but I had to make a clean break, one that didn't make Anwyn think I had abandoned her, but one that also didn't give her any hope that I'd return.

"A month before the wedding, I had my chance. Once again the sea was rough and the waves battered the boat. When we were several miles out to sea, I made sure my father watched me lose my footing during a crashing wave, falling overboard and into the deadly water. There were no life jackets back then. Being that far out to sea in rough weather was a certain death sentence - at least to one who wasn't a Berserker. Once I was under the water, I 'zerked and swam away from the boat. I made my way back to land and met up with Scottie at a prearranged location. As far as everyone I had ever known was concerned, I was dead. Just another fisherman swallowed up by the sea."

Rhys sat down next to me. There were no tears in his eyes, but they looked hollow and empty, still haunted by memories of long ago. I reached out and put an arm around him. At first he stiffened, but then he relaxed and leaned into me. Together we sat in the cold under a clear sky full of stars, each of us absorbed by our thoughts.

"Did you ever go back?" I asked.

"I did," he said. His voice held a note of resignation. "It was thirty years later. My parents had died by then. My younger brother was grown and had turned our tiny fishing boat into a fleet. He had a good life."

"What about Anwyn?"

"She married my best friend. They had six children and over a dozen grandchildren. I hadn't planned on seeing her. We had been chasing a Havoc across Wales, and the temptation was too great. I promised myself that I wouldn't try to find her, but as I walked down by the quay I saw her. She looked older, but she was still beautiful. Her eyes still had that twinkle and her lips still looked like they were ready to smile at the least provocation."

"Did she see you?"

Rhys frowned. "Yes, she did. For one moment our eyes locked, and then I turned away and walked behind a shop. She didn't follow."

"That must have been hard." I said.

"It was hard," Rhys said. "But it was good. It forced me to confront the fact that she was no longer mine. She was happy and her heart belonged to another now. There was no place for me in her life. Intellectually I had always known that, but seeing her for the last time made it real."

I hesitated before asking my next question. I wasn't sure if it was too personal, but Rhys seemed to be in a talkative mood and who knew when that was going to happen again?

"Do you regret your choice?"

Rhys studied my face with his piercing eyes. I had no idea what he was looking for or whether he found it, but he did answer.

"I guess it depends on what you mean. Do I regret leaving Anwyn? Absolutely. Leaving her was the hardest thing I ever did. Not a day has gone by that I haven't second-guessed my decision. I wish with my whole heart that it hadn't been necessary. But I also know with that same sense of surety that I did the right thing. So, if by regret you mean 'would I make a different choice knowing what I know now', the answer is no. I'd make the same choice every time."

I had always known that there was more to Rhys then met the eye, but it was nice to get a glimpse of it. Now I understood some of that pain I had seen that day when our eyes met in class.

"Thanks," I said.

Rhys gave me a curious look. "What for?"

"For sharing with me," I said. "Those are some very powerful memories. I'm sure that talking about them wasn't easy. I feel like I know you a bit better now." I laid my head on his shoulder.

"It was good to talk about them," Rhys said. "There aren't that many people on this earth who can relate. It was nice."

"What about the fun stuff?" I asked. "Tell me about some of your fun experiences as a Berserker."

For the next hour we talked about the places Rhys had gone. He had visited nearly every country in the world, some of them were so long ago that they'd had different names at the time. He had traveled to all seven continents and had climbed the ten highest mountains in the world. It made a nice diversion after the seriousness of our previous conversation.

Rhys was telling me about the time he and my dad had fought off a pack of Bringers in the Sahara desert when Dad came back to the camp.

He handed me a small GPS unit.

"What's this for?" I asked.

"I've programmed in the location of the drall," he said. "It's time."

The plan was for Rhys and me to 'zerk and sneak in to Goblin Valley through the back side where there were no roads and less chance of being spotted. The drall was on the far side from the main entrance and parking lot, so there was a good chance we could get in and out completely undetected. Plus, this late at night the main entrance was closed and there was very little security in the valley itself.

"Aren't you coming?" I asked.

Dad shook his head. "I can't run like you two can. I would just slow you down. Rhys knows what he's doing. Besides, while you two are gone, I'm going to get everything ready for your bonding."

Not that anyone had yet bothered to tell me how the bonding was going to work, but the large suspended cauldron did at least give me an idea of what I was going to have to do – a disgusting, creepy idea.

Given my nervousness about upcoming events, finding the emotion in me to 'zerk was easy. Once we had begun glowing, Rhys and I both sprinted into the wilderness following the GPS to our destination. I was used to car GPS units that gave me turn-by-turn audio directions. This one just showed the distance between us and our destination and the direction we needed to go.

We dashed through the night, past rocks and scrub brush. The berserking heightened my awareness of the temperature around me, but because we were moving so quickly, my body was able to stay warm.

When we were only a few miles from our destination, Rhys

reached out a hand and said "Stop".

He pointed toward the sky. I had been so focused on following the GPS that I hadn't looked up. With my enhanced Berserker vision, the stars were more clearly visible than I had ever dreamed possible. Blazing pinpricks of light filled the sky. Growing up in Washington, I had never seen the stars this bright before. I wasn't sure if it was the clouds, the elevation, or the light pollution, but all I knew was this was beautiful.

We only stopped for a moment before turning back to the task at hand. We followed the GPS needle, now traveling slightly uphill. Up and up we went, our forward vision limited because of the rise, until we reached the top and looked out over Goblin Valley.

It was easy to guess how this place had gotten its name. A huge valley at least a mile deep and two miles wide stretched out before us. Dotting the landscape within were thousands of tiny rock formations. Well, they looked tiny from up here, but some of them were the size of small houses. The strange mushroom shaped formations were everywhere – like an army of goblins. It was beautiful in a strange alien-landscape sort of way. It almost looked like someone had taken a piece of mars – or at least how I pictured it – and transplanted it here. It seemed too strange to belong to earth.

But I knew there were no aliens or goblins here. Just a drall, and my job was to harvest an arm.

Lucky me.

We descended the rim of the valley and onto the floor. We ran through the goblins, weaving in and out of the strange formations.

The GPS guided us to an open spot ringed by eight or nine small goblins – by small I mean they were the size of cars rather than houses.

"We're here," I said.

The air was still and quiet, without the loud calls of the frogs and other wildlife I was used to. My ears picked up plenty of sounds, but much softer than I had expected, and to me it felt almost eerily silent.

"Is this the right place?" I asked. "I don't see anything."

Rhys smiled. "This is where your dad said it was, so I am sure it's here. It's just a matter of luring it out of its den."

"How do we do that?" I asked.

"With this," said Rhys. He pulled out his varé and handed it to me. "I don't know if it's the scent or some other method, but drall are attracted by the presence of a varé."

I took the varé and opened it up. As if on cue, a creature seemingly made entirely of tentacles leaped out of a hole next to one of the rock formations. I dropped to my knees, barely managing to avoid it as it leapt past me. At least a hundred tentacles writhed on the creature's round body. Some of the tentacles were long, clearly long enough to be harvested for a varé, but others were smaller, only a foot or less in length. I had imagined the skin of this creature to be slimy, like an octopus. I couldn't have been more wrong. The drall's skin was rough and cracked. Every inch of the creature was covered in rock. It looked as though it had been dipped in glue and then rolled in gravel.

As the drall leaped at me again, I caught sight of a wide mouth that instead of teeth seemed to be filled with sharp rocks. I pivoted and held up the varé for defense. This seemed to enrage the drall. It flattened its tentacles and propelled itself towards me, rolling like a tumbling boulder.

I leaped out of the drall's path. How did I ever survive before without a Berserker's speed and strength? I landed next to Rhys, who stood leaning against a rock formation, disturbingly unconcerned. "Are you going to help?" I yelled.

"I can't," he said. "You have to do this on your own to bond your varé." He gave me an apologetic smile. Good thing for him it looked sincere.

"What am I supposed to do?" I asked.

"Cut off an arm."

"Thanks. I figured that part out," I said. "How? It won't stay still."

Rhys punched a large rock and it shattered into fragments. "Feed it rocks," he said.

"Rocks? Is this some sort of joke?"

"Look out!"

I had been so intent on Rhys' rock lecture that I didn't notice the drall roll around behind me. Pain blossomed up my back as the drall connected with one of its arms. The jagged rocks tore through my coat and gouged out furrows of flesh. They must be a living part of the drall if they could slice me like that. I screamed and lost my footing in the dirt, falling to the ground with the all the grace of a pigeon covered in cement.

The drall leaped into the air and pointed all its tentacles down, attempting to impale me.

Rhys threw a large rock at it, trying to distract it, but the drall completely ignored him and continued its plummet. I rolled to the side, and almost got away. None of the tentacles pierced me, but one of them did pin the shoulder of my coat to the ground.

I jerked my body as hard as I could and ripped the coat, freeing myself. Scrambling to my feet, I pulled out the varé and faced the drall, prepared for its next attack.

I needn't have bothered. In attempting to impale me, the drall had managed to drive the majority of its tentacles deep into the ground and was now stuck, unable to pull itself free.

I circled around until I found the mouth. Now that it was still I could see four tiny eyes above it. I raised the varé, ready to drive it through the drall's mouth and hopefully kill it.

A hand caught my arm. Rhys stopped me. "What are you doing?"

"Me? I'm trying on prom dresses." I said. "What does it look like I'm doing?"

"Don't kill the drall," said Rhys. "There are only a few left in the world. Cut off an arm and let's get back to camp."

"Isn't killing monsters part of the Berserker job description?" I asked.

"Not these," he said. Rhys picked up a few pieces of rock and tossed them into the drall's mouth. It chewed the rocks with the noisiest crunching sound you could imagine. It was like listening to someone eat Grapenuts while using a megaphone.

It almost seemed as if Rhys liked the creature. Me, I personally had a hard time getting past the whole trying to impale me incident and wasn't feeling much love.

"Cut off an arm and let's go," said Rhys. He pointed at one in the back left side. "This one looks to be your size."

I swung the varé and sliced off the arm. It fell to the ground, writhing and flopping, like a fish out of water. When I picked up the tentacle it was moving so much that it was difficult to hold properly. It was also much heavier than it looked. I was pretty strong as a Berserker, but this arm was noticeably heavy.

Once I had moved the arm out of the way, Rhys pushed against the side of the drall, freeing some of its legs. Using its newly freed tentacles, the drall frantically began digging the rest of itself free.

"Let's go," said Rhys. "You don't want to be anywhere close when this guy gets loose."

We ran off into the night and out of Goblin Valley. The trip back was much slower than the trip in. The thrashing arm seemed to grow in strength as we ran. Or in my case, tried to run. The thrashing kept knocking me off balance.

After I had dropped it for the fourth time, Rhys said, "I would offer to carry it for you, but if anyone else touches it the bonding can't happen and the entire trip would be a waste of time."

After the tenth time the tentacle had thrashed out of my grip, I realized my coat was completely in tatters from the sharp rocks attached to the tentacle. It was a lot like trying to hold a moving chainsaw blade.

I began to wonder if this wasn't some sort of cruel Berserker initiation rite. A joke they all played on the newbies. Fortunately for Rhys, he didn't seem to be enjoying my frustration and pain so I didn't whack him with the tentacle. If Eric had been there with his mocking smile, I probably would have lost it.

We followed the GPS back to the camp where Dad had a roaring fire going under the cauldron, which was now filled with boiling water. When he saw the ripped up state of my coat, arms, face, and well... everything, he rushed over to us.

"Are you okay?"

I threw the tentacle on the ground where it continued thrashing. How long was it going to take for this thing to die? "I'll live." I said. "What's next?"

"Boiling."

I looked at the thrashing tentacle. "You can't be serious. How are we going to keep that thing in the pot?"

"We will be doing nothing of the kind," said Rhys. He released his power and the glow faded around him. "You will be doing it. Remember, we can't touch it."

What I wanted to do was change out of these clothes and crawl into a sleeping bag and crash for a dozen hours, but it didn't seem like that was going to happen anytime soon.

"Fine. Let's get this over with." I picked up the tentacle. Dad and Rhys backed away as if I were infected with a disease rather than just carrying a nasty severed tentacle. I struggled to hold it still while it thrashed wildly in my arms. I stumbled over to the pot and dumped the tentacle in.

The boiling water turned bright green and a cloud of steam erupted. The tentacle thrashed even harder and emitted a high-pitched keening sound. I took a step back. It sounded like it was still alive and we were torturing it.

With a splash, the tentacle flipped out of the pot and onto the ground. Rhys jumped out of the way to prevent it from touching him. I quickly picked it back up and found that with the added effect of boiling heat it was even less pleasant to hold than before. I dumped it back into the pot before it could burn my hands too badly. This time I picked up a thick forked branch from the pile of firewood and used it to hold the tentacle in the water.

After a half hour or so, the thrashing began to die down. I relaxed slightly. It seemed that the worst was over.

Dad and Rhys came over to inspect the progress. By now the tentacle was just twitching slightly. I gave it a good jab with the forked stick just in case it was even thinking of jumping out again.

Dad approached with a large serrated knife and informed me that now I needed to cut the flesh off to reveal the bone below.

I fished the tentacle out and laid it on a camp table set up near the fire. I took the knife and began sawing at the thick hide on the tentacle. It was difficult to cut through, but after a few minutes I hit bone and was able to start peeling the flesh away. It peeled off in a single piece, like a sleeve turned inside out, revealing the bones that I knew would form my varé.

Next Dad and Rhys showed me how to carve down the larger bones at the end to form a hilt for the sword and the release button.

After that, I filed the bones along the blade to make them sharper. When we were done, I looked at what I had built. It was a beautiful piece of work even if I did say so myself. As far as I could tell, it was indistinguishable from Rhys' and my dad's varés. I pressed the button and the sword rolled up into a small disk.

I grinned. "Is that it?" I asked.

"Not yet," said Dad. "Now comes the actual bonding."

"Hold the sword out in your hands and close your eyes," said Rhys. "What you need to do now is to search for the varé. I don't know how else to explain it. You should be able to reach out with your mind and feel it. Once you feel it, push out and put a bit of yourself into it."

I closed my eyes and held out the sword. It seemed to pulse and shift in my hand as if part of it were still alive. I reached out, looking for... something. At first I felt nothing, except stupid. Could the instructions have been more vague?

But before I could open my eyes and accuse Rhys and Dad of playing a joke on me, I felt the first inklings of the varé. It was still alive. Severed, boiled, and skinned, but it still held a tiny spark of quickly-fading life.

I reached out and with my mind pushed into the varé, feeling the connection arise. While I knew what I was supposed to feel, the descriptions I had heard were utterly inadequate to the experience. It wasn't a sense I could describe, but it was similar to the feel of a nearby Berserker using his powers, or the sensation of Bringers encroaching – only not so evil and gross.

Joyful.

That was how the varé felt when we connected. It welcomed me and allowed my essence to suffuse it. Peace and happiness flowed back to me. Rather than joining with something new, it felt as if I had regained a lost limb.

I opened my eyes and saw Rhys and Dad smiling at me.

"It feels wonderful," I said.

I stepped back and flicked open the varé. I swung it in a graceful arc. They had been right about the control. The varé was no longer an inanimate object in my hand, but a living part of me. I could manipulate the blade as well as I could my limbs. I instinctively knew how close or far away it was to an object. After a few more practice thrusts I leaped into the air, swung the varé in a complicated pattern, and brought it down toward the cauldron. I stopped it at the last second, a mere fraction of an inch above the back metal.

Complete control over the blade.

Now I understood why Dad had been so insistent that I bond to my weapon as quickly as possible.

I couldn't wait to get back and start training.

CHAPTER 14

THE ONLY WOMAN IN THE WORLD

A s I got ready for school Monday, I had a new addition to my purse. Up until now, my EpiPen had been the only item I always kept on me - in case of bee stings. Now the varé had also earned a permanent spot. Never again would I be caught unprepared.

The weather was hot for Washington, especially given that it was mid-November. Usually by now the temperature had dropped to the low 50s with lots of rain. This year it was staying in the upper 60s and 70s. We were also getting hardly any moisture – a rare occurrence in this area. At least that was the case for a fifty mile radius around Woodbridge. The weatherman on the news was unable to explain why this high pressure system was still lingering and causing such unusual weather patterns in the area.

I mentioned it to Rhys and Eric when they picked me up for school.

"It's Osadyn," Eric said.

"Osadyn," I repeated. "What would he have to do with the temperature?"

"Do you remember what you felt when he first attacked you?"

I thought back to the day I had followed Rhys and Eric home. "Nausea," I said. "I felt sick to my stomach." I didn't mention the fact that I had actually vomited all over the side of the road.

"What else?"

"Heat. It was like I'd opened an oven door."

"Exactly," said Eric. "All the Havocs bring heat with them. It's usually just a small area because they move around so much, but since Osadyn is staying here, it seems to be causing some unanticipated effects."

"That's an interesting theory," said Dad walking into the kitchen. "This may be the first time that a Havoc has stayed in an area for so long. Hmmm." He paused and looked thoughtful.

"What is it?" asked Rhys.

Dad shook his head. "Nothing – for now anyway. I want to do a bit of investigating to be sure."

Eric groaned. "Fine, Scottie, be that way." He turned to me, completely changing the subject. "Can I see your varé?"

I pulled the circular disk from my purse and handed it to him. With a deft flick he opened it and began to examine it.

He ran a finger along the sharpened blade. "Not bad," he said. "The balance feels good, too." He flicked it closed and handed it back to me. "That's a nice weapon you have there. I personally can't wait to see it in action."

***

When we pulled into school there was a crowd standing in the parking lot. Two freshman were in the center rolling on the ground and attempting to beat each other senseless while the crowd egged them on.

Without even a glance at each other to coordinate their plans, Eric and Rhys waded through the crowd and pulled the thrashing freshmen apart. The clustered students booed and jeered, but when it became clear that the fight was over, they quickly dispersed. Eric and Rhys were left holding two struggling freshmen who were doing their best to get back to pummeling each other.

"What's going on?" asked Rhys.

"I hate him!" shouted the smaller of the two. His shirt was ripped at the shoulder and he had the beginnings of what would be a spectacular black eye.

The other freshman surged forward, pulling Eric off balance.

"He started it!"

While he was somewhat larger, he didn't seem to have gotten off any better. A cut on his scalp dripped blood down his face and his shorts were split down the backside, revealing plaid boxers.

Eric lifted the kid into the air. "Well, we're stopping it," he said. The boy's eyes grew wide and his furious anger gave way to fear as he realized the position he was in. Eric set him down facing the school. "Get to class. Or better yet, go see the school nurse," he said and gave him a nudge. The boy looked back resentfully, but did as he was told.

After the boy was out of sight, Rhys released the second freshman. He glared balefully at Rhys. "I would have had him if it hadn't been for you." He walked toward school. When the boy was almost inside he turned around, yelled a couple of semi-articulate swear words, and ran off.

Eric shook his head. "See, this is why being a good Samaritan just isn't worth it."

There were three other fights during school that day and the entire atmosphere felt tense. Everyone was on edge, ready to blow up at the least provocation.

It wasn't just that day, either. For the next two weeks, the fighting continued to escalate. Even the teachers were not immune. They were grumpy and irritable, giving out detentions with little provocation.

The whole atmosphere made school practically unbearable. Fortunately, I had my after-school varé training sessions to look forward to. Rhys supervised the majority of my instruction, with Dad and the other Berserkers helping out here and there.

Rhys taught me the various defensive positions and blocks. We worked on posture, the proper way to hold the blade as well as the underlying theory of combat with the varé.

I wasn't sure if it was because I had bonded to the varé or because I was a Berserker – or maybe both together - but learning the moves Rhys taught was much easier than I had expected. Rhys had only to show me something once, and I was able to replicate it easily.

After I had the basic movements and theory down, we moved into more advanced practical applications with other instructors. With my dad, I had slow-speed sparring matches where I had to explain each move choice as I attempted to attack or block. With Rhys, I had real-time sparring where I had to put together combinations of attacks and blocks together in a seamless flow.

With the rest of the Berserkers, I had the opportunity to fight against other weapons and adapt my moves to the weapon wielded by my opponent. Because we were bonded to our weapons, we were able to spar at nearly full-speed without any danger of accidentally hurting each other.

When Thanksgiving break came around, I was grateful to be out of school for a few days. The tension in the halls was practically palpable. Several fights a day were now the norm. And it wasn't just the school that was affected. The crime rate in Woodbridge skyrocketed with more violent attacks in a one month period than in the previous five years combined. Dad finally let us in on his theory that Osadyn's presence was not only responsible for the heat, but for the increase in violence as well.

"It's because of his primary power," Dad told me and Rhys after a training session.

Rhys looked thoughtful and nodded. "That could be it," he said. "I've only seen his primary power used on targets within his field of vision, but you're saying that it could be another side-effect of his presence?"

"Exactly," Dad said. "Something is manipulating emotions on a massive scale. I don't think it's a coincidence."

"What's a primary power?" I asked.

Dad blinked and looked at me, then shook his head as if clearing it. "Sorry, Madison. I sometimes forget you're still learning about all this.

"Each Havoc has a unique ability. We call that its primary power. Osadyn's power is emotional control and manipulation. Fear, paranoia, lust, hatred, doubt: Osadyn can make anyone feel these emotions, or the opposites, but that's much rarer."

"That's why Osadyn has been so difficult to bind," said Rhys. "The few times we have gotten close enough, he's turned us against each other."

"Only those emotions?" I asked.

"No," said Dad. "He has control over the full range. But he certainly prefers some emotions over others."

"What about the other Havocs? What are their primary powers?"

"I'll take this one," said Rhys. Dad shrugged, acquiescing. "Thuanar, Aata's Havoc, has the primary power of invisibility. It can also conceal objects and people. Navitan, Shing's Havoc, drains living things of energy. Margil, Eric's Havoc, accelerates decay. It also has a limited control over the dead." I shuddered, thinking of an army of undead zombies attacking me. "And Pravicus, your Havoc, has the ability of mental domination. It can bend people, even Berserkers, to its will."

"So, all the crazy stuff going on is because of Osadyn?"

"I think so," said Dad.

Which meant it was all happening because of me. Osadyn was only staying in one place to get me. He was waiting for me to be alone so he could free Pravicus. The longer that took, the worse things would be. Winter Solstice felt like it was years away instead of less than a month.

"How can we keep waiting?" I asked. "If this keeps up, people are going to die."

And suddenly Dad was there, pulling me into a hug. He held it for a long moment and then let go, looking at me very intently. "I know this is hard for you," he said. "But what Osadyn does isn't your fault. It's because of you that we even have a chance to bind him. Yes, the fact that you are here and too well-guarded for him to attack means he will stay close by and will likely cause more people to die. But you have to understand that he will kill wherever he goes. There may be a few more deaths now, but you have to weigh that against all the lives that will be spared when he is finally bound."

Rhys nodded in agreement. "Believe me, no one wants Osadyn bound more than I do, but we've tried going directly after Osadyn before. It doesn't work. This time we will make him come to us and believe me, we won't waste this opportunity.

***

For Thanksgiving, we invited all the Berserkers and Binders to our house. It still seemed strange to have Mom both know and not know what was going on, but the haze seemed to be working. Mom interacted with everyone and seemed to genuinely like them, but never spoke about their powers or why they were with me so much.

Eric seemed to have gone out of his way to charm my mother. He helped out in the kitchen, preparing the turkey and making the mashed potatoes. While she was around he seemed like the most perfect well-mannered boy – not the way I generally perceived him. I wasn't sure what he was up to until Mom started talking about what a nice boy he was and hinting that if I showed a bit more interest he might ask me out.

I wasn't sure whether to laugh or rip out my hair in frustration.

After Thanksgiving dinner, we all sat outside enjoying the weather. At first I felt guilty since I knew the warmth came from Osadyn and was surely causing serious problems with the local environment, but the pleasant temperature was too inviting to pass up.

When I mentioned my difficulty to Shing, he looked at the sky for a moment before responding. "Is it wrong to make something good out of something evil?"

Before I could come up with an answer, Mallika sat down by me. "I have a proposal for tomorrow morning," she said.

I glanced at Shing. He didn't seem to be waiting for an answer to the question he'd posed, so I turned my attention back to Mallika. "I'm intrigued. What's up?"

"I know your father wants you fully weapons-trained before the Winter Solstice, but that training has come at the expense of teaching you about the relationship between the Binder and Berserker. I haven't pushed too hard since we were waiting to find your Binder, but I don't think it can wait any longer. Tomorrow morning, I would like Kara to give you some basic lessons on Binders."

"Sure," I said. "If you think it's that important, then I'm in."

Mallika nodded. "Good. I'll let your father know the plan. Kara and Aata will pick you up tomorrow at eight o'clock."

***

The next morning I accidentally slept in and had to rush to get ready on time. I didn't have time to really do my hair, so pulled it back into a ponytail and threw on a hat. I don't wear hats often, but this one was really cute, and I had bought it for just such an occasion.

Kara and Aata picked me up in the Range Rover and drove me back to the Berserker house. Aata, Kara, and Mallika were the only ones there. Shing, Rhys, and Eric had gone out scouting locations for setting our trap for Winter Solstice.

We went upstairs to a rather bare room with wood floors and mirrors covering the walls. It looked like it was intended to be some sort of exercise room, or dance studio, but right now it was completely empty except for a couple of wooden ladder back chairs.

Not the most comfortable of accommodations.

Aata lingered, as if reluctant to leave, but Mallika gently took him by the arm and led him out of the room. "I'll just be downstairs," Aata said as Mallika escorted him out and closed the door behind them. "Let me know if you need anything."

Kara rolled her eyes and gave me a lopsided grin. "They may be Berserkers, but that doesn't stop them from being boys, no matter how old they get."

Thinking back to Eric's efforts to get on my mom's good side, I couldn't help but giggle. Being with Kara felt like I had a girlfriend again. Ever since Amy started dating Cory, I hadn't seen much of her. Of course, I had been rather busy myself, so it wasn't entirely her fault.

"Of course, you are in a bit of a unique situation," Kara said.

"What do you mean?"

Kara raised an eyebrow. "You're a Berserker," she said. "A female Berserker."

"So?"

"So? Isn't it obvious? Think about it from these guys' perspective. You saw how reluctant they were to tell you about the aging process for a Berserker. They weren't pretending to be worried. They've all felt its effects. It's hard to have a relationship when you know you'll live for hundreds of years while your loved one grows closer to dying every second."

"And that's if they don't shun you and think you're some sort of monster," I said, thinking back to my dad's and Rhys' stories. It wasn't the first time this had crossed my mind. Hearing Rhys talk about his fiancé and how he had left her was enough to get me thinking about what kind of relationships I might have - or more to the point - not have.

"Exactly," said Kara. "Now you can see why Rhys and Eric are always competing for your attention. From their perspective, you are the only woman on earth. Literally. Or at least the only one they can hope to have a lasting relationship with."

"I guess," I said. I could certainly see Eric's interest. I would have to be blind to miss that. Unfortunately, any interest on Rhys' part was certainly more subtle. So subtle I wasn't even sure it was there. Just because I was the only person available didn't mean that he was interested in me. Besides, did I want to be desired just because I was the only option? How pathetic was that?

Kara's ears perked up at the tone of my voice. She looked me in the eye and smiled. "Okay, something's going on. Spill." The excited tone in her voice forcibly reminded me of Amy and her Machiavellian take on dating.

"No, it's nothing," I said. "You're right. I've definitely seen Eric's interest, and I've kind of seen Rhys' show some interest, but...."

"But not as much as you would like?" Kara asked, her eyes too knowing.

I nodded.

"I knew it!" Kara said. "You do like Rhys."

I nodded again and blushed, then shook my head. "I don't know," I said. "I guess it doesn't really matter since Rhys doesn't seem to feel that way about me."

Kara rolled her eyes and slumped back into one of the chairs. "Are you serious?" she asked. "Are you that blind? Just because Rhys isn't as outgoing as Eric doesn't mean he's not interested. Rhys is just a little more introverted. Trust me, if you show some interest he will definitely reciprocate."

My heart started thumping at those words and the excitement was enough that I began to pre-zerk. The world around me grew crisper.

"Really?"

"Really," Kara said. "I've been with these guys long enough to see what they're usually like. Your arrival has gotten them all worked up."

"All of them?" I asked.

"Well, sort of," she said, a thoughtful look on her face. "Shing's been around for so long that he is physically more than twenty years older than you – so I think he sees you as a little girl. And as for Aata... well, he's already interested in someone else."

At that instant all the pieces clicked into place. "You?" I said. "You and Aata?"

Kara giggled and smiled before putting a finger to her lips. "Shhh. It's a secret."

"Why?"

"Because we want a bit of privacy for one thing. But the real reason is we don't want to hear the lectures and judgments."

"What do you mean?"

"Berserker - Binder relationships are heavily frowned upon. It was discouraged before your parents got married, but because of how that ended it has really become taboo."

"So, no one knows?"

"Well, Aata knows, obviously, and so does Mallika, but none of the others do. At least, I don't think so."

Kara spent the next half hour telling me how she and Aata first met and expressed their feelings to one another. It was a familiar conversation, one I'd had with other girl friends countless times. The details were always different, but the discovery and sharing of feelings was always exciting. For a few brief moments I forgot about being a Berserker. I was just a normal girl talking with a friend about the guy she likes.

Until Kara looked at her watch.

"Uh-oh! I'm supposed to be teaching you about the Binders and here I am blathering on about me."

And then it was back to the Berserker world.

At first I was disappointed when our girl-talk ended, but as Kara began teaching me, I discovered that the role Binders play in protecting the world from Havocs was fascinating.

Just as Berserkers are always male – until I came in and ruined that club – the Binders are always female. Unlike Berserkers, Binders live a normal lifespan, aging and dying like any other person. They don't have flashy powers, super strength, or extraordinary senses, but they do have their own skills and role to play.

It is through the Binder's power that the Havocs are contained. The Binder uses the Berserker's blood to tie the Havoc to a location and push it out of synch with our world. Once bound, only the Berserkers and Binders can see the Havoc, and no one can interact with it.

"Once a Havoc is bound," said Kara, "you can walk right through it and not feel a thing."

"What else can Binders do?"

"Binders have two other abilities – casting a haze and weaving a snare. A snare is a net of energy able to trap a Havoc, rendering it temporarily immobile."

"Why haven't we done that with Osadyn?" I asked.

"It's a slow process," Kara said. "A snare powerful enough to hold a Havoc for only a few minutes can take days to weave. You can't just weave one when the Havoc is there. You have to do it days in advance. Since we don't know ahead of time where a Havoc will be, snares aren't really that useful.

"The haze, on the other hand, is something we use a lot. Glowing men battling massive monsters isn't exactly a subtle process. To keep our work out of the public's knowledge, Binders can cast a haze to separate a piece of knowledge from the conscious mind. The information isn't erased, it's just impossible to access."

I nodded. "I remember Mallika casting the haze on my mom. How exactly does it work?"

"It's a two-part process," said Kara. "First, the Binder casts the actual haze."

"Is that the blue stuff that came out of Mallika's hands?"

Kara nodded and gave me a piercing look. "How do you know that?" she asked. "Has Mallika covered this already?"

"Know what?"

"The color of the haze."

I shrugged. "I saw it."

Kara held up her hands. "Do you see anything now?"

"Just your hands. Why?"

"How about now?"

This time, blue mist came out of Kara's hands. I took a step back, not wanting to have any contact with it.

Kara dropped her hands and the mist disappeared. "You really saw that?" The open happiness that had been on her face only moments before was now gone, replaced by a look of concern.

I stayed where I was, unsure whether I'd offended her. "Yeah, I saw the mist," I said tentatively. "Is that bad?"

"I don't know," she said. Her eyes darted towards the door. "I don't think so. It shouldn't be. I'm going to get Mallika." She practically ran out of the room leaving me alone and wondering what I had done wrong.

It didn't take long before Kara had returned with Mallika. "Tell her what you told me," Kara said.

"I saw the blue mist when you put a haze on my mom," I said.

Mallika raised her eyebrows in a surprised expression that seemed out of place on her normally stoic face. "Interesting." She turned to Kara. "I'll take it from here," she said.

Kara nodded and walked to the door. She turned and gave me a small wave before closing it behind her.

With a few quick strides, Mallika stood in front of me and looked me up and down. "You, Madison, are quite the conundrum," she said. "A female Berserker who can also see a haze casting. Hmmm. I guess I should have thought to test you for this before, but in my defense, this is completely new territory."

"Test me for what?"

"To see if you are a Binder, of course."

Now it was my turn to be surprised. "But I can't be a Binder. I'm a Berserker. It's impossible to be both, right?"

"A few months ago I thought it was impossible to have a female Berserker," said Mallika. "I think the word 'impossible' has lost some of its absoluteness, don't you?"

There was really no way to argue with that, so I sat down in the chair to take Mallika's test.

"We already know you can see a haze," she said, "but can you see a snare?" She raised her arms high into the air and splayed her fingers. Black, thread-like tendrils oozed out of the tips of her fingers. They dripped to the ground and began weaving themselves into a thicker rope. After a moment Mallika stopped and looked at me. "What did you see?"

When I finished describing everything I had seen to her, she nodded thoughtfully. "That just leaves binding," she said. "Unfortunately, I have no way to test that here." She pursed her lips, looking thoughtful. "I don't think there's any other way. I'll have to send for the Sarolt stone."

"Sarolt stone?"

"It's the true test of both a Binder and a Berserker. Although generally it isn't used on Berserkers because the signs of power are rather obvious. But I'm afraid that it will take a while to get it here. Or rather, to convince the Binder Conclave to send it. They hold a rather tight rein on the objects of power and don't send them abroad without an exhaustive and lengthy discussion."

"Ok, hold on a second. There's a Binder Conclave?" I said, my voice rising. "What's that? And why haven't I heard anything about objects of power before now?" I had to exercise quite a bit of control to keep myself from shouting.

Mallika put an arm around me. "Madison, I know it's been a shock becoming a Berserker. If we consider that you may also be a Binder, then the hard truth is that there's no way you can fully understand your new roles all at once. We're not hiding anything from you to make you frustrated or as part of some evil plot. We're simply trying to give you the information you need to know when you need to know it so that it will make sense to you.

"We've been keeping the political structure of the Berserkers' world in the background because until now, it wasn't important for you. And to be honest, it still isn't. Our top priority right now is to prepare you for Winter Solstice. Everything else, including whether or not you are also a Binder, is secondary. Okay?"

I dropped my chin, feeling like a spoiled child who just threw a tantrum.

"Okay."

I still didn't like getting blindsided by new information all the time, but listening to Mallika I could at least understand the reasoning behind it.

Mallika smiled at me. "Good. The last thing we need right now is a distraction to take away from that preparation. Until we get confirmation from the Sarolt stone, we should keep this between you, me, and Kara. Agreed?"

"Agreed," I said.

I stayed in the room after Mallika left, staring at my reflection. It had been long enough since my transformation last summer that I no longer wondered who the stranger in the mirror was, but as I looked at my reflection, I couldn't help wondering what other changes might be in store.

CHAPTER 15

ANAPHYLACTIC SHOCK

I spent the next few weeks reflecting on everything I learned during my one brief Binder lesson. Mallika seemed to think it best to ignore the signs of my being a Binder, at least until there was proof. As nice as that sounded at the time, it was hard not to think about it. Was I really both a Binder and a Berserker? Did that mean I would age normally? Could I learn to cast snares and hazes, or could I only see them? What else was different about me that I took for granted as being normal Berserker powers?

As Christmas break approached, so did finals. For the first time in my life, I didn't hear a single word from my dad about buckling down and studying. As far as he was concerned, I only stayed in school to keep up the appearance of normality. My real education revolved around self-defense and the swiftly approaching Winter Solstice.

To that end, I continued my after-school weapons training, and even added some early morning meditation sessions with Shing. Shing taught me how to control my berserking and it wasn't long until I could move from normal, to pre-zerk, to full 'zerk at will.

As for the varé, I was learning faster than I had dreamed possible. By the time Thanksgiving break was over, I had mastered all of the basic positions, blocks, and stances. Now we were working on combinations of attacks and planning three or four moves in advance.

Rhys and Dad were impressed with my progress. Dad said I was a natural and Rhys said it had taken him more than a year of practice to get to the point I was. I walked on air for the rest of the day.

The weather continued to get warmer. The temperatures went to record highs. The normally green vegetation was drying up as the lack of rain and excessive heat took their toll. Dead brown began to replace lush green as the dominant landscape color. The county had put in water restrictions, and for the first time ever water was being rationed.

The weather wasn't the only thing running hot. The news was full of assaults, murders, attempted murders, and practically every other possible crime of passion. Osadyn's influence was like a disease, slowly contaminating more people each day. I tried not to feel guilty when I watched the news reports, but every time I saw a story about another murder, I felt sick inside. No matter what the other Berserkers said, it was my fault this was happening.

I went through the motions of school, but my heart wasn't in it. I stopped studying as the big day grew closer and my preparation escalated. I expected my grades to go down, but surprisingly they stayed pretty much the same. I had always been pretty good at taking tests, and one of the side effects of the pre-zerking is unusual mental clarity and recall.

I asked Rhys a few surreptitious questions and discovered that enhanced memory was another power unique to me. I also suspected it was the real reason behind my quick mastery of the varé.

By the time school ended for Christmas break, I was ready to be done. Preparations for the big fight had gone into overdrive. Aata and Shing were working on building some new type of weapons that would help keep me safe, while Dad and Rhys spent quite a bit of time out scouting the ideal location of our battle.

The first morning of Christmas break, I was supposed to go out with Eric and Aata to practice combat in wooded terrain. When Eric arrived in the Mercedes alone, I knew something was up.

"Where's Aata?" I asked.

Eric shrugged. "He had some other things to take care of. I told him where we'd be, and he said he'd catch up with us later." He slipped out of the car and opened my door with a formal bow. "Hop in, my lady."

I couldn't help but laugh at his bizarre mixture of formal and slang. Which, judging from the big grin he gave me, was exactly what he was hoping for.

Eric pulled out of the driveway and gunned the car down the road. The acceleration threw me against the seat and took my breath away. I had forgotten just how fast this car could go.

When we got onto the highway, I quickly realized that I had never seen how fast the car could really go. Eric floored the gas and we practically flew across the pavement. Within seconds the speedometer blew past 100 mph and continued higher. When we reached 150 mph, I yelled at Eric to slow down, but he just laughed.

"Don't worry," he said. "A car wreck can't hurt you."

185 mph.

"But it might kill whoever we crash into!" I yelled as Eric swerved between two cars at a speed that made them seem like they were standing still.

197 mph.

With a sigh, he lifted his foot from the gas pedal and the car began to slowly decelerate to a normal freeway speed. Very slowly.

We drove south into Portland and then east into the Columbia River Gorge, one of my favorite places in the world. The river ran through a massive canyon with high, tree-lined walls on either side. Waterfalls decorated the landscape every few miles and the view was simply breathtaking - at least when the weather was normal.

Even this far away, the effects of Osadyn were painfully visible. The once green gorge was definitely more brown than usual, and the usually flowing waterfalls were mere trickles.

Eric took an exit, drove into a parking lot, and parked next to a Jeep with a jacked up suspension and massive tires.

"Time to switch," he said, and hopped into the Jeep.

It didn't take long to see why he had switched vehicles. The Mercedes could go fast, but it wouldn't have made it past the first switchback as Eric pulled off the pavement and began driving on dirt roads.

To be honest, I wasn't sure which was scarier, Eric flying down the freeway at almost 200 mph, or Eric driving up switchbacks practically on two wheels as we ascended the gorge walls. Instinctively, I reached over and grabbed his arm, but I immediately dropped it when I saw the smirk on his face.

I was not going to play into his plans.

At the top of the path was a beautiful meadow overlooking the Columbia River. The view was breathtaking. I had lived in this area my whole life, but I had never been any place like this before.

Eric grabbed my hand and pulled me into the middle of the meadow where there was a large blanket and picnic basket waiting for us.

"Hmmm. I wonder how this got here," he said, feigning curiosity. He opened the basket which was full of food and drinks. "It seems a shame to let this go to waste," he said and began setting up a meal.

"Aren't we supposed to be practicing combat in wooded terrain?" I asked.

Eric raised his eyebrows and gave me his best wounded expression. "Of course we are," he said. He gestured to the trees on the edge of the meadow. "And so we will, don't worry. I just thought you might want a bit of sustenance before we begin."

I should have known he would try something like this. I would be willing to bet anything that Aata either had no idea where we were or that Eric somehow bribed or blackmailed him into not coming with us.

"If you're not hungry, we can certainly practice first and then eat later," Eric said, his eyes wide and innocent – well, as innocent as Eric can be. "Whatever you prefer."

Despite myself I couldn't help smiling. I knew I shouldn't. This was frivolous and we should be practicing, not having a picnic. But the reality was it felt kind of good to take a bit of a break. I just wished it could have been Rhys I was here with instead of Eric.

"Fine," I said, "but after we finish eating we need to practice, okay?"

"Absolutely," said Eric with an overly sincere expression. "As soon as we finish eating, we will get right to it." His lips twitched and I could tell he was trying not to smile. He was up to something, but I was conflicted on whether or not I wanted to stop him.

He reached into the picnic basket and pulled out several bundles of food. "I didn't know what you would be in the mood for, so I brought a few contingency dishes. Are you in the mood for fancy or more of a traditional picnic?"

I admit I was curious about what the fancy option entailed, but it was strictly academic. My taste buds were more or less back to normal, but I still didn't have much of an appetite for exotic spices and flavorings.

"Traditional," I said.

He nodded as if he had been expecting that answer. He reached into the picnic basket and pulled out a pair of sandwiches piled high with vegetables, a container full of sliced watermelon, two slices of apple pie, and two bottles of ice cold root beer. It all looked delicious. He couldn't have picked out a better meal if he had read my mind – or asked my mom. Which was almost certainly what he had done.

We sat in silence for a while, eating and enjoying the cool breeze. I even went crazy and kicked off my shoes and socks, enjoying the sensation of wind on my toes – and hoping my feet didn't stink too badly. We were far enough away from Osadyn that the temperature was a good fifteen degrees cooler than in Woodbridge, and the gentle breeze was nothing short of pure bliss.

I waited for Eric to start up a conversation, but for the first time since I'd met him he seemed content to simply sit and enjoy the moment.

Which, of course, made me intensely curious. Was what Kara had said true? Did Eric see me as his last chance at having a long-term relationship? Was he doing this simply because I was the only female Berserker, or would he have been interested in me even if I were normal? Did I even want him to be interested?

The problem was that I hardly knew Eric. Yes, I had seen the façade he put on for everyone to see, but the more I watched him the more I thought the real Eric might be someone different, deeper - and hopefully less abrasive.

It was time to do a bit of investigating.

"Okay, Eric," I said, "tell me about you. I've known you for several months now, but I still know next to nothing about you." Okay, so it wasn't very subtle, but with Eric I doubted the subtle approach would have worked, anyway.

Eric rolled onto his back. "Story time, huh?" He took a deep breath. "The truth is that I don't like to talk much about me, or the old me anyway." He turned his head to look at me. "But for a girl as pretty as you, I am willing to make an exception."

I groaned. "Is the story going to include the number of times you've used that line?"

With an indignant sniff, Eric rolled back over. "If this is how I can expect to be treated..." he said.

I picked some grass and threw it at him. The wind was blowing the wrong way and most of it blew back onto me. Eric laughed and sat up.

"You really want to know?" he asked. "It's not a very fun story. Kind of a mood killer. That's why I usually try to pretend my past never happened."

I shrugged. "I thought those who ignored the past were doomed to repeat it?"

"No, no," said Eric. "Those who don't learn from the past are doomed to repeat it. I've learned from it, now I'm trying to forget how I learned all those valuable lessons. See, it's really more of a repressed memory thing."

"Oh, I see. Well, I'm still interested, so if you're up for it I would love to hear it."

Eric flashed me a grin. "If you insist. But if you find yourself hopelessly depressed afterwards, don't blame me. I tried to warn you."

"I promise not to blame you."

"Okay. You've been warned. I was born in rural Indiana right before the Great Depression. My father was a farmer who had come to the United States from Ireland with his family when he was just a few years old. He had grown up poor and worked extremely hard to pull himself out of poverty. He managed to provide for his wife and - once I came along - four sons. When the stock market crashed he didn't initially think it would affect him. But when the banks collapsed, his loans were called in, and the price he could sell his produce for plummeted. Within a matter of a few months he lost everything, including the farm he had spent his life building.

"We moved to Indianapolis because my father was offered a job there. Only by the time we got there, someone else had been hired. My father was a proud man and continued trying for several years to support us, but the few jobs he could find were extremely hard labor, and he died of a heart attack when I was ten.

"Without our father around, my brothers and I were forced to beg and scrounge to get by. Mom found temporary work washing laundry, but it barely covered the rent of the broken-down apartment we lived in.

"It was during this time that I met Sophie. She was poor like us, but there was something different about her. In the midst of all the hunger and squalor, she always seemed to find something to be happy about. Being around her made life tolerable. She was my first love. Sappy, but true. For the next five years we were best friends and somewhere along the way became more.

"When World War Two broke out, I knew this was my chance to make something of myself. I lied about my age and joined the army to go fight the Germans. The pay was $50 a month, which was a lot of money for me. I proposed to Sophie before I left and promised that I would marry her when my service was up."

Eric stopped talking and gave me a searching look. "Do you still want me to go on?" he asked. "It only gets more depressing from here."

He hadn't been lying about this being a depressing story. But now that I was into it, I wanted him to keep going. "I want to hear more," I said.

With a shrug Eric continued. "I'll spare you the gory details about my first year in the army. Let's just say I saw plenty of combat and killed a lot of people. Apparently I had a knack for killing people because I was given a position as a squad leader.

"All this time I kept writing to Sophie. She was the only thing that kept me sane. I kept her most recent letters in my pocket so I could reread them. While I was gone, she joined in the war effort and took on work in a factory, helping to build weapons. Each letter, she told me she loved me and that she was waiting for me to come home to her.

"My mom passed away while I was in Germany, but I didn't get the letter until two months later. I will never forget that day, because it was not only the day I found out my mother died, but it was also the first day I 'zerked.

"I had gotten the letter that morning and we were ordered to move out in the afternoon. There was no time for grief - just the sick knowledge that I was now an orphan. As we marched, we were caught in an ambush. We ran for cover in the trees off the main road, but by the time we got there, most of my squad had been killed or injured. I had taken a bullet to the leg, and I could see that it had nicked an artery. We tried to put pressure on it, but the bleeding wouldn't stop. There were too many other wounded to take care of who could be treated, so I was left alone to die.

"It was then that I felt an anger like I had never felt before. The unfairness of it all was just too much. My mother was dead, and now I was going to die in the middle of a war and never see my Sophie again. It seemed like too much to keep inside and my anger boiled over.

"I began to glow and the pain in my leg went away. The bleeding stopped and the wound healed. But at the time I didn't notice because I wasn't exactly thinking clearly. Pure, raw emotion dominated my brain. All rational thoughts were thrust away.

"I don't recall much about my initial 'zerk. When it ended I realized that my wound was healed, and that everyone within a mile radius was dead – enemy and friends both. In my rage, I had somehow killed them all."

I gaped at Eric, unsure how to respond. He had slaughtered all those people? His own friends? How could that have happened?

"I don't blame you for staring at me that way. Believe me, there is no accusation you could make that I have not already made against myself."

"I wasn't accusing you," I said. "It was just that I..." I had no idea what to say that wouldn't sound horrible and make the situation worse.

"It was a lot of years ago," said Eric. "I can't change what I've done, but I do find comfort in knowing that I did not consciously choose to kill those people. My body may have been the instrument of their death, but my mind was not the driving force behind it.

"I've since learned that it is not uncommon for the first 'zerking to be violent and uncontrollable," he said. "But that is cold comfort to me. I was so repulsed by what had happened that my mind was unable to process it. I huddled in a ball and waited to die. Instead, I was found the next day by the reinforcements who had come to our defense. As the lone survivor I was given a medal and put into another squad.

"War is confusing and scary enough without also dealing with emerging Berserker powers, but I didn't have a choice. I vowed that I would make up for the lives that I took. That I would master this power and use it to kill our enemies. If I could only kill enough of them, I was convinced that I could make up for what I had done to my friends.

"During the next few months, I learned how to control the 'zerk. I snuck out past our patrols at night, seeking enemy camps. I killed everyone I found without hesitation or mercy. They were not people to me - they were my chance at redemption.

"I didn't stop killing until Scottie and Rhys found me. They explained what I was and what was happening to me. They wanted me to come with them, to abandon my fellow soldiers and to fight mysterious monsters that I had never seen or heard of. They said my powers were meant for saving the world from enemies more powerful than the dictators I was fighting, that I wasn't meant to kill humans with these powers. But they didn't know how many people I had already killed. I was afraid to tell them – or anyone for that matter – what I had already done. Besides, following them meant leaving my Sophie behind forever.

"I couldn't do it. I refused to go with them and threatened to expose them when they wouldn't go away." Eric gave me a sour grin. "We kind of got off on the wrong foot.

"They finally left me, but it was clear they would keep in touch in case I changed my mind. From that point on I stopped using my powers to fight enemy soldiers. I realized that more deaths could never make up for the lives I had taken.

"When the war was over, I went back home to Sophie. I remembered what Scottie and Rhys told me about the aging, but I didn't care. It didn't matter to me if she got old. Did they really think my love for her was that shallow? We would make it work."

I heard a tiny buzz and looked over to see several bees floating from flower to flower. My first instinct was to move away from them. I was so allergic that a bee sting could potentially kill me. But I was afraid that if I made a big deal about the bee Eric might stop his story, and I wanted to hear the rest. I had my EpiPen in my purse, so I sat tight and tried to ignore the buzzing.

"We got married a few months after I returned. I was able to put my memories of the war atrocities behind me and for the most part, we were happy. At least that's what I told myself. Sophie's extreme optimism once again made life bearable. For five years everything was fine – until my oldest brother came for a surprise visit.

"I hadn't seen him in almost ten years and his shock at my appearance opened Sophie's eyes to the fact that I wasn't aging. When she confronted me about it, I told her what had happened to me. To my surprise she embraced it with the same enthusiasm that she had for everything. She encouraged me to work with the Berserkers and fulfill my responsibilities to the world.

"For the next twenty years we lived together happily. We never stayed long any one place. After a few years in a city we moved on. It was tough for Sophie to constantly move around and leave her friends. I at least had the Berserkers for friendship, all she had was me. And I was gone most of the time.

"Fortunately, money wasn't an issue because the Berserker before me had been quite good at investing his resources. When I came on board, I inherited more money than I had ever dreamed of owning."

"Wait," I said. "What's this? You inherited money from the Berserker before you?"

"Oops," said Eric, not sounding very regretful. "Let's just pretend I didn't say anything about that."

"Eric." I gave him my best glare.

"Okay, but remember you didn't hear this from me." He gave me a conspiratorial wink. "Your Dad doesn't want you thinking about this part yet. Berserkers have been around for a long time and in that time have fully taken advantage of the miracle of compound interest. Basically, we're all filthy rich. Since we also live long lives, we have to take on multiple legal identities; so all the money is put into a trust for each of the Havocs. That way the money is not attached to an individual and the Berserker can access it for hundreds of years by using multiple identities. When a new Berserker comes on, the trust is transferred to him. It's one of the perks of the job."

Eric picked up a leftover piece of watermelon and popped it in his mouth. He closed his eyes, savoring it. When he opened his eyes again, he chuckled.

"It's not as great as it sounds," he said. "Money gets boring after a three or four decades. When you can have anything you want, acquiring material possessions loses a lot of the thrill."

I really wanted to pursue this topic, but I figured I could grill Kara about it when we got back. "So what happened next?"

Eric hesitated. "It gets really boring after this, and even more depressing," he said. "Let's just stop here."

Did he really want to stop? I studied Eric's face to see if this was just another of his ploys for attention, or if he really had dealt with too much pain today. "I guess we can stop," I said. "If the memories are too painful for you."

"That's not it," said Eric. He stared into the sky for a few minutes without saying anything. The he took in a deep breath. "I suppose we might as well finish the story," he said. "There's not much left. In nineteen sixty eight Sophie was diagnosed with stomach cancer. We began treatment immediately, but the cancer was too far along. She died six months later. The end." He picked up a bottle of root beer and tilted it up to drink down the last few drops. He looked rather cavalier about the whole thing, but I could see through his façade to the pain below.

"So Sophie, who was good and sweet and kind, died an early death, while I, who had more murders to my name than all the famous serial killers combined, continued living looking practically no older than I had when we first were married."

I opened my mouth to speak, but nothing I could come up with seemed to be adequate, so I closed it. When he had said his story was depressing, I had figured he was exaggerating or at least being somewhat dramatic – it was Eric after all. I had no idea what kind of guilt and horror he had been living with all this time.

And just like that, in an instant, my entire perspective of Eric changed. The jokes and bravado now were visible for the defenses they were.

Eric laughed, and I jumped, not expecting that reaction.

"I warned you," he said. He stood up and stretched. "But please don't get all sentimental on me," he said. "I'm not going to break down and cry or anything."

I started to deny it, but he gave me a look that said he knew exactly what I had been thinking.

"Please," he said. "Do us both a favor and spare us the lies. Yes, what I just told you was painful, but it's old pain. The wounds have healed and while they may have left scars, they made me stronger and are part of who I am today."

He walked over and reached out a hand, pulling me to my feet. I felt the cool grass poke up between my toes.

"Unless, of course, you wanted to try and kiss it better?" he said, his usual gleam back in his eye.

Talk about knowing how to ruin a moment. I pushed him away, but since I wasn't even pre-zerking, all I managed to do was to push myself backwards. I took a step back to regain my balance.

Big mistake.

I felt the pain immediately. I didn't have to look to know what had happened, but I couldn't help it. I lifted my foot up and there in the soft arch of my foot was a red mark with a tiny back dot in the center.

I had stepped on a bee.

For most people, this was just a minor annoyance. Not for me. I had only been stung once before. I was eight at the time, and it had nearly killed me. I wasn't allergic to very many things, but what I lacked in quantity, my body made up for in horrible throat-constricting quality.

Immediately, I felt my breath tightening. I gasped as panic flooded through me. I managed to point to the Jeep and croak out the word "purse".

Eric ran to the Jeep and grabbed my purse. I fumbled through the contents until I found the EpiPen. By now, great black dots were floating across my vision and I desperately fought to cling to consciousness.

I pulled off the cap and slid the injector out of the tube, but I couldn't seem to get my fingers to pull off the safety release. The black spots in my vision grew larger and larger until they completely engulfed me.

***

Pain. Searing pain in my thigh.

My eyes flew open, and I saw Eric pull the EpiPen away from my leg. My thoughts were jumbled and confused. Why was I on the ground? Why had Eric used my EpiPen?

And then I 'zerked.

But this was no ordinary 'zerking. Horrible burning rage coursed through my body. An anger stronger than I had ever before felt. I wanted to break, destroy, kill. I was like a child on a makeshift raft being hurled along on top of a tidal wave of emotion – I had no control and no way to stop myself.

I leapt to my feet, my Berserk-enhanced muscles feeling tight and powerful. There was nothing I couldn't lift, nothing I couldn't destroy. I was power, rage, and destruction in human form.

In the back of my mind I vaguely noticed Eric 'zerking, but I didn't really care. I rushed to the trees and ripped up a tall pine as easily as plucking a blade of grass. I swung it into the other trees, watching the wood splinter apart.

I gloried in the destruction.

A hand gripped my arm and in one motion I yanked myself free and turned toward my attacker. It was Eric. Anger surged through me. He was supposed to be my friend, and now he betrayed me?

I grabbed him and lifted him off the ground. With all the force I could muster, I hurled him into the trees hearing the satisfying crack of flesh connecting with wood.

I turned around, looking for something else to destroy.

Powerful arms gripped me from behind, pinning my arms to my waist - or at least trying. With hardly any effort I threw out my arms, breaking the grip of my attacker.

I spun around with my elbow out, catching Eric in the head. He flew across the meadow, smashing through three trees before finally stopping thirty yards away.

He pulled himself shakily to his feet. He shook his head and then charged, tackling me. We slid across the ground, digging a big furrow as grass and flowers were thrown to either side by our passing.

We ended up by the picnic blanket. I turned my head and saw that my purse had been knocked over, spilling the contents on the ground. A bone disc caught my eye. I brought up my legs and kicked Eric off of me. While he flew through the air, I grabbed the disc and pressed the button to open my varé.

Eric lay sprawled on the ground, partially supported by a tree he had slammed into but had not completely knocked over. His eyes widened as he saw me charging towards me. In addition to all the sounds and sensory input, a new smell reached me.

Fear.

I thrilled in it.

I flung myself at Eric, swinging the varé down for a killing blow.

But instead of the inviting feel of my blade slicing through flesh, I heard a hard crack and felt the bone jarring impact of the varé being stopped short.

Eric held his bone staff over his head, blocking my varé. The strain of exertion was etched upon his face. I was stronger than him.

And I would kill him.

"Madison," he said, his voice breathy and weak. "Please don't. You don't want to do this."

But he was wrong. I did want to do this. I wanted to kill and destroy.

Didn't I?

And like a candle guttering out in the wind, my anger was gone. Completely and entirely, without any traces or a gradual calming.

I dropped the varé as the 'zerking left me and I once again returned to my normal self.

Collapsing to the ground I cried, huge gasping sobs wracking my body. What had I done? What had happened to me?

After a few seconds, Eric lifted me up and pulled me into an embrace. We stayed like that for several minutes before he pulled back to look at me.

"Are you back?" he asked.

I nodded. "I think so. What happened?"

"I'm not sure," said Eric. "You were trying to use that injector thing and passed out, so I figured it out and injected you. Then you went - pun completely intended - berserk."

"But the anger and hate," I said. "I've never felt that before."

"Never?"

"No, never."

"Interesting," said Eric.

"Interesting? Why?"

"Because anger and hate is what all Berserkers feel. Except you, apparently. I wonder why?"

"If that's what you feel when you 'zerk, then I don't know how any of you do it. How do you keep from killing everyone around you?"

"Like I told you before, the first 'zerks tend to be the worst, then you learn to think through the fog of anger and to keep your mind clear."

Eric let me go and picked up his staff, compacting it once again.

"What was in that injector anyway?"

"Epinephrine – adrenalin," I clarified. "I'm allergic to bee stings and the EpiPen keeps me from going into anaphylactic shock and dying."

"Adrenalin, huh?" Eric said, his eyes were distant, clearly thinking. "That makes sense."

"What makes sense?"

"The adrenalin triggering the 'zerking. Strong emotions always accompany a 'zerk. It's possible that a Berserker's powers are activated not by the emotions themselves, but by adrenalin in the blood. I've never really thought about it because our powers seemed more like magic than science. Still, it doesn't seem like a particularly pleasant experience. I mean, the side effects seem a bit extreme."

I blushed. "I'm sorry," I said, knowing how lame it sounded. How could I even begin to apologize for almost killing Eric in a mad fog of hate?

Eric grinned and shrugged. "Don't worry, it's not the first time a girl has flown into a rage and tried to kill me. I doubt it will be the last."

I couldn't help but laugh. It felt good after the stress of what had just happened. But the laughter quickly turned back into tears.

Eric lifted my chin. "Hey, no crying," he said. "Besides, look at the bright side – you completely missed the Jeep. Now we don't have to walk home."

CHAPTER 16

THE LONGEST NIGHT

T he final few days before the Solstice flew by in a blur of preparations. Dad and Rhys had selected an isolated hilltop about fifty miles northwest of Woodbridge to set the trap, Shing and Aata were working on some sort of new weapon for me to use, and Mallika and Kara were preparing to cast a snare.

The plan was to put me in an isolated spot in the middle of the woods that would be easily defensible - then leave me stranded by myself. Since Osadyn clearly wanted my blood, we hoped that once I was alone he would come for me. When he attacked, I just had to stay alive long enough for the rest of the Berserkers to come back and fight him.

The real trick was to figure out how to lure Osadyn out of hiding. I had to appear vulnerable enough to be tempting, but avoid the whole blood draining thing.

Rhys still didn't approve of the plan to use me as bait. At first, his over-protective attitude annoyed me, but the closer we got to the

Winter Solstice, the more I began to think he might be the only sane one here.

The day before the Solstice, we all drove out to the site for a walk through. There was no access road to get there, so we parked at a trail head several miles away and traveled in on foot. Mallika and Kara were already at the site casting the snare, so Dad was the only one who couldn't 'zerk. I offered to carry him, but I could tell by the expression on his face that the thought of being carried by his sixteen-year-old daughter wasn't very appealing. He opted to ride with Aata instead.

Together we ran through several miles of dense forest. From the looks of things, this place definitely met the isolated requirement - I couldn't even get any cell phone reception. There were no paths, tracks, or other signs of human use.

Until we got to the hill.

The hill stretched out a quarter mile and rose about fifty feet in elevation at the highest point. It had once been completely covered by trees, but now they had been cleared away, leaving the top of the hill littered with stumps and holes. The excavated trees had been sharpened like stakes and stuck into the ground at an angle, facing outwards. The base of the hill was surrounded by a large trench and a wall of dirt. It looked vaguely like a sand castle a small kid might make at the beach – only life sized.

We walked over to the trench and climbed the earthen wall. Looking down I could see that the Berserkers had dug the trench seven or eight feet down and ten feet wide. Inside the trench were a series of black rope-like tendrils – a snare.

"The first line of defense is the dirt wall surrounding the hill," Dad said. "It's not much, but since we were digging the trench for the snare, we figured we might as well leave it there."

We climbed over the wall and walked across the trench on a makeshift plywood bridge that had been laid across the top. We walked in a circle, following the trench until we found Mallika and Kara. Kara was in the trench, her arms out, fingers splayed wide with black tendrils oozing outward, and sweat pouring down her face. Mallika sat outside the trench nearby, looking exhausted. Her face was gaunt and her eyes red-rimmed and bloodshot. I knew she was much older than I was, but this was the first time I had seen her look old. Rhys hurried over and began whispering to her, his eyes questioning. I wanted to join him and to check on Mallika, but there was something about their whispered conversation that seemed private, a matter between Berserker and Binder, so I stayed back.

Dad continued talking so I stayed with the tour while Rhys assessed her status. "The second, and most important, line of defense is the snare. We will cover the entire trench with plywood and dirt. It should be strong enough to let the Bringers past, but weak enough to collapse when Osadyn tries to cross it. Once he has crossed, he will be stuck in the snare and we can bind him." He looked back at Mallika and Rhys. "Assuming that our Binder can maintain consciousness?"

"I'll be fine," said Mallika. Her voice sounded strong and confident, even if she did look like she would keel over if someone accidentally breathed too heavily near her. "Casting a snare is never easy, and this is by far the largest snare I have ever seen done, or even heard of being attempted." She straightened and glanced back at Kara, who had her eyes closed in concentration. "But we will be done in time."

Dad led the way to the sharpened stakes sticking out of the hillside. "The stakes, like the dirt wall are here simply to slow down the fight so you don't get overwhelmed before the Berserkers arrive. Bone would be better, but since we cleared the top of the hill to give better visibility, Shing pointed out the defensive use of the cut down trees."

We walked up a little higher, but still a good hundred feet from the top of the hill. Here there was a ring of boxes every couple of feet, circling the entire hill. Each box was made of metal and roughly a foot in every dimension. Holes had been dug into the sides of the hill and the boxes partially buried so that only one side was fully visible.

"These," said Dad, "are your main line of defense. A little surprise that Shing and Aata developed – a bone bomb. Each box is packed with an explosive charge, but in addition the charge, the boxes are filled with hundreds of bits of sharpened bone. When the charge goes off, the bone will fly forward tearing, whatever's in front of it to bits."

"We tested it on a few Bringers this week," said Aata. "It was beautiful!" He winked at me. "They'll get the job done, no worries."

"The optimum range is approximately ten feet," said Shing. "If you detonate it too far away and you don't get the proper force, but too close and you will not get a good dispersal."

Dad held up a small box. "This is the detonator. I'll show you how to use it later."

We climbed to the top of the hill and looked out at the surrounding forest. Ignoring the destruction of the hill we were on, the view was spectacular. Because of the heat, the trees had held onto their leaves much longer than usual, and the foliage was just now changing colors.

But tomorrow would be different. Tomorrow this would no longer be a peaceful place of beauty, but a war zone. I was trying to remain calm, but now that the time was almost here, I was nervous. I had felt nauseated all day, and now my stomach felt like it had angry weasels fighting in it.

"And the final line of defense," said Dad, "is you." He gave me what I knew was supposed to be a reassuring smile, but it just made my stomach weasels writhe more fiercely. "Your job is to fight off the Bringers until Osadyn comes after you. If all goes according to plan, Osadyn will fall through the covering of the pit and into the snare. Then we can bind him and put all this behind us."

For the next half hour, Dad and the other Berserkers discussed where they would be waiting and what strategies to use once they arrived. Since it really didn't require any input from me, I joined Mallika and Kara near the trench. Mallika had traded positions with Kara and was now down in the pit weaving the snare. Kara lay collapsed on the ground with her eyes closed. She was breathing –

barely – but that was the only way I could tell she was alive.

I watched Mallika for a few minutes as the thin black tendrils oozed from her fingers. I felt an energy coming from her. It was part of that new sense I had developed that let me know when Berserkers were using their powers, or when Bringers were near. The feeling I got with Mallika casting the snare was different than either of those, but somehow familiar.

Closing my eyes, I held out my hands with the fingers splayed apart as I had seen Mallika and Kara do. I concentrated on the feeling I was getting from Mallika and I imagined black tendrils coming out of my hands. After a moment I felt a strong pulsing throb in my fingers.

I opened my eyes. Thick black cables an inch in diameter were shooting out of my fingers. I was so startled that I lost concentration and the cables broke off, dissipating into black smoke. I glanced around, but Kara still appeared half dead and Mallika was so focused on her weaving that she hadn't noticed my experiment.

I wanted to ask what I had done. Why had I sent out thick cables rather than slender tendrils like Mallika and Kara? What good were thick cables when I needed fine tendrils to weave a net? Clearly I had done something wrong, but I had no idea how to correct it and Mallika and Kara were already so overwhelmed that it would be selfish to ask them to finish the snare and train me in my new Binder powers.

Rather than disturb them, I made my way back over to Dad and the Berserkers, who were still going over strategy.

Dad glanced over when I joined the group and gave me a quick smile. "Good, you're back. Aata is going to show you how to work the detonator."

I sighed. I loved my dad, but I didn't like his tendency to get all über-bossy when dealing with Berserker matters. I knew he had my best interests at heart, but when he got stressed he started barking out commands rather than including me in the process.

Aata showed me the small black box that controlled the bone bombs. His explanation was perfectly adequate, but he kept looking over in the direction of Kara and Mallika. I could tell he was worried.

"She'll be fine," I said, working hard to keep the smile off my face. It was cute to see how much he cared.

"What do you mean?" he asked, a startled look on his face. "What are you talking about?"

"Kara," I said. "She'll be fine. You keep looking over at her. I was just there and Mallika was taking her turn while Kara slept."

"Well," he said, clearly unnerved that I had called him out about Kara. "Yeah, I mean, uh, of course she'll be okay. I was just checking to see the status of the snare."

"Okay, Aata, the snare will be fine," I said.

Aata fixed me with a penetrating gaze before a huge grin erased his serious look. "She told you, didn't she?" he asked.

"She may have mentioned something about her feelings for a certain Berserker, but I can't seem to remember which one she was referring to..."

"I'm worried that Kara and Mallika are extending themselves too far on this," he said, the seriousness returning to his expression. "I know this is our best chance and we have to put everything into it, but it makes me nervous."

We spent the next few hours finishing the preparations. Once Kara and Mallika had finished the snare, the rest of us laid sheets of plywood across the trench, completely covering it. We then piled on dirt, and by the time we were done, you couldn't tell that there was a trench there at all.

We carried Kara and Mallika back to the cars – Aata conveniently ended up carrying Kara – and everyone went home to clean up, rest, and meet up at our house for dinner that night.

After we ate, Eric pulled me aside.

"I just wanted to thank you for the other day," he said. "I haven't talked about that for years, and I appreciated you listening to me." His lips quirked into a smile. "Even if you did try to kill me."

Before I could think of a response, he leaned over and kissed me on the cheek. Then he left. I watched him walk away, my thoughts and emotions spinning around like debris in a hurricane.

If I lived to be a thousand – which as a Berserker didn't sound so farfetched any more – I doubted I would ever understand boys.

***

The next day was the calm before the storm. All the preparations had been made and there was nothing to do but wait. Shing, Aata, and Rhys came over that morning, while Eric stayed behind to watch over Mallika and Kara as they slept.

I was glad he wasn't there because I still didn't know what to do about Eric's kiss - it was technically a kiss, as lips were involved, even though it was just a peck on the cheek. Clearly he was interested in me, but I didn't really feel the same way about him. He was reckless, crazy, irreverent, and arrogant. But all that seemed to be a façade hiding the real Eric who was vulnerable and sweet. I finally got a glimpse of that Eric, but it was just such a small part of my experience with him that it was hard to ignore the brash exterior.

At three o'clock Dad announced that it was time to go. Everything was already packed, so there was nothing left to do but to say goodbye to Mom and leave.

I found her in the living room reading a book. As I sat down next to her, she smiled at me and put her book down.

"I've got to go now, Mom," I said. I leaned over and put my head on her shoulder. "I love you."

She reached a hand up and placed it against my cheek. "I love you too," she said. "Where are you going? Anywhere fun?"

Not by a long shot, I thought. In fact, where I was going was about as far away from fun as you could get - unless you liked putting yourself in mortal danger.

"Up north," I said. "It's a Berserker thing."

At the mention of Berserkers Mom's eyes glazed over and the haze kicked in, keeping her from understanding what I was telling her.

"It's kind of dangerous," I said, pulling Mom into a hug. "And to tell you the truth, I'm really scared."

Mom squeezed me back and then said something that surprised me. "I trust you Madison," she said. "I know you will do the right thing." She gave me a kiss on the cheek, and picked up her book.

***

I rode shotgun with Rhys driving the Range Rover and Aata in the back. Dad and Shing took the truck.

We drove in silence, the reality of what we were attempting to do weighing heavily on us. The scenery flew by too quickly and the miles seemed to melt away before us.

My cell phone rang, startling me out of my drive-induced trance. It was Amy.

Grateful for the distraction, I answered the phone. At first I thought we had already left cell phone range because all I heard was incoherent noises.

"Amy?" I said. "Are you there?"

The noise died down and I heard several sniffs. It suddenly all clicked into place - she was crying.

"Madison?"

"I'm here, Amy. What's wrong?"

The crying intensified. "Cory and I broke up," she said, only partially understandable through the crying.

"Why?" I asked. "What happened?"

"We got into a fight," Amy said. "He had been so angry lately, and

I told him he needed to treat me better or I was going to find someone who would."

I closed my eyes, the beginnings of a headache suddenly appearing. "Then what happened?" I asked.

"Then he started shouting at me," Amy said. She gulped in a few breaths before continuing. "I got so angry that I started hitting his chest and shouting back at him. Then he shoved me down onto the sidewalk." The sobbing intensified. "I scraped my hands when I landed, and I hurt my wrist."

"Where are you now?" I asked.

"Home." She let out a few more sobs. "I need you, Madison," she said. "I just need to be with someone right now. Can you come over? It's been so long since we've done anything together. I miss you. Please?"

My heart ached to hear Amy so upset. My every instinct was to help her. She was my best friend; I couldn't just leave her like this. I opened my mouth to tell Rhys to turn around, but then I stopped.

What about Osadyn? What about the deaths he had caused? Yes, my friendship to Amy was important, but she would still be there when I got back – if I got back. This was a once in a lifetime chance to finally bind Osadyn. Could I really throw that away?

I remembered Rhys' story about leaving his fiancé and faking his own death in the name of duty. My own father had given up family and friends to become a Berserker. How could I do any less? Besides, the effects of Osadyn's continued presence was more than likely the cause of her and Cory's relationship trouble. The best way to help her

289

was to do what I had planned and stop Osadyn.

"Listen, Amy, I can't," I said. "I'm heading out of town right now. Amy?" But there was no response. I looked at my phone and saw that the call had been dropped. We had moved out of range of the cell tower, and I had no signal.

"Is everything all right?" asked Rhys.

I put my phone back in my purse and took a deep, calming breath. There was nothing I could do right now. "It was Amy," I said. "She just wanted to talk, but I lost the connection."

And possibly lost a friend too.

***

After we arrived, everyone stayed long enough to help me set up camp on the top of the hill and go over the lines of defense one more time. It wasn't a real camp with a tent and sleeping bags because there was absolutely no chance of any sleep happening tonight, plus we didn't want anything large on the hill blocking my visibility. But we did build a big fire with lots of extra wood, and put out a camp chair for me to sit in while I played my role as bait.

Dad gave me a hug. In the light of the fading sun his eyes seemed overly bright. "I am so proud of you," he said. I held the embrace, knowing it would likely be the last comforting thing I would feel for the rest of the night – or possibly forever.

"I love you, Dad," I said.

"I love you, too," he said, and gave me a gentle squeeze.

"Remember the plan, and keep yourself safe."

I blinked back tears. "I will."

Shing and Aata wished me luck, and then it was time to say goodbye to Rhys. I stood there looking awkwardly at my feet, unsure what to say.

"Good luck," Rhys said.

I looked up into his eyes and saw the concern there. "Thanks."

For an awkward second neither of us moved, but then Rhys reached out and we hugged. Only, to call it a hug didn't come close to adequately describing the reality of it. It would be like calling a majestic eagle a bird, or the ocean simply salt water.

Maybe it was the imminent danger, or something else about our circumstances, but as we embraced it was both thrilling and comforting at the same time. New, yet somehow familiar. It was as though we were meant to be together, two separated halves coming together for the first time - inevitable, wonderful, perfect.

I ached as we pulled apart, knowing it was necessary, but not wanting to let go. Letting go meant that he would leave. That I would be left alone in the dark to await a monster.

Not wanting my dad or the other Berserkers to see my reluctance – Dad would call the whole thing off if he thought I'd changed my mind – I stepped away from Rhys and turned away, walking back to the top of the hill and sitting in the chair. From there I waved to them as they drove off, leaving me alone. I felt a bit like Andromeda from Greek mythology chained to the rock, awaiting the Kraken.

Only this Andromeda wasn't chained, and she carried a wicked bone varé.

For the next several hours I waited as the sun set and the moon rose. Supposedly, since it was Winter Solstice, the 'zerking would be more powerful and the full moon would make the Binding stronger. I hadn't 'zerked yet today because Dad and Rhys said that by 'zerking I somehow made myself more visible to Osadyn.

But now that the time was right, visibility was exactly what we wanted. I stood up and concentrated, reaching inward toward my emotions. Given the impending battle, it was not difficult to 'zerk.

I felt the glow envelop me – a rushing tidal wave of emotion, almost overwhelming. Like the time I had used the EpiPen, the emotions were stronger, more violent, but I refused to let them master me. I pushed them down, keeping my control, but taking in the power.

Alive. There was no other way to describe it. I wanted to run, jump, and play – or destroy something. Anything to work off the extra energy.

But I knew that I needed to concentrate right now. I had to be vigilant, searching my feelings for the approach of the Bringers, to be ready for Osadyn when he came – if he came.

So I waited patiently, examining the remote detonator that would set off the bone bombs, going over the practice forms with my varé, and thinking about Rhys.

Had he felt the same sort of sense of loss that I had as we parted? Did he even feel the same way about me? I knew that Kara seemed to think so, but Rhys was always so polite and formal, that I couldn't tell what his level of interest was.

Especially with Eric around.

I liked Eric. He was funny, devious, and he had an emotionally vulnerable side that he didn't show very often, but he always demanded to be center stage, to have all eyes and attention on him. Rhys was so much less assuming I had no chance of gauging his feelings unless we were alone together.

And so the hours passed. The sky grew blacker, the stars grew brighter, and the moon hung low overhead, a great yellowish ball casting bright shadows in the dark night.

I sensed them before I heard them. The tiny niggling feeling of something unnatural – evil. I stiffened, the 'zerk intensifying. They were here. Bringers – hundreds of them by the feel of it.

I paced the top of the hill, varé extended, anxious to begin but afraid of the potential outcome. How long would I need to hold out on my own? How long would it take for Osadyn to appear and for the Berserkers to come to my aid?

Three Bringers rushed out of the woods, clearly ahead of the pack. They topped the earthen wall, and raced over the covered trench.

They weaved through the ring of stakes and onto the bomb-filled slope. I considered detonating one, but it seemed a waste to use it on only three Bringers, so instead I waited and watched.

The trio approached me cautiously, the slimy mouths in their elongated heads gaping with all sorts of nasty juices that I had no desire to know the nature of. The last time I had faced them, I had my dad's old varé. It hadn't been pretty, but I had defeated them.

The outcome this time was much different. I killed all three of the Bringers with only two strokes. The movements were natural, effortless. Partly it was because I was bonded to this weapon and had been trained in its use. But I could also feel the effects of the Winter Solstice. It not only magnified my speed and strength, but also enhanced my innate sense of how to attack the Bringers, turning me into a lethal killing machine.

The first three were just a drop in the ocean of what was to come. Even as they dissolved into black goo, I saw more Bringers burst from of the forest.

The next wave consisted of twenty Bringers. Again I considered using the bone bombs, but I didn't for two reasons: First, I could sense more Bringers nearby and wanted to save my ammo. Second, I needed to do something, and killing the Bringers with my varé felt really good right now.

While I had in no way reached Rhys' level of mastery with the varé, I had learned very quickly. My varé flashed as the enemy approached, slicing through multiple Bringers at a time. I slashed, I spun, I danced a gruesome waltz of death. The varé was my partner, and together we sliced through the crowds – quickly, effortlessly.

I stood in the midst of the carnage, my varé out, ready for attack, only to discover that I had no opponent. I blinked in surprise. I wasn't quite sure how I had killed them all. In some ways my mind had been on autopilot while my body followed the training that had been drilled into it.

And then I felt it. Not Osadyn – it was too early for that – but a massive sense of darkness. This time it wouldn't be a few Bringers, or even a couple of dozen. It would be hundreds, maybe thousands.

Black shapes exploded out of the forest and rushed against the earthen walls, pouring over them like the tide washing onto the shore. I held my breath as they rushed over the wall and onto the boards covering the snare, praying the boards would hold.

They did, and the wave of Bringers advanced up the hill. The uphill climb and the wooden stakes slowed them down. Pressed by those that followed, several Bringers were impaled on the stakes, thrashing furiously before melting off into goo.

I grabbed the detonator box and waited for the Bringers to get closer. One hundred feet. Fifty feet. Twenty. Finally they were close enough that I detonated the first bone bomb.

With a deafening thunderclap, the first bomb went off, vaporizing the Bringers within a ten-yard radius and spraying deadly bits of bone for another twenty. The Bringers screeched and spread out to the sides.

Right by the other bombs.

This time I detonated two bombs simultaneously. The noise was horrific. Between the earth-rattling boom of the bomb and the high shriek of the Bringers' death cries, I knew I would be replaying this night in my dreams for years to come. But the bombs got the job done, wiping out several hundred Bringers in an instant.

And so it continued. As the Bringers advanced, I exploded the bone bombs, decimating their numbers. Unfortunately, I ran out of bone bombs with at least a hundred Bringers left on the hill.

Now came the hard part.

I held my varé at the ready, positioned to attack. I had to destroy these Bringers. Only once Osadyn saw that its Bringers could not capture me would it come for me personally.

As the Bringers approached, I pulled in all the energy I could. I felt the extra power that was there from this one day and I opened myself to it – fully, completely. I let it envelop me.

When the Bringers arrived, I was ready. I was no longer Madison – Berserker in training. I was death, destruction, and chaos incarnate. As I surrendered to the energy around me, I exploded into action: cutting, slashing, stabbing, and killing.

The first Bringers to arrive were killed in an instant, dissolving into goo before they hit the ground. Never before had I moved so quickly, killed so efficiently, or felt so alive! My motions were effortless, graceful, and automatic. It was as if I were detached from my body, watching from above as it sliced and killed the Bringers. I cheered myself on, loving every minute of it. I wanted to shout for joy, to sing, anything to express my feelings.

And then it came.

Darkness.

Not the dark feeling brought on by the Bringers, but the true-black darkness of a Havoc – Osadyn. He pushed his way through the trees, cracking them like a child snapping twigs. When he came into the open, a wave of heat washed over me, followed by an almost overwhelming feeling of nausea.

I faltered in my dance of destruction and a Bringer grabbed me from behind, wrapping its arms around me and lifting me off the ground. Its hot fetid breath surrounded me as it opened its jaws wide and lowered them over my head.

I struggled to escape. I was far stronger than the Bringer, but with my arms pinned I had no leverage to use that strength. There were only a few dozen Bringers left now. If I could just get my arms free, I could kill them.

But I couldn't. Other Bringers swarmed in and grabbed my arms and legs, immobilizing me and knocking my varé to the ground. As the Bringer's head descended over me, the last thing I saw was Osadyn climbing over the dirt wall.

The hot, moist membranes of the Bringer's mouth surrounded me. The muscles of its esophagus constricted, pulling me down. I tried to move my arms and legs but there were at least a dozen Bringers holding me. I wanted to scream, but I couldn't even breathe to take in air.

And then as I was halfway down the Bringer's throat, I heard a loud crash, an almost deafening roar, and the squeals of frightened Bringers. Despite my unspeakably gross predicament, I wanted to cheer – Osadyn had fallen into the snare. Several of the Bringers let go of my legs and arms, giving me just a fraction of freedom.

But it was enough.

Immediately I threw my arms out, breaking open the jaws of the Bringer who was swallowing me and smashing anything my fists could reach. When I had enough room, I dropped to retrieve my varé, swinging it around behind me to kill the Bringers who were coming at my back.

Fatigue was setting in. My struggles to escape the clutches of the Bringers had taken more out of me than I thought. I stumbled, but recovered in time to cut a Bringer neatly in half before moving on to the next. How much longer until the other Berserkers came? I couldn't last much longer on my own.

Between killings I had time to glance at Osadyn. Just as we had planned, he had fallen through the plywood and into the trench. The black bands of the snare clung to him, stretching as he struggled to free himself, but for now they held. We needed Mallika or we would lose this opportunity to bind Osadyn.

To my immense relief, from the south I felt their welcome presence as they ran towards me. So did the remaining Bringers on the hill. Twenty of them ran to protect Osadyn while the rest attempted to recapture me.

Like a welcome sunrise, the Berserkers burst out of the trees, their glow brightening the hill, making everything easier to see. Shing and Aata came out of the woods first, wielding their bone weapons, followed by Rhys and Eric carrying Mallika and Kara.

Shing met the Bringers head on with his Tiger Hook swords, swinging them in a deadly arc. Aata used his Mere club to bash in the Bringers' heads.

Rhys and Eric put down the Binders and jumped into the fray, Rhys wielding his varé and Eric his staff. Together the four of them made quick work of the remaining Bringers, pushing them back up the dirt embankment.

Aata pressed forward, running after them.

"No!" I yelled, but it was too late.

Like a praying mantis on demonic steroids, Osadyn's claws flashed out, grabbing Aata and pulling him down into the trench.

I finished the six remaining Bringers near me in two strokes and ran down the hill, pulling up short near the ensnared Osadyn. The last thing we needed was for both of us to be captured.

By the time I got there, the Berserkers had gathered around Osadyn and Aata. Osadyn held Aata tight, a massive claw enveloping his neck. If Osadyn pinched his claw closed, Aata would be decapitated. He might be a Berserker, but he was clearly in Osadyn's power.

But Osadyn did not kill Aata. He looked at me, and in that moment I saw an image – the snare was gone and Osadyn was letting Aata go. Instinctively, I took a step back and shook my head. I suddenly didn't feel so good.

Aata's face had gone white, and he stopped 'zerking, his glow faded to nothing. His eyes were filled with fear. Fear and sadness. He stood completely still - not struggling, not even moving. His eyes met Mallika's and he mouthed the words, "Do it."

At that moment, an overwhelming sense of peace come over me. A calmness, completely out of relationship to everything going on around me. For some odd reason, I found it difficult to continuing 'zerking – the emotions I depended on were fading, relaxing.

Once again, I saw the image in my head of the snare disappearing and Osadyn releasing Aata. But this time I didn't back away. I peered into Osadyn's eyes and found him staring back at me. Not a creature driven by hunger or the need to kill: I saw intelligence there, a mind, a want.

Once again images flashed into my mind, one, then two, then a dozen. They ripped through my brain like tissue paper - there was too much information, too quickly. The pain was unbearable, and I screamed, pressing my hands to my head, trying to keep it from exploding.

Abruptly the images stopped, and I knew what Osadyn wanted.

"If we release the snare, Osadyn will let Aata go," I said.

Everyone looked at me with expressions varying from open skepticism – Shing – to sheer terror – Kara.

"How do you know?" asked Rhys, not taking his eyes off of Osadyn.

"He's sending me images, or impressions. I'm not really sure," I said, "but they're coming from Osadyn. He wants to bargain."

Kara looked at me with tears streaming down her cheeks. "Are you sure?"

But before I could answer, Aata spoke.

"Don't do it," he croaked, his voice raspy and harsh. "We may never get a chance to bind-" he cut off in mid sentence as Osadyn tightened his grip.

"The Havocs have never communicated before," Shing said. I couldn't tell if he meant that he believed me or not. Given his look of skepticism, I was going with the not.

"But the fact remains," said Mallika, "that Osadyn has not yet killed Aata, so there may be truth in what she says."

"So after a couple of thousand years, Osadyn finally decides to get chatty?" said Eric. "I'm going to have to go with Shing on this being unlikely. Why now?"

"Because Madison is both a Binder and a Berserker," said Mallika.

For a moment, there was complete silence. Even the wind in the trees and the animal noises seemed to fade into nothingness.

Then more images from Osadyn - my head felt torn in two. I dropped to my knees as the pain overwhelmed me, and instantly Rhys was there, draping my arm over his shoulder to lift me.

"We have to decide now," I said. "He won't wait much longer."

Aata stared up at us, and began to really struggle. "Don't do it," he said, his voice so hoarse, it was barely a whisper. "Remember your oaths."

Rhys nodded and then spoke, "I will do what it takes, whatever it takes, to fight for our cause." It had a memorized, ritualistic feel to it, and the other Berserkers nodded in response.

Aata seemed to relax as he saw that the Berserkers were not going to give in. I had a hard time wrapping my brain around the fact that he looked so peaceful knowing that he was going to die. That even though there seemed to be a chance to save him, he would rather die than give up this opportunity to bind Osadyn.

My body began to tremble, and I felt the tears flowing down my cheek. Rhys pulled me even closer and whispered into my ear. "I know it is hard," he said. "But some things are worth dying for."

I nodded. Of course I understood – intellectually. But it is one thing to academically know that something was worth dying for. It was quite another to see it happen – to let it happen.

And then I heard Kara sobbing. She looked down at Aata and reached out a hand feebly towards him. He mouthed the words, "I love you," and then closed his eyes, waiting for the inevitable.

Kara turned to me, terror in her eyes. I tried to look brave, but she must have seen in my face that I was not going to interfere with Aata's wishes.

"No!" Kara shouted. She was hysterical, her voice rose in pitch and grew louder. "I won't let this happen! I love you!"

It happened in an instant. Kara raised her arms above her head and slashed them down to her side. Aata's eyes flew open as he realized what she was doing. He didn't have time to do more than open his mouth in an expression of horror before it was over.

Kara's hands finished moving. The black bands of the snare fell apart, disintegrating into mist, leaving Osadyn free.

Before anyone could react, Osadyn dropped Aata and leapt out of the trench. In three bounds, he had cleared the top of the hill and was speeding into the darkness.

Shing, Rhys, and Eric raced after Osadyn, but even with the incredible speed of Berserkers, it was clear they would not be able to overtake him.

With Rhys gone, I managed to stay on my feet for a good half a second before collapsing to the ground. My head felt like it had spent the past few hours being beaten by a two by four full of nails.

I managed to roll to my side in time to see Mallika and Kara rush to Aata's side. He appeared to have lost consciousness, and Kara lifted his limp head into her lap. She stroked his face and rocked back and forth, tears still streaming down her cheeks.

Bits of whispered conversation made their way to my ears. I couldn't piece them together, but I had the distinct impression that Mallika and Kara were at the beginning of a spectacular argument. The fog of pain in my head made it difficult to think, but after lying on the ground for a minute, I finally realized that the battle was over and there was nothing left for me to do, so I stopped fighting and embraced unconsciousness.

ACKNOWLEDGEMENTS

A HUGE thanks to Sabine Berlin who called me up after reading the first chapter and insisted I finish the book. Her chapter-by-chapter critiques helped me figure out how to write a 16-year-old girl and gave me motivation to keep writing.

Thanks to editor extraordinaire, Nancy Fulda, for removing thousands of words and inserting hundreds of better ones in their place.

Thanks to Aaron Williams and Jana Bitton for using their OCD tendencies to weed out typos and other errors, as well as providing general encouragement and appropriate kicks in the rear.

And thanks to early beta readers Natalie Williams and Shelly Tuohy (I haven't forgotten my promise to you), who showed enough enthusiasm to convince me to publish it.

Thanks to Tian Mulholland for using his many graphical talents to create an extraordinary cover. I am in awe of his skill.

I also want to thank my parents for making me a reading addict at a young age and enabling my addiction throughout my life.

And finally, thanks to my ancestor Arngrim "Berserkur" Grimsson whose name triggered the beginnings of this story.

ABOUT THE AUTHOR

BRANT WILLIAMS never outgrew YA literature and thinks almost any book can be improved by the addition of magic, superpowers, or monsters. He graduated from Brigham Young University with a Bachelors degree in Psychology and a Masters Degree in Organizational Behavior. He lives near Portland, OR with his wife and four beautiful children who make him smile. This is not the first book he has written, but it is the first one he has made public.

UNBOUND (THE HAVOC CHRONICLES BOOK 2)

NOW AVAILABLE

CHAPTER 1

I awoke in a bed that wasn't mine, rays of sunlight filtering through large windows framed by thin, lacy curtains. For a moment I simply lay there, not sure where I was, or how I had gotten there.

Then I heard shouting and the previous night's events came flooding back: The endless torrent of Bringers. Osadyn and Aata. Kara releasing the snare. Although I didn't recognize the room, I figured I was in one of the many bedrooms in the Berserker house.

With more effort than should have been necessary, I swung my legs over the edge of the bed and onto the floor.

The world spun, a dull ache pulsing at the back of my head. Nausea rose in my stomach, so I put my head in my hands, concentrating very hard on not projectile vomiting all over.

After a moment the worst of it appeared to be over, and I felt strong enough to stand. As I got up, I realized I was wearing a long nightgown that was definitely not mine. I had no recollection of how I got into it, but I sure hoped it was Mallika or Kara who put it on me.

I followed the sounds of arguing downstairs and into the large living room with the massive stone fireplace and overstuffed leather furniture.

Aata and Kara were locked in a massive shouting match, and from their appearance had only recently gotten out of bed themselves.

I took a step back, not wanting to intrude on their conversation, but there wasn't a place I could go in the house where I wouldn't overhear them screaming at each other. Unsure of what to do I simply stood there, out of sight, just around the corner.

"I was trying to save your life!" Kara shouted.

From my brief glance into the room, Aata had looked positively furious. I wouldn't have been surprised if any second he 'zerked.

"You had no right!" he shouted back.

Back and forth they yelled, Aata furious that Kara had released the snare and freed Osadyn, and Kara upset that Aata was angry at her for loving him enough to save him.

"It wasn't your choice to make!" Aata said. "I put my life on the line when I joined the Berserkers. We all did when we took the oaths. Some things are worth dying for."

"I couldn't just let you die," said Kara. "I love you!"

A crash and the sound of splintering wood reverberated through the house. "And that's why Berserkers and Binders should not get involved with each other!" shouted Aata. "I told you from the beginning that this would lead to trouble. Now you've ruined our one chance to capture Osadyn. All his future deaths are on your head!"

Heavy stomping footsteps crossed the floor. The front door was yanked open and slammed shut, shaking the house.

With Aata gone, the decibel level dramatically dropped. But the sound of Kara's muffled sobs pierced the silence, bringing tears to my own eyes.

I rushed into the living room and found her collapsed on the couch, sobbing uncontrollably. I sat down next to her and pulled her head onto my shoulder. I didn't say anything; I just held her and stroked her hair, brushing the stray strands out of her face.

Eventually Kara's sobs began to subside. She looked at me with tear-filled eyes and a sense of hopelessness. "He... he hates me, Madison," said Kara, and the sobs began again.

There was nothing for me to say, so I simply continued stroking her hair and making gentle hushing noises. Looking around the room, I saw a splintered hole in the floor and a broken chair. The frame had been split, the leather torn, and the stuffing was half out. I guessed it hadn't been Kara who had done that.

To be honest, I wasn't too happy with what Kara had done myself. I understood it – what if it had been someone I loved there – and in her position I probably would have done the same thing. But this morning, in the harsh light of day, just the thought of Osadyn getting away made me feel queasy about Kara's choice. Who knew how many people were going to die because we hadn't stopped him when we had the chance?

I was rescued from my comforting duties by Rhys, Shing, Mallika, and Eric arriving home with food for breakfast.

When Mallika saw us on the floor, her face changed from its normal stoic expression to one of pity. She reached down and pulled Kara to her feet. She and Eric guided Kara up the stairs to her bedroom, the crying growing fainter as they closed the door behind her.

The rest of the day was rather subdued. Aata didn't return and no one knew where he might have gone off to. Dad showed up around lunch time and gave me a big hug. He tried to cheer me up by telling me how brave I had been, but all I wanted to do was forget that last night had ever happened.

Once I had gone back home, I tried to call Amy and repair the damage I had done to our relationship by not being there when she desperately needed me. Unfortunately, she had already left to visit her Grandparents' farm in a tiny town in Kansas that we knew from past experience did not have cell phone reception. There was no way to contact her and make it right so it would have to wait until I saw her again at school.

If we needed proof that Osadyn was gone, the weather was all the evidence we needed. The temperature dropped down to a much more normal fifty degrees. Then, as if making up for being so warm, on New Year's Day, we got a couple of inches of rare snow that managed to last the entire afternoon before melting.

In addition to the temperature drop, the local news – which for the past few months had been full of assaults and murders – now seemed to be nothing but a non-stop holiday love-fest. Unlike the snow, that was a welcome change.

With Osadyn gone, there wasn't much reason for everyone to stay put. Yes it was possible – even probable – he would come back and attack, but the Berserker council wanted at least some of the

Berserkers to once again go on the hunt for him.

There were many days of arguing and debate while the Berserkers tried to decide who should go and who should stay. They finally decided that Shing, Aata, and Eric would leave to actively search out Osadyn. There wasn't much they could do without Rhys' blood and Mallika's binding power, but it was to be purely a reconnaissance trip for the time being. Kara would stay because it was best for Kara and Aata to be apart for a while, and Rhys and Mallika would stay here because Osadyn might begin targeting me again.

With the logistics decided, Shing, Aata, and Eric left just before school started again, leaving the Berserker house feeling much emptier than before. While I was sad to see them leave, in some ways it was a relief. Aata's departure removed a source of tension and meant that Kara would now leave her room.

And, if I was honest with myself, I was eager to spend more time alone with Rhys now that Eric could not monopolize my attention.

The first day at school, I immediately sought out Amy to beg her forgiveness. I found her at her locker, her usual vivacious smile gone, replaced by a night-of-the-living-dead zombie-ish blank expression.

"Amy, I'm so sorry!" I blurted before she even had time to speak. "We were driving out of town when you called and we just left cell phone range. I tried to call when I got back but you were already in Kansas, and I couldn't get a hold of you. But I did leave several messages."

Knowing Amy for as long as I have, I knew she couldn't hold a grudge for very long, but I thought for sure she would pout and make me do a bit of pleading for forgiveness before thawing out. To my surprise, she gave me a smile and a big hug.

"I know," she said, and squeezed me tight.

"You do?" I pulled back to get a better look at her. This wasn't like Amy. Something was going on here.

"Yeah," she said. "The night I called, Rhys came by a couple of hours later to tell me he had dropped you off at an Aunt's house, and he told me how upset you were that we hadn't been able to talk. He stayed and listened to me babble on about what a jerk Cory was for almost an hour." She gave a sigh and leaned back against her locker. "It's too bad the boy is so clearly smitten with you, or else I would go after him myself."

Rhys had gone to see Amy while I was in the forest? Why hadn't he told me? It would have saved me a lot of worry if I had known.

Amy must have seen some of the concern on my face. "Oh, don't worry about him, that boy is crazy about you. I mean what kind of uber-perfect boyfriend would think to do something that sweet?" Her eyes tightened. "Not Cory, that's for sure."

Boyfriend? The word bounced around my head like a hummingbird with ADD, never staying still long enough for me to analyze it. Did he really tell Amy he was my boyfriend or was that Amy making one of her usual – shockingly accurate – assumptions?

While Amy turned back to her locker and continued getting her books, I took in a few deep breaths. The last thing I needed now was to trigger a 'zerk in the middle of school. "Did, he, uh actually say that word?" I asked.

"What word?" Amy asked, not looking up from her preparations.

"Boyfriend." It came out rather higher-pitched squeakier than I had intended. I knew the minute the word came out of my mouth that I had said too much.

Amy looked up, a wicked gleam in her eye. I had her attention now. She paused and appeared to give the matter some thought. "I'm pretty sure," she said. "Does it really matter? I mean the boy has love-sick puppy written all over him." She gave me her most devious smile. "Unless you don't want him, of course?"

"No! I, uh..." I was too flustered to find words. Of course I wanted him. Who in their right mind wouldn't want someone like Rhys? But I still had those nagging feelings of self-doubt. I knew how I felt, but we had never actually talked about a relationship before. For all I knew any relationship we had could all be in my imagination. I didn't want to presume.

"Yes," said Amy, this time with a genuine smile.

"Yes, what?"

"He said the word 'boyfriend.'"

A warm giddy feeling washed over me. Our special moments weren't all in my imagination! He did care about me. That wonderful, almost magical, connection wasn't just some pent up schoolgirl fantasy playing out in my head – at least not entirely.

"Yeah, yeah," said Amy, closing her locker. "But keep in mind since you and Rhys are an item, that means Eric is now up for grabs, and I'm ready for a serious rebound."

We took a few steps down the hall before I answered her. "That might be difficult to do, unless you're looking for a long distance relationship."

Amy stopped and crossed her arms. "What do you mean?" she asked. "Spill."

When it had been decided that Eric would join the hunt for Osadyn, we knew we would have to come up with a good story to explain his disappearance. Eric wanted us to tell people he had been sacrificed by a ritualistic cult, but as usual we all ignored his suggestion.

"Eric is going to a military academy in Virginia for this semester," I said.

Amy gaped at me. "Military academy? Like the kind of places where they shave your head and make you run ten miles with a heavy pack in the middle of the night?"

I shrugged. "Something like that," I said. "I don't know all the details - it was rather sudden. Rhys told me he kept breaking house rules and something bad happened on Christmas Eve so they sent him there to learn some discipline."

Once the initial excitement of new gossip was over, Amy seemed to deflate. "Well, so much for rebound option number one," she said. Suddenly she brightened. "Hey, why don't we forget about boys for a while and do something together, just the two of us?" she suggested. "Like old times."

"You really want to go back to old times?" I asked. "You and me as spokespeople for the hopelessly undateable? I'll pass, thanks."

"Not that," she said. "You and me go and have a girls' night out.

No boys allowed."

"Sure, why not?" I said, with what I hoped was an enthusiastic voice. Actually I could think of several really good reasons why not, the foremost of those being my desire to spend time with Rhys, but Amy was my best friend. She was trying to be tough, but I could tell she still needed me.

"This will be fun!" Amy put an arm around my shoulder. "Look out world, Madison and Amy are going out on the town."

Over the next few days we solidified our plans. I was hoping for a laid back evening spent watching romantic movies and crying our eyes out, but Amy wanted to "get out and do something." We settled on dinner and shopping in Portland Friday night.

Getting permission to do that was not so easy. Dad and Rhys were both against it, but that made me all the more determined to make it happen. I had spent the last several months under constant surveillance. Osadyn was gone – it was time for my parole to begin.

"Can Rhys at least come with you?" Dad asked. As much as I liked the idea, I knew Amy wouldn't want it, so I shot that idea down in a hurry.

"This is a girls' night, Dad," I said. "Not only would Rhys hate it, but the entire point of this trip is to do something fun without any boys around."

I was glad I had started early, because it took most of the week to wear them both down. But my logic was sound: Osadyn was clearly gone – significantly colder temperatures as proof – and I was a Berserker, which meant it was safer for me to wander around downtown Portland than it was for Dad.

By Friday night they had given in – if not willingly – to my demands, and Amy and I drove my mom's car down to the Pearl District – a sort of urban-chic hipster neighborhood with plenty of art galleries, shopping, and restaurants.

Amy wanted Thai food so we went to a little place off of Hoyt street that had recently opened up. Amy was more adventurous and tried one of the spicy dishes, but I stuck with my usual Pad Thai. I hadn't eaten Thai since I had become a Berserker and I hoped it wouldn't be too strong for my enhanced sense of taste.

Despite the fact that Amy had wanted this to be a girls' night out with no boys, she sure had a hard time not talking about them. She told me all about Cory and how he had gradually gotten meaner during the semester until that last night when he had shoved her down.

"And now he has the nerve to call up begging for forgiveness," she said, and thrust her fork into a piece of chicken as if it had personally offended her.

I tried to persuade her to give him a second chance, especially since I knew it was partially my fault he'd been acting that way. But without revealing the key fact that her boyfriend had been influenced by the prolonged presence of a monstrous demon, I didn't really have much of a case.

After dinner we walked through the streets looking in shop windows and occasionally going inside for a closer look. In the end we didn't buy anything because the prices for everything were unbelievable. We were used to shopping at the mall and everything here was quite a bit more expensive.

I remembered Eric's revelation that as a Berserker I'd inherited some sort of trust fund, but I hadn't heard any mention of it since, and Dad certainly hadn't brought it up. So, in the meantime I was going to have to continue in my teenage poverty.

After a while Amy got discouraged by the prices. She had never had much money and was hoping to find a good bargain for the last of the income from her summer job. To take her mind off of clothing, I suggested we stop at Powell's Bookstore. To my surprise, Amy agreed.

We hopped on the MAX, Portland's light rail, and rode over to Powell's, one of my favorite places in the world. To call it simply a bookstore didn't do it justice. They called it the City of Books, and that wasn't much of an exaggeration. It took up an entire city block and extended several stories upwards. It was my own personal haven. I could spend hours there and never get bored.

Together we wandered through the rooms browsing through thousands of titles packed onto row after row of shelves.

By the time we'd finished, it was getting late and we decided to head home. A thick fog had rolled in while we were inside, turning the night eerie and damp. The night air surrounded us and coated us with moisture as we walked back to the MAX stop.

With the fog as thick as it was, we accidentally missed our stop and had to get off one stop farther than we'd intended. It was only a few blocks so we decided to walk rather than wait for a train back.

"Thanks for tonight," said Amy as we walked. "I know you have better things to do than hang with me, but it felt good to be back together again. No boys getting in the way of our sisterhood."

Before I could reply, a large man stepped out of a nearby alley holding a knife in his hand. He wore jeans and a black hooded sweatshirt pulled over his head, obscuring his face.

"What are two attractive young ladies doing out here all alone at night?" he asked, casually holding his knife as if he were simply going to use it to clean his nails. His voice sounded merely curious, but it was glaringly obvious he was trying to intimidate us with his presence and physical size.

Amy hesitated, but I grabbed her arm and began to steer her around the man. The sound of a click from behind brought us up short.

"The man asked you a question," said a raspy voice from behind. Amy let out a soft gasp as a second man stuck the barrel of a gun in my back. She looked up at me, her eyes bulging and terrified. As girls living outside of the city, this was the kind of situation we had been warned about our entire lives but never actually expected to encounter.

I tried to turn around, but the man grabbed me by the back of the neck and steered me towards the alley. After the first moment of initial shock I became more annoyed than anything. I was a trained Berserker. I had fought Osadyn and hundreds of Bringers and come out with hardly a scratch – I didn't count the fact that I had practically passed out from exhaustion afterwards. I could take out both of these creeps with nothing more than my thumb.

The only thing that prevented me from 'zerking right then and there was Amy. As a Berserker I was bullet proof – at least in theory, I hadn't ever tested it out – but Amy wasn't quite as durable. If I 'zerked, the guy with the knife might hurt Amy out of panic. Also, I might have a hard time explaining to her the whole glowing freak thing.

Behind me I heard Amy's muffled squeal as the man with the knife dragged her along into the alley with us. The man with the gun shoved me up against a wall, and the man with the knife did the same to Amy.

The man with a gun held me and Amy at gunpoint, while the man with the knife retrieved a paper bag and pulled out a roll of duct tape. He placed it over our mouths and bound our hands behind our backs.

While this was happening, I took a closer look at the man with the gun. He seemed to be in his thirties with long brown hair and a scar on his neck almost like a gruesome necklace. He wore jeans with a dark sweater.

But the thing that struck me the most was his eyes. Cold and hard, they showed neither mercy nor pity. His mouth was turned up into a smile – the sick creep was enjoying this.

He noticed me watching and leered at me, licking his lips in hopes of frightening me. And if I were a normal girl it almost certainly would have worked. But I was anything but normal. I gave him my best flat stare to show him that I would not be intimidated.

"Oh, you are a feisty one," he said walking closer to me. "This is going to be fun."

While he was distracted with me, Amy had been scooting closer to the mouth of the alley. Her mouth was taped and her hands were bound, but her legs were still free. When the man with the gun moved towards me, she took the opportunity to run.

Continued in
Unbound (The Havoc Chronicles Book 2)

CPSIA information can be obtained at www.ICGtesting.com
Printed in the USA
LVOW101441140613

338656LV00015B/629/P